WHO CAST THE FIRST STONE?

THADDEUS BARRY—A righteous crusader ready to stamp out dirty books and free speech . . . and mad enough to stamp out Reverend Randollph.

THEA MASON—A gossip columnist who kept files on the past of every man in town . . . and whose next exposé could ruin Reverend Randollph.

ADRIAN HOLDER—Samantha Stack's boss at WCHG-TV, he wanted to star in her personal life, but once she married Reverend Randollph, he'd be out of the picture.

LUCIA DE BEERS—An unhappy wife who found solace in a bottle of Southern Comfort . . . and a son who went . . . Johnnie Jr. fell in . . . ife.

CLAREN— . . . ndollph residence, . . . st table in the Midwest . . . until a clever killer made him a purveyor of death.

When a killer adds Reverend Randollph's name to his death list, C.P. sees that a seminary education never taught him to spot a psychopath. But his special skill at understanding human nature might provide the puzzled pastor with a solution to this devilishly dangerous case.

Other Avon Books by
Charles Merrill Smith

REVEREND RANDOLLPH AND THE AVENGING ANGEL
REVEREND RANDOLLPH AND THE FALL FROM GRACE, INC.
REVEREND RANDOLLPH AND THE WAGES OF SIN

REVEREND RANDOLLPH AND THE HOLY TERROR

CHARLES MERRILL SMITH

 AVON
PUBLISHERS OF BARD, CAMELOT, DISCUS AND FLARE BOOKS

This is for Warren Bayless, agent and friend, whose enthusiasm for the first Randollph mystery inspired me to keep writing them.

AVON BOOKS
A division of
The Hearst Corporation
959 Eighth Avenue
New York, New York 10019

Chapter One

On the last afternoon of his life John Wesley Horner watched the weak February sun struggle through the thick stained glass of his study's mullioned windows, and congratulated himself on the salubrity of his present state.

Those colors, with which the windows patched the polished walnut of his desk top and stamped irregular patterns on the heavy beige carpet, seemed to symbolize the sequences of his life, he reflected. At least his recent life and career.

There was the blue, cold and cheerless. And the melancholy amber. They stood for the period back in Phoenix, the months he wished he could wipe from his memory and expunge from his personal history. He'd had everything going for him—large congregation, prominence in the city, beautiful parsonage, excellent salary for a clergyman.

But then he'd gotten mixed up with that pious crook, Alton Dinwiddie.

Dinwiddie had joined the church, organized a businessmen-for-Christ club, talked about his investments and his Lord in the same sentences. Horner had the feeling that Dinwiddie was a phony. But the old boy gave the church a block of stock in his

investment company. The dividends were excellent, and Pastor
Horner spoke with enthusiasm about Dinwiddie's generosity to
the church. He did not mention that Dinwiddie had also given
the pastor a block of shares. He knew he shouldn't have accepted
it. He knew he shouldn't have concealed the fact that he owned
it. If he hadn't owned those damned shares he could have been
forgiven. People would have said, "Well, he's just a naive man of
the cloth taken in by a con artist who supported his church
handsomely. He didn't make anything on it."

But he had made something out of it. And when Dinwiddie
disappeared with some three million dollars from the sale of
bogus stock to rich members of Horner's congregation, Horner
had tried to keep it a secret that he'd been given those shares.
That rotten muck-raking reporter had found out somehow, and
he'd made it sound as if Horner were an accomplice in the
scheme to fleece the members of his flock. And that's what had
turned the congregation against him.

Of course, he hadn't been in cahoots with Dinwiddie. Or had
he been? He had smelled fraud from the first. He'd thought about
investigating Dinwiddie. But when those dividends came rolling
in he'd forgotten about his suspicions. Or was it that he just
didn't want to know?

He blotted the ugly days and weeks from his memory. The
investigation. Pleading for himself as an honest fool. Being
cleared without dissipating the cloud hanging over him. The
realization that he was through in that congregation. The dark
blue days. The amber days.

But the chunks of colored glass laid down lighter and brighter
swatches on the desk and carpet. Hot orange. Cheerful crimson.
Calm green.

Thank God he belonged to a denomination in which a bishop
made the final decision as to who would be pastor of what
church. The Church couldn't kick you out, even if it wanted to.
And the denomination didn't want its pastors—especially pastors of large and prominent churches—turned out in scandalous
circumstances.

Fortunately for him, Horner thought, at any given time there
were plenty of pastors who, for one reason or another, needed to
move to greener pastures. Many of them were incumbents in

large churches. So the bishops worked out deals, trade-offs, three- and even four-corner switches. Problem pastors changing chairs, so to speak.

And that's how he'd ended up at Alexandria Hills, a growing upper-middle-class suburb northwest of Chicago. The congregation wasn't so large as the one in Phoenix. The people here didn't have as much money as his people in Phoenix. But they weren't poor. And if the climate was rotten, the parsonage was very nice. Not to mention the dividends he'd saved from Dinwiddie's fake stock which had helped buy his wife all new furniture. And a Chevy Camaro.

Best of all, though, he'd made a connection with the Chicago Times and started a column called "Pastor Horner's Corner." Corny title. Corny column, really. He'd discovered that he had a knack for writing homey sentiment and pleasant pieties. What was more important, there was a really big market for such stuff. The column was already syndicated, and the list of subscribing papers was growing almost daily. His name wasn't a household word like Billy Graham or Norman Vincent Peale—but he was just getting started. So his bad break had turned into a good break. Or, as he preferred to think of it, he had emerged from the darkness of the deep colors cast by the blues and browns and maroons. He was now walking in the brightness splashed on desk and floor by slabs of yellow-gold glass, and which he thought of as the sunshine of God's approval.

Saturday afternoon. Tomorrow's sermon done. He spent Saturday afternoons going over the letters inspired by last Sunday's "Pastor Horner's Corner." He answered them all. Mostly he wrote a 1 or 2 or 3 on a letter and put it in the out basket. His secretary would know, then, which stock answer to use. Sometimes a letter required a few lines which couldn't be handled by any of the stock answers, so he scribbled a short note in the margin.

Big pile of mail today. Last week's column had been popular. He slit an envelope with a gold opener made to look like a dagger.

> Dear Pastor Horner:
>   I think it is just marvelous how you spend every Saturday evening at the hospitals bringing cheer to the sick . . .

There were a lot of letters very much like that. He'd known there would be. He'd described, in the column, how he had this Saturday-evening routine, rigidly adhered to, for all the years of his ministry. After dinner he'd drive to one of the city's hospitals and call, not on members of his own congregation, but on people who had no pastors to comfort them and pray with them. He'd even put in a list of the hospitals he called in—"Last week I visited Columbus Hospital; this week it will be Wesley Memorial, next week . . ."

Actually, he'd only been doing this since he started writing "Pastor Horner's Corner." It was a glorious idea for the column, but it was also a pain in the neck. Some pastorless patients appreciated his visits, but most of them growled at him or swore at him. He usually made it as short and sweet as possible; he planned to drop the whole thing as soon as he decently could.

He slit another letter. It was a cheap dime-store envelope with no return address. He got many like it, but the address was usually handwritten. This one was typed. The single sheet inside was ruled notebook paper. There was a poem typed on it.

Little Jack Horner came here from Phoenix
Where he had quite a slice of the pie.
He put in his thumb, and pulled out Dinwiddie's plum,
And said, "What a good boy am I!"

Little Jack Horner now writes from his corner
And folks say "How holy he is!"
But Little Jack Horner's just a pious performer
And one day he's bound to get his.

Horner's warm euphoria turned to a chill of fear. He had learned to live with the uneasy awareness that someone might some day smear his good name, hard-earned and richly deserved, by bringing up the Phoenix unpleasantness. He thought of this potential disaster as being smeared rather than as having his past exposed. After all, he hadn't done anything really wrong. He'd just been too trusting, too innocent in the ways of crooked businessmen. Was he going to have to pay for this well-intentioned mistake forever? Everything was going so beautifully.

He knew that a malevolent informer, twisting and distorting his honest error, could bring him down.

Soon, though, the cold chill of fear was driven out by a hot anger. Well, by God, they'd better not try to smear him! He'd fight! He'd sue! He had a great platform in his column, a weapon with which to bludgeon them bloody! He began to compose a column in his head:

"Dear friends, it is with sadness I have to tell you that even those of us who have only love in our hearts do make enemies. Unwanted enemies to be sure, who out of some black motive—jealousy or hate or plain meanness—want to do harm to those who seek to do good. This is now happening to me, and I want to tell you about it. . . ."

He felt a surge of relief. He was in the driver's seat this time. He slit another envelope, a pink one.

> Dear Pastor Horner,
> Your Godliness shines through everything you write . . .

He felt lots better.

John Wesley Horner came out of the doors of Wesley Memorial Hospital and turned up his coat collar against the damp cold wind blowing in from the lake. He walked down the street to the parking lot, then diagonally across the lot to his car. Someone was sitting in the passenger seat in the car next to his, and he thought they must be pretty cold if they'd been sitting there long. But, in the fashion of city people, he paid little attention to other human beings about him.

Pastor Horner bent over to insert the key in his door lock. It is doubtful that he even heard the crack! crack! crack! of the three small-caliber bullets that slammed into the back of his brain.

Chapter Two

Cesare Paul Randollph, former professional football player, doctor of philosophy, ordained clergyman, tied his tie and thought about life. More precisely, he thought about his own life. More precisely still, he thought about the strange and unexpected corners his life had turned in just a year.

Less than a year ago he had been leading a serene existence as professor of Church history in the seminary which was his graduate-school alma mater and which was washed by the benevolent breezes off the Pacific. Then had come the invitation from his friend and former dean, now the bishop of Chicago, to spend a sabbatical year as interim pastor of Chicago's Church of the Good Shepherd.

If ever a church was misnamed, he had discovered, it was the Church of the Good Shepherd. He doubted that a sheep had ever been within ten miles of the place. Maybe in the days when Chicago was a trading post and the church a mission to the Indians it had been a rural parish. But there was nothing bucolic about it now. It was housed in the first three floors of a high-rise office building occupying some of the most expensive real estate in Chicago's Loop. You wouldn't even know it was a church unless you noticed the discreet bulletin board sunk in the masonry beside the heavy brass doors which opened into a lobby of tile and marble and banks of elevators. Or unless you craned your neck and saw the incongruous Gothic pinnacle capping the building, rather like a fat inverted exclamation mark, proclaiming, "You aren't going to believe it, but this is a church."

Actually, the location of the church was a combination of Christian piety and shrewd business—a sort of Protestant ethics in action. As the cost of Loop land per front foot escalated with the rapid growth of Chicago the businessmen of the congregation found themselves, every Sunday, calculating the worth of the property on which their gloomy old Romanesque church squatted. The amount, increasing by the year, was so astounding as to give them pain every time they came to church and thought about it, which made it impossible for them to worship the Lord in the beauty of holiness.

So they built the office-building-hotel-cum-church. The rentals and leases brought in gratifying sums of money, and the sturdy businessmen-members felt a lot more spiritual when attending divine worship.

Almost as an afterthought they built a two-floor penthouse-parsonage in the octagonal base of the Gothic tower which, although the rooms were a bit odd-shaped, was luxurious and spectacular.

"It will help attract a first-class pastor to our church," one of the trustees had said. "And anyway, it's just unused space."

When he'd accepted the bishop's invitation, Randollph reflected, he'd given the fates a chance to whack him around. It had turned out pleasantly, on the whole. He'd expected to stay the interim year and return to teaching on the Pacific shores. But, as of last week, he'd resigned his professorship. Next week he would be named permanent pastor of the Church of the Good Shepherd. And he was surrendering his independent bachelor life. In an hour or so he would be married to a beautiful red-haired divorcée ex-Presbyterian agnostic named Samantha Stack, who was Chicago's most popular television talk-show hostess. All this was change aplenty, in twelve months, for a man in the autumn of his youth or the springtime of his middle years.

"Good Shepherd is not a normal church, C.P.," the bishop had said a year ago, when cajoling Randollph to be *locum tenens* for twelve months.

"What's a normal church, Freddie?" he'd asked.

"Oh, small, hard-pressed for money, underpays its pastor."

"And Good Shepherd?"

"No money problems. Large endowments. Excellent revenues from its hotel and offices. I'm not sure that's good for a church, but it does make life easier for the pastor."

"Large membership?"

"Not especially. Old families. Prestigious Protestants of Chicago. But they live in the suburbs."

"Who comes to church?"

"Visitors. Conventioneers a lot of them. You're near the big hotels."

"So I'll be preaching to a crowd rather than a congregation."

"If St. Peter could do it, so can you," the bishop had replied cheerfully. "After all, he didn't have a Ph.D., and you do."

The chapel, appended to the nave of the Church of the Good Shepherd several years after the original construction, is Gothic. Fake Gothic, to be sure, but expensive and quite lovely. It is in heavy demand for smallish weddings and is one of Chicago's chic places to be knotted into the bonds of holy matrimony, if your guest list does not exceed a hundred people.

The chapel even has a pipe organ, built especially for it. Tony Agostino, Good Shepherd's organist, was playing a medley of appropriate wedding music which covered the rustlings and whisperings of fifty or sixty guests. Tony struck up something from Purcell, and Lieutenant Michael Casey said, "All right, Doctor, it's time to go."

Randollph had felt a little strange asking Lieutenant Casey to be his best man. They weren't close friends. They didn't even call each other by their Christian names. However, when the time came to select an attendant Randollph realized that the homicide detective was the nearest thing he had to a male friend in Chicago. All of his buddies, pals, and peers were in California. Most of them were teachers at the seminary and thus prevented by indigence from making the trip for what was just a small wedding.

Randollph and Casey took their places at the chancel rail. The bishop and Dan Gantry, number one associate pastor at Good Shepherd, came in at the same time, looking solemn in their robes and white stoles and carrying their little black ritual books.

Tony pushed the organ up a notch. Thea Mason, tall and tan and—Randollph thought—just a trifle hard-looking, came down the aisle. Waiting till Thea took her place at the chancel was Samantha Stack on the arm of John DeBeers.

"I don't have a father, and I don't need to be given away since I was given away once before, but I want to be escorted in, and John DeBeers is not only my boss but a man I like," Sam had said, explaining her choice to Randollph.

Tony Agostino boosted the organ again, and Randollph watched Sam and DeBeers come down the aisle. It was like one of those dream sequences you see in movies now and then. It was real and unreal. He didn't even see DeBeers. What he saw was the most beautiful, interesting, desirable girl in the world floating— that's how he thought of it—floating toward him. She was dressed in a rust velveteen suit with loose-fitting jacket, straight skirt with a kick-pleat, cream scoop neckline crepe-de-Chine blouse, and rust pumps with tie straps and spike heels.

This was how the account of the wedding in the papers would describe the bride. Randollph couldn't have described her outfit to save his life. His quarterback's eye could survey a defense and in a mini-second know exactly where every man was, what each was planning to do once the ball was snapped. Now all he could see was a vision without detail, without specifics.

The vision arrived at the chancel rail and beamed a self-possessed smile at Randollph. DeBeers left the chancel to sit by his thin, sullen wife. The bishop cleared his throat and said, "Dearly belovèd, we are gathered here in the sight of God, and in the presence of these witnesses, to join together this man and this woman in holy matrimony. . . ."

Then, Dan Gantry said, "I require and charge you both, as you stand in the presence of God, to remember that love and loyalty alone will avail as the foundation of a happy and enduring home. No other human ties are more tender, no other vows more sacred. . . ."

Randollph was vaguely aware of saying, "I, Cesare, take thee, Samantha, to be my wedded wife . . . ," of exchanging rings, and walking up the rough stone steps to the altar where the bishop pronounced them man and wife. Of kneeling with Samantha and joining the congregation in the "Our Father"—with Samantha saying "forgive us our debts" because that's the way Presbyterians were taught to pray it, instead of "forgive us our trespasses"—of the bishop's blessing, of kissing the bride and camera lights winking at them as they walked the short aisle. Samantha's arm in his. It crossed his mind that from now on he would be more patient with bridegrooms surrendering their bachelorhood under his official eye. He was now better able to understand their confusion, their zombielike state, and even why some of them came fortified with a snort or two against the shakes.

Randollph felt no need of the champagne which a cute young uniformed maid Clarence Higbee had hired for the occasion was offering to the guests. He was still slightly dazed from the wedding ceremony. But the bride was having a splendid time. She was waving an empty glass to punctuate the animated conversation she was carrying on with a covey of guests. Randollph took two glasses from the maid's replenished tray and joined Sam's group.

"Refreshment for the bride," he said, handing Sam a full glass and taking her empty one.

Sam dazzled him with a smile into which he read love, affection, pride, happiness, and a hint of wanton sensuality. His knees felt weak. No other woman in all the world could affect him this way. He'd kept company with enough beautiful women to know.

Sam wasn't feeling weak. "Welcome to our little professional gathering, C.P.," she said. "Do you all know my newly acquired husband, retired quarterback and noted man of the cloth, C.P. Randollph?"

"I do, of course," John DeBeers said. Actually, Randollph thought, I've only met him once. He liked DeBeers, though. Partly because Sam liked him and partly because he had personal charm. Sam had said he was fifty-five years old, but he didn't look it, with his thick blond hair and a body stocky with muscles and not fat. Sam had told Randollph he was a health nut. He looked it.

"And so do I." Thea Mason interjected. "In fact, I want to rent him for a week when the honeymoon's over. I like big jocks with dark hair. I'm not keen on the clergy, but I'll overlook that."

"You keep your hands off," Sam said. "The honeymoon's not going to be over—ever."

"Hey, that's good! I'll put it in tomorrow's column. 'TV star says honeymoon with handsome preacher won't ever end.'"

"As soon as this lady quits babbling I'll tell you that I'm John DeBeers, Jr." The slight dark young chap didn't look a bit like his father. "I'm anchorman on WCHG-TV news—Dad's station. Sam's station. Nepotism, of course. Please don't call me Junior. Call me Johnnie. People call Dad John."

"I'll remember," Randollph said.

"I was in love with Sam. Still am. Hope you don't mind."

Randollph summoned up a gracious reply. "I should think that every man would be in love with her."

"How sweet!" Sam chiped in. "But with Johnnie it was lust, not love. He just wanted to get me into bed."

"There's that, of course," the younger DeBeers said.

"And you an ex-seminarian," said a small girl with a madonna face. "Tut-tut." She turned to Randollph. "I'm Marva Luscome, anchorwoman—or should I say anchorperson—on WCHG-TV. That makes me coworker with this other anchorperson."

"You went to seminary?" Randollph wasn't much interested in the answer.

"Roman Catholic."

"Oh, you're Catholic?"

"No. Not anymore. Momma is. Very Catholic. Old-world pious-type Catholic. Dad's Protestant—was Protestant. He isn't much of anything anymore. Neither am I since I decided I couldn't hack the priesthood."

"Probably got some girl pregnant, and got kicked out," Marva said with a smile that would have graced a saint.

Young DeBeers reddened and was momentarily flustered. "You've got a nasty tongue, Marva girl."

"So people tell me. Nice to have met you, Reverend Randollph." She moved away.

"Well, nothing wrong with a little healthy lust, I always say." Thea Mason covered the awkward pause.

"My, what would your daddy say if he could hear you? Her daddy was a Baptist preacher," Sam explained to the others.

"He'd say, 'Let us pray for the soul of this poor sinner,'" Thea answered. She turned to Randollph. "That's why I don't care much for the clergy, Reverend. Show me a child of a strict, hell-fire preacher and I'll show you a church-hater."

"That's often the case, I expect." Randollph couldn't think of any other reply, and he didn't want to argue the point.

"And poor!" Thea was steamed up now. "Get kicked out of one rotten lousy little church and drag on to one even worse. Talk about cheap Christians! I could write a book! Paid every slick evangelist that held a revival for Daddy a potful of money. But for us?! Lowest salary they could get by with. 'Plenty of preachers glad to have your job for what we're paying you, Reverend,' the deacons would say. 'Afraid we can't raise your salary this year.' And the horrible parsonages—"

John DeBeers interrupted her. "We all have our childhood horror stories, Thea. My father wasn't a clergyman, but he was a strict Dutch Reformed layman. Dutch Reformed Christians are strong on guilt. Preach about it all the time. You're finally convinced that you really are guilty. Come along, Reverend, and meet my wife—that is, if your wife will excuse us."

"I'd like to meet your wife, but would you omit the 'reverend.'" Randollph hoped he didn't sound testy.

"Oh? Why?"

"It's not a title. It's an adjective. It modifies minister or doctor or father."

"You're right, of course," DeBeers said. "But everyone calls a clergyman reverend. Doesn't common usage make it acceptable?"

"Not with me," Randollph said. "I have this personal crusade to eliminate it. Put it down to an idiosyncrasy. I've been called reverend three times in the last few minutes, which accounts for my acerbic lecturing."

"I call him reverend when I want to irritate him," Sam said brightly.

"And what do you call him when you want to excite him, Sam old girl?" Dan Gantry asked as he joined the group. He looked unnatural in clerical garb, Randollph thought. He was carrying a round-bottom cocktail glass with ice cubes floating in amber liquid.

"You'll never know, buster." Sam punched him in the belly. "Where'd you get the booze?"

"Clarence gave it to me. I said, 'Clarence, I've worked hard today. And champagne makes me sick on an empty stomach.

And, since I got on this collar I look like a Church of England rector, so I ought to smell like one, don't you think?' So Clarence says, 'I have a bottle of Glenlivet single-malt Scotch whiskey which I consider an estimable spirit. Would that do?' So he gave me a slug."

John DeBeers set his champagne glass on a table. "Would somebody introduce me to Clarence? Who is he?"

Randollph cleared his throat to answer but Sam beat him to it. "I found him for Randollph when the poor guy—Randollph, that is—was looking for a cook and housekeeper, back when he was single. He was about to hire a woman, the dope. A young woman. Well, young enough." She looked fondly at Randollph. "Clarence Higbee is a darling, finicky little Englishman who won't work for anyone unless he considers them worthy of his efforts. He considers me worthy."

"About that whiskey," DeBeers said. "That is, if Reverend—I mean the reverend doctor—is willing to postpone meeting Mrs. DeBeers—"

"Come with me," Dan said, and led him off.

Clarence Higbee had been careful to ask about the cost of the wedding buffet before he planned the menu.

"Clarence," Sam had told Randollph, "will always think of the clergy as living in genteel poverty. That's what the Church of England clergy do, don't they?"

"Unless they marry money."

"Well, Clarence is the most devoted follower of the Church of England on either side of the Atlantic. He wants you to tell him that cost is no consideration."

"I'll tell him."

"And, C.P., I'll chip in."

"Don't be foolish. I didn't spend all the money I made playing football."

"I know, darling. But your staunch Protestant soul sometimes cringes at the sight of sinful extravagance."

"Only at some extravagances. I'll tell Clarence to go all out."

Clarence had gone all out.

There were three uniformed maids with him behind the buffet table which was set in the dining room with the glass wall that

practically forced you to peer down on Chicago's business
district. The guests in front of the table, though, were peering at
the assortment of foods.

"Galantine of veal, m'lord," Clarence responded to a question
from the bishop. "Breast of veal cooked with pork sausage and
strips of ham, seasoned with pistachio nuts and various spices,
and garnished with aspic. A most flavorful cold meat. As is this
Boeuf à la Mode en Gelée."

"And what goes into it?" The bishop asked.

"Larded beef strip marinated in brandy seasoned with garlic
and pepper, then arranged with vegetables in the gelée. There are
hot dishes, also," Clarence added. "Eggs baked in tomato shells
for those who want to feel they are having breakfast. Scallops and
shrimp in pastry shells"—he indicated a silver chafing dish in
front of one of the maids. "Chicken à la King, my own recipe. . . ."

Randollph knew the names of all the dishes because Clarence
had gone over the menu with him. Eggs stuffed with caviar.
Shrimp in cucumber boats. Avocado and mushroom salad. An
exotic-looking green salad. Smoked Scottish salmon. Cold
chestnut soufflé with chocolate sauce. Trifle. Lemon mousse.
And more, and more. Hot dishes. Cold dishes. Sweet. Sour.
Hearty. Delicate. A culinary answer to any conceivable taste.

Randollph's staunch Protestant soul, educated to distrust
sensate pleasure, did cringe a little. What would the prophet
Amos think of all this? Probably not much, Randollph decided. A
line from the gloomy old herdsman of Tekoa poked into his
thoughts: "Woe to those who are at ease in Zion."

On the other hand, they'd said Jesus was a glutton and a
boozer. An exaggeration, but a thought to comfort.

He'd better circulate and be a good host, Randollph reminded
himself. It was a role in which he was not quite comfortable. The
bright banter of the smart set came easily to Sammy. She could
churn it out with no visible strain. But he had to work at it.

"One of your problems, C.P.," the bishop had said, "is that you
respond to people with interesting minds."

"So why is that a problem, Freddie?"

"Because the number of people with interesting minds is, in
any given group, very small indeed. Not every one you deal with
as a pastor will fascinate you with their conversation. You are

spoiled. You are accustomed to the companionship of the bright people who make up the faculty of a graduate school."

"Some of them are a little strange."

"That's what makes them interesting. People who can be typed and classified are predictable. You know how they are going to react, what they are going to say. They do not have interesting minds." The bishop sighed. "On the whole, being a pastor—especially of a church like Good Shepherd—is an exciting kind of life. But a pastor must also develop the ability to sustain boredom. You have to learn how to simulate interest when people are blathering away about their adventures in the stock market, or the unprecedented success of their children, or their latest business triumphs. These are subjects which you will find tedious, but you must learn not to fidget or get a glazed look in your eye."

Randollph grinned at the bishop. "Why, Freddie, I'm shocked that a pious bishop would counsel his clergy to be hypocrites."

"Nonsense, C.P.," the bishop replied cheerfully, "it is this kind of well-intentioned and compassionate hypocrisy that keeps us from cutting each other's throats. All successful pastors are quite good at it."

It required plenty of compassionate hypocrisy, Randollph thought, to carry on a conversation with Mrs. John DeBeers. He had taken it upon himself to find her and make himself agreeable. It wasn't easy. Mrs. DeBeers apparently was mad at life.

"Have you seen my husband?" She asked truculently.

"I believe he went in search of a glass of whiskey," Randollph said. "Or perhaps he's at the buffet. May I get a plate for you?"

"Not hungry." Mrs. DeBeers was, though, slaking a thirst. "You can get me a refill on this." She handed him her empty champagne glass. "He's probably chasing some chippie."

"What?" Randollph was startled.

"Anything in skirts." Mrs. DeBeers burped discreetly into her handkerchief. She'd reached a state of mawkish intoxication, Randollph perceived, in which she'd be telling him things he didn't want to hear, and which, when sober, she'd wish she hadn't. Her thin, lined face was the badge of a beauty gone sour. Was that turned-down mouth a biography of a miserable marriage? The streaks of gray in the black hair, too many and too early, stigmata of some grievous wound to the spirit? He was about to find out. Randollph prepared to simulate interest and avoid a glazed look in his eyes.

The man who broke into the unpromising conversation was very tall—at least six five, Randollph estimated. And exceedingly thin. About Randollph's age.

"Lucia, Johnnie's looking for you," he said to Mrs. DeBeers. "There's a girl he wants you to meet."

Mrs. DeBeers brightened up. "Thanks, Adrian, I'll find him."

"You looked like you needed rescuing," the tall man said, offering his hand. "I'm Adrian Holder, news director at WCHG-TV. Technically, I'm your wife's immediate superior. But stars don't have bosses. Was Lucia telling you about her sad marriage? She usually does after she gets a little smashed."

"I think she was about to tell me when you came along. Thanks."

Holder wandered on. Randollph made an effort to chat with every guest, but was relieved when they began the exodus. He was surprised to see Sam put on her coat. She stood on tiptoe to kiss him.

"Before you can bed the bride," she whispered, "she's got to go to the station and tape her ever-popular talk show. Won't take long. Write a sermon or something."

Clarence had arranged for a team of professional cleaners to rid the penthouse-parsonage of the mess made by the wedding guests. Randollph admired their competence. He was amazed at how quickly their machines sucked up the mush of spilled food and gravel of broken glass from the deep-pile grassy green carpet. By the time Sam returned from the studio the place had been restored to its usual unsullied condition and the cleaners had gone.

Clarence, dressed in a dark, British-cut business suit and looking strange to Randollph's eyes which were accustomed to seeing him in the uniform of striped trousers, morning coat, and bat-wing collar, was preparing to leave. He handed Sam a typed paper.

"This is a list of comestibles I've prepared for you during my absence, madam. I'm sure you will find the supply sufficient. Everything's in the large fridge, clearly labeled and stored conveniently."

"Cassoulet," Sam read from the paper. "Lobster Newburg, Chicken Honduras, Beef Stroganoff—Clarence, I'll get fat as a pig!"

"I doubt that, madam. Notice that I've included a supply of crêpes. They may be used for the Newburg or the chicken. I've chosen menus that aren't harmed overmuch by refrigeration, though they won't be as savory as if they were fresh. And now I must be going. My cousin is meeting me downstairs and will be driving me to Wisconsin. I've never been to Wisconsin."

"Come back on schedule," Sam admonished him. "I married Randollph because he promised you'd always be here to look after us, you know."

The master bedroom of the penthouse-parsonage, half octagon in shape, was green and gold and luxurious because Matilda Hartshorne, wife of the incumbent pastor when the penthouse had been built into the tower, had seen to its furnishing—and she liked green and gold and luxury. The oversized bed had a bookcase headboard. The long green sofa was fronted by a slate coffee table sufficient to accommodate a small banquet. There were two chairs upholstered in white brocade with gold thread, the color of the carpet, laced through it.

"Whoever would have thought that I'd come to live in luxury by marrying a preacher," Sammy said. "My, this carpet feels good to a barefoot girl!"

"Dan Gantry says this bedroom looks like a high-class whore-house," Randollph, stretched out on the bed, said.

"How does he know? And you wouldn't know, would you Randollph?"

"Only from what I've seen in the movies," Randollph said. "Why don't you come closer?"

Sammy undid something at the shoulder and her robe fell in a soft pile at her feet. She was naked.

"Euclid and me," Randollph said softly.

"What?" Sammy moved toward the bed.

"Euclid alone has looked on beauty bare," Randollph said. "And I have too."

"How lovely!" Sam said, "Even if this isn't exactly what Edna had in mind when she wrote that line."

"Come here," Randollph commanded.

"Yes, master." She stretched out beside him. "I'm ready, and you can rough me up a little if you like. I'm not fragile. I won't break."

This, it went through his mind, is why they coined the word "ineffable." This ultimate melding with the one you loved. This unsortable mingling of tenderness and lust and affection and desire sharp as pain. This natural act so spiritual that it expressed the inexpressible. This blind, driven coupling which made sense out of God and creation. This animal experience through which the meaning of life could be glimpsed. This ecstasy which built to an explosion of sensation and revelation.

Sam nibbled at his ear. "My God, Randollph, you do know how to make a girl happy! Where did you learn? No, don't answer that. I don't want to know. Let's go heat up some of Clarence's Beef Stroganoff. That'll renew our strength, and we can come back up here and do it again."

Chapter Three

Father Ludwig Gropius was tired and dispirited. Normally the Saturday evening mass was the moment in the week he liked best. St. Mary and All Angels' Church, a red-brick barn in a decaying inner-city neighborhood, was always filled on Saturday nights, with people standing in the aisles. The incense, odor of holiness; hundreds of candles fighting the darkness, and losing out somewhere in the black vastness below the vaulted roof, a symbol of the light of the gospel in a dark and sinful world; the reassurance of the lovely Latin; all this usually served to salve his soul.

But not tonight.

Ludwig Gropius was much in the news these days. On television. In feature stories.

"Slum Priest Fights Vatican Reforms" was the caption on a recent story. Some of the others had been: "Father Gropius Sticks to the Old Ways"; "Catholics Flock to Hear Mass in Latin"; "Priest Bucks Ecclesiastical City Hall."

He'd had an unusual career, Father Gropius reflected, as he popped the wafer on the tongue of an expensively dressed man in his sixties who—the priest guessed—was a wealthy banker or lawyer from Lake Forest, led to this distasteful and dangerous part of town by a piety as conservative as his politics.

Father Gropius had entered the priesthood late. He'd been fortunate to have been assigned to a parish of his own, even one as unpromising as St. Mary and All Angels'. He'd worked hard ministering to his diminishing flock. He'd flogged money out of the chancery for a medical clinic and counseling service. He'd begged and borrowed to keep the crumbling old church in repair.

Then Vatican II had happened.

Father Gropius ignored the order to say the mass in English. His parishioners spoke Spanish and Italian and Polish. The old ones only knew enough English to get by. They'd just be confused and disturbed by religion in English. They didn't understand a word of Latin, of course, but they knew it was the language of heaven.

What had amazed Father Gropius was that, suddenly, his obscure parish began attracting city-wide attention. There'd even been a story about it in the religion section of *Time*. He was a celebrity of sorts.

At first, Father Gropius had continued the mass in Latin for what seemed to him sensible and practical reasons. Then, all the publicity attracted both worshipers and money. There was a hunger, apparently, in many a Catholic soul for the old ways. The uncertainty of the times, maybe, needed the certainty of the familiar. A people whose religion was founded not on faith but on custom desperately needed "the blessed mutter of the mass." St. Mary and All Angels' was the only spiritual filling station in the city where this fuel of faith was for sale, so business was very good indeed.

At first Father Gropius had defended his adherence to the old ways on the practical grounds that they suited his parish. But he soon sensed that the affluent faithful who flocked to his grimy old church for mass wanted to be told that this was what God wanted. So he told them. Then, like the confidence man who finally falls for his own line, Father Gropius began to believe that he was doing what God wanted. He began to think of himself as the heroic defender of the true faith, battling alone in a sea of secularism which threatened to quench the fires of holiness. He was a knight of the church, sword drawn against the ordained ribbon clerks and slick accountants in clericals who cared only to keep the ecclesiastical shop open. It even crossed his mind that, in some future century, he might be canonized. *St. Ludwig the Faithful*. It had the right sound to it.

But not tonight.

Because he was so frequently in the public eye these days his mail was always heavy. Most of it encouraging. Much of it filled with extravagant praise for his courage and devotion. Nearly all of it with money for the church. An occasional nut letter, of course. That was to be expected.

But there'd been two letters today that had upset him.

One was from the secretary to the auxiliary bishop. Would Father Gropius attend upon the bishop at two o'clock next Thursday? It was phrased as a request, but of course, it was an order. The auxiliary bishop was the cardinal's hatchet man. The cardinal was the godfather. He gave the order. But he didn't dirty his own hands with the execution. And execution it would be. The cardinal hadn't bothered Father Gropius early on. So long as it was only an obscure parish which continued the mass in Latin for a handful of poor parishioners, who cared? But when the media had smelled a good story, there had been suggestions from headquarters that Gropius change his ways. Then warnings. The bishop had dropped one shoe. A prudent priest would have backed off then. But Father Gropius had gone too far. He was trapped by his publicity and his need to go on leading the antireform movement. Trapped by the acquired conviction that he was defending the true faith. Trapped—though he did not understand this—by a flaw in his soul which craved the cleansing of personal suffering; which coveted the salvation awarded to a martyr.

But for all the unexamined motives wiggling around in the recesses of his spirit, he was a practical man. He knew they had him trapped. There was a kind of exquisite torture in giving him almost a week to ponder his errant ways before the auxiliary bishop dropped the other shoe. They'd ask him to promise to change his ways, of course. But since he couldn't do that, they'd probably remove him from his parish. Order a lengthy spiritual retreat in some monastery in the middle of nowhere. Assign him to some office job in the chancery. He could be effectively emasculated in any number of ways.

He could submit, or he could defy the bishop. Defiance would mean carrying on outside regular channels. He'd have to find his own church building. Organize a parish. He knew he'd get plenty of people, good conservative Catholics, to back him, finance him, follow him. But he really didn't have much stomach for defiance. That French bishop had gotten away with it. But he was a bishop. A parish priest would have a tough time of it. Still, defiance was the most appealing of the unappealing routes open to him.

The other letter had cinched his depression and sense of despair. It had come in a cheap envelope, address typed. In it, a single sheet of dime-store paper had a poem typed on it.

> You may talk o' gin and beer
> It's what the folks are glad to hear
> When their righteous padre says they should avoid it;
> But when it comes to slaughter
> Take a snoot of laughing water
> An' a souped-up car with Lester Ludwig in it.
> Now in Newark's awful grime,
> Where young Lester spent his time
> A drinkin' and a-raisin' holy hell,
> The finest man by far
> Though he was black as tar
> Was a social worker name of Jimmy Bell.
>
> I shan't forget the night
> When Jimmy crossed, and with the light
> But Lester came a speedin' down the street.
> He'd been slakin' a keen thirst
> And so he thought a burst
> Of speed to beat the light would be real neat.
> Jim Bell lifted up his head,
> And Les hit him, an' he bled,
> And he coughed, and screamed—and beat
> His hands upon the curbing
> Which to Lester was unnerving
> And he blasted off, face white as any sheet.

Bell! Bell! Bell!
You are not in hell
But by the livin' Gawd that made us
Lester Ludwig's going east
Though he's now a pious priest
Hell's the only fitting place for Father Gropius.

That had been a long time ago. He'd been young and wild. He'd
left the bar too drunk to drive. It was a rainy night, and dark. And
Jimmy Bell was black as the night, wearing a black raincoat, and
impossible to see. He'd hit him. And he'd run away. But they
found him easy enough. Matched the broken glass to his car.
Bell's blood on a fender. Jimmy Bell was a saint in the black
community, and feeling ran high. But whites were running
Newark back then. And his father, a lawyer, had political
connections. He hadn't been able to get his son off altogether, but
he'd gotten by with six months and a lecture from a friendly
judge.

But his life was shattered. He'd killed a man. He was an ex-con.
When, a year later, his parents' car had been hit by a drunken
driver and they'd both been killed, he took it as the judgment of
God. He changed his name, legally, from Lester Ludwig to
Ludwig Gropius. He'd gone to college, made top grades. Then he
applied for admission to seminary—applied under his new
name. His records contained nothing about his past as Lester
Ludwig.

Now someone had found out. He wondered how, but it didn't
really matter. He wasn't legally culpable. He'd served his time,
though six months was hardly commensurate with his crime. But
if the auxiliary bishop got hold of this information he'd use it for
blackmail. He wished now he'd come clean when he entered
seminary. Back then, he'd been afraid that the Church would
reject him if it knew he'd been in jail. Actually, just the opposite
was true. An ugly, sinful, even criminal past was almost an asset
to a clergyman. The worse the sin from which you had been
saved the better for your ministry. You could capitalize on it. You
could write a best-selling book about it.

But he hadn't come clean. He'd foolishly concealed his past.
And now he was stuck with it. If the newspapers got hold of the

story he was done for. His only way out would be to claim that his change of name and concealment of his crime had been the decision of a shock-and-grief-disoriented young man. People might forgive that. People were inclined to overlook the foolish choices of the young. He could say his vocation as a priest was a form of atonement. Yes, that sounded good. And for all he knew, it was the truth.

The line at the confessional booth was abnormally long tonight. Father Gropius didn't like confession after the Saturday-night mass, but there were Sunday-morning masses, and some people worked all day Saturday and couldn't get to confession until evening.

But it was just about over. This, he thought, was the last confession. He'd learned the trick of hearing confessions without really hearing them. They were so boring. So many of them to do with sex.

"I masturbated six times this week."

"I let a boy put his hand inside, you know, uh, my panties. . . ."

"I refused my husband his marital rights. . . ."

"I went with a whore. . . ."

Father Gropius sometimes wondered about the Almighty's wisdom in His arrangement for the perpetuation of the species. Surely God could have foreseen that it would be a messy, animalistic, guilt-ridden business. On the other hand, sex had a lot to do with keeping the Church in business. If you took away all the confessions of sexual misbehavior most priests would be underemployed. Maybe God knew what He was about, after all, when He created Eve.

He hoped this last confession of the evening would be something nonsexual. Even though he listened to all the dirty stories the confessors told him with only half his mind, and passed out penances like popcorn, he'd like to close up shop tonight with a good spiritual taste in his soul. A spat with a neighbor. Unkind words with a fellow worker at the plant. Jealousy of a friend's new car. Even a small embezzlement was preferable to another woebegone recounting of a marital infidelity. He waited for the unseen sinner to begin.

"Father, forgive me for what I am about to do," the voice said. A blue-steel barrel poked through the thin baize that curtained priest from sinner. Father Gropius, in the last moment of his life, recognized it as a silencer like the bad guys used on the TV crime shows.

Chapter Four

Captain John Manahan had Lieutenant Casey on the carpet. Or as close as he dared come to putting Casey on the carpet. Manahan was Casey's superior, sure. He had every right to be mean, nasty, overbearing, unfair, and obnoxious in his treatment of the lieutenant. That's how things worked in the police department. If you got your ass chewed out by the commissioner you chewed the ass out of the guy just below you.

But you had to be careful with Casey. Casey was the golden boy. Casey had polish. He knew how to handle wealthy and important people. He had been to college. The commissioner appreciated Casey's gift of knowing the right word to say to big taxpayers. Casey was more important, in the eyes of the commissioner, than Manahan. The captain was bitter about that.

But he concealed his bitterness. He sighed for simpler days and said, "Mike, you see Thea Mason's column this morning?"

"No, I haven't, Captain."

Manahan resettled his pudgy posterior in his stuffed leather desk chair and said: "Listen to this." He began reading from a newspaper folded three times: "'Thea Hears'—that's the name of the column."

"I know."

"Well, she hears, and I quote: 'The Reverend John Wesley Horner, and Father Ludwig Gropius, both recent murder victims, were shot by the same gun. And both received, shortly before they were murdered, poems sent anonymously which predicted they would be killed. Do we have a madman loose in Chicago bent on killing clergymen? Thea hears that the poems, in each case, referred to some unpleasant secret in the preacher's past. Is the murderer a righteous avenger? Are priests and ministers with something to hide to be the target of a Holy Terror?'" Manahan slapped the paper on his desk. "Commissioner thinks you told this Mason dame about the poems and the gun. You bein' in charge of the investigations. He's madder 'n hell. This was supposed to be reserved information."

Casey knew the captain was lying. He didn't doubt that the commissioner was mad, but it was Manahan at whom the official wrath was directed.

"I didn't tell her," Casey said simply. No point in arguing with a blockhead like Manahan.

"You know her, don't you?"

"Yes, I know her. It's my job to be on good terms with all kinds of people from the media. That doesn't mean I told her."

"Then who did tell her?" The captain made an effort to speak more genially.

"How do I know?" Casey shrugged. "All sorts of people knew about it. Sergeant Garboski knew. The photographer knew. The meat-wagon boys probably heard about it. The lab men, some of them knew. The stenographer who photocopied the poems knew—about the poems anyway. People like Thea Mason have spies and informants everywhere."

Captain Manahan grunted. In a properly run world policemen would have the right to censor what went into the newspapers. If people like Thea Mason printed stuff detrimental to the work of the police they'd be thrown in jail. But it wasn't a properly run world. The Mike Caseys were running it instead of the John Manahans.

"Let's wring it out of whoever did it. This has got to stop."

"May I suggest, Captain, that maybe it's better for us to have this information made public?" Casey made an effort to be diplomatic.

"What! Hell no! Why?"

"Because whoever did it may do it again. He may have a hit list of—of clergymen with some kind of guilty secret."

"So?"

"We can't call every priest and preacher in Chicago and say 'Do you have something to conceal about your past?' But if they have an idea why this killer is doing it they can protect themselves. Or try to. If they get a poem in the mail they can call us and we'd give them protection."

"You want a press conference and make all this public?"

"That's what I'd recommend. It might save a life."

Manahan blew his nose on a dirty handkerchief. "Uh, I'll think about it and let you know."

Casey was glad that at least the captain didn't say anything more about trying to find out who had leaked the information to Thea Mason. He was curious about it himself, but knew that—short of the rack or thumbscrews—they'd probably never find out.

Chapter Five

Randollph liked the scruffy elegance of the office Good Shepherd provided for its pastor. It was referred to as the pastor's study, but it functioned more as a room where the Lord's business was transacted than as a retreat where Holy Scripture was probed for revealed truth appropriate for transmission to next Sunday's congregation. Fumed oak paneling fenestrated by slashes of stained glass; furnished in expensive but slightly tatty brown leather sofa and chairs suitable to a stuffy gentleman's club; a massive brown desk, complete with brown leather executive chair which had been selected to accommodate the generous rump of the Reverend Dr. Arthur Hartshorne, Randollph's predecessor (for a quarter century) at Good Shepherd, all contributed to an ambience of sober comfort. Actually, the room had depressed him at first. But by replacing the dingy old brown rugs with crimson carpeting Randollph had brightened up the place and offended Miss Adelaide Windfall, church secretary, whose tenure had been lengthy, and who considered any artifact installed by Dr. Hartshorne, even a carpet, as sacred.

"Addie's a good old girl," Dan Gantry had explained to Randollph on his first day at Good Shepherd, "but bossy. Been here so long she thinks she's the head honcho—which, come to think of it, she probably is."

He could never hope to earn the sexless affection Miss Windfall held for Dr. Hartshorne, Randollph knew. Dr. Hartshorne, a folksy raconteur whose sermons consisted almost exclusively of tales from the life and works of Arthur Hartshorne, and who spent most of his time between Sundays speaking (for generous fees) to luncheon clubs and business conventions, was viewed by Miss Windfall as the paradigm of the clerical profession.

If, out of loyalty to Dr. Hartshorne, she had been disloyal to him, Randollph would have fired her. But Miss Windfall respected the office of pastor of Good Shepherd, even if she disapproved of Randollph's colored shirts and natty but uncleri- cal-looking haberdashery; even though he had come to Good Shepherd a bachelor vulnerable to sins of the flesh and the ample supply of husband-hunting females in the congregation; and even though he had now burdened himself with a bride from the socially tacky world of showbusiness.

So they'd struck up a working relationship based on tradition and a wary mutual respect. Miss Windfall knew things about the Church of the Good Shepherd that a replacement would not learn in less than twenty-five years. She knew where every member belonged on the social and economic scale. She knew where the handles of power were located. She knew who was rich but not influential, and who was influential but not rich. She knew who was cantankerous and who was pleasant. She knew who could be counted on to get the job done when you put them on a committee, and who couldn't. She knew almost everything there was to know about the members of Good Shepherd except which ones were good people and which ones weren't. Miss Windfall had never developed the ability to make this kind of distinction because the qualities of goodness or badness were irrelevant to the efficient operation of a church. What counted, as Miss Windfall had learned early in the game, was who had the clout. Miss Windfall could calculate to a fraction the clout-rating of any member of the Church of the Good Shepherd.

So when Miss Windfall buzzed him on the intercom Randollph knew that either there was some administrative emergency beyond her range of authority, or someone of sufficient stature to merit his time and attention wanted to see him. She might not cherish him, but she served him with professional competence.

"The bishop is here to see you," she announced through the crackle of the imperfectly wired intercom.

"Send him in."

"I am in, C.P." The bishop shut the door behind him and crossed over to the sofa. "Miss Windfall needs to diet." He patted his belly. "But then, so do I."

"Pleasingly plump, Freddie. Just pleasingly plump. You, I mean. Not Miss Windfall. I'm glad to see you, but surprised. I thought the drill was for the pastors to go to the bishop, not the bishop to the pastors."

"When the pastors come to me it's either because I've summoned them to discuss some mess they've gotten themselves into, or to ask them to do something for me—or more accurately, the church. I, of course, put this in the form of a request, but they know it's really an episcopal order. Or they come to see me because they want me to do something for them. Occasionally, it's nice to be what is the slang expression—'laid back'—and just drop in for a visit. Especially when all I have to do is to take the elevator from my office down to yours." The bishop propped well-shined black scotch-grain oxfords on the heavy wood coffee table in front of the sofa. "But the real reason I came by was to mark your first day as the permanent pastor of Good Shepherd. It's in the morning papers."

"I'd forgotten, and I haven't read the paper yet."

"It's on the sports page. 'Con Randolph, former Los Angeles Rams quarterback, named to pastorate of Loop Church,'" the bishop quoted from memory. "'They called him Con because he could make you believe he was going to do what he wasn't going to do, or that he wasn't going to do what he was going to do.'"

"You know, Freddie, I was proud of that nickname when I was playing. But 'Con' doesn't strike me as a fitting tag for a pastor."

"Oh, I don't know, C.P. Most successful pastors have a bit of the confidence man in them."

"Freddie, I'm shocked!" Randollph grinned at his old friend. "I don't recall you teaching us that in the seminary."

"Of course not, C.P." The bishop was unruffled. "I'd never put

it that way publicly. I'd use words such as 'diplomatic' and 'tact.'
But they mean the same thing. They mean you con people into
thinking what you aren't necessarily thinking."

"I suspect this is leading up to a lecture in church administration."

"It is," the bishop said. "Never having served as a pastor before
your interim year here, you'd probably be unaware that now I've
named you the permanent pastor-in-charge all your pastoral and
professional relationships have suddenly changed."

"I can't believe that, Freddie. Why?"

"Because up until today, it was assumed you'd be going back to
your teaching at year's end. You didn't have to worry overmuch
if you offended a rich parishioner or got some unfavorable
publicity, or made a decision which went against what some
influential member had urged you to do. You'd be leaving soon
anyway. They couldn't hurt you. But you're staying. And that
changes everything. They can get at you. It is essential for you to
keep the good will and hearty support of a solid majority of the
power structure that runs Good Shepherd. You have it now. But
there will be times that it will take the tricks of a confidence man
to keep it."

"You didn't explain all this to me when you asked me to take
this job, Freddie."

"Of course not. Would you have listened?"

"But—"

The bishop held up his hand to stop any interruption. "I saw to
it that you were named to this post because it is a difficult job and
you are ideally suited to it—"

Randollph did interrupt this time. "Freddie, be honest, did you
have this in mind when you persuaded me to come here as
interim?"

The bishop was unperturbed by the accusation. "Good administrators always have many things in mind, C.P. I had this
prominent pulpit, and I didn't have anyone at hand suitable to
fill it. I needed administrative breathing space. Your coming as a
year's interim provided it. Of course, the thought had occurred to
me that if you proved successful, and if you liked it—" The
bishop spread his hands as if to say, "What could I do but name
you to the pulpit?"

"Freddie, you know you got me to sign on so I could stay here and marry Samantha, because then she wouldn't have to abandon her career."

The bishop rose to go. "God works in mysterious ways His wonders to perform," he said. "You no doubt look on your path crossing Samantha's as a fortuitous circumstance. I am permitted—since you are the ideal answer to my problem at Good Shepherd—I am permitted to look upon it as the dealing of a benevolent Providence. Or, if you want to be pious about it, who can say it isn't the work of the Holy Spirit?"

"Freddie, Freddie!" Randollph couldn't help laughing. "So I'm to be tactful and devious in discharging my responsibilities. Aren't you advising me to be a hypocrite?"

"Not at all, C.P. Just don't engage in every battle that is offered you—and there will be plenty. Save your ammunition for the battles over genuinely significant moral and spiritual issues. There'll be no lack of them, either." He headed for the door. "But enough episcopal wisdom for this day. I have an appointment with a pastor who wants me to find him a job in Florida."

"Will you?"

"He'll have to get in line. The bishop of Florida tells me he has a list of applicants stretching from Jacksonville to Miami. A lot of our pastors feel called to serve the Lord in Florida or California—especially as the cold months come on us."

Randollph had discovered that the best way for him to go at the tasks laid on him by virtue of his pastorate at Good Shepherd was to follow the work patterns of professional football.

The Christian calendar corresponded to the schedule. Advent, which began the Christian year, was like opening the season with four consecutive games against Dallas, Oakland, Miami, and Pittsburgh. Advent generated much emotion. Tradition whipped up feelings. It was exciting. But it wasn't easy to come up with fresh plays (or sermons) for these occasions. It had all been done before.

Then, after Christmas, a letdown. Something like a couple of games against New Orleans or the Chicago Bears. All the sermons were important. But easier to handle. The semiliturgical Protestants of his denomination didn't pay much attention to the seasons of Epiphany or pre-Lent.

But Lent was upon the preacher almost before he'd shaken the

tinsel out of his homiletical hair. It was another series of
exhilarating but tough games—six Sundays plus Easter, and
you'd better have a series of sermons, like game plans, to meet the
challenge of the occasion.

Randollph organized his week thinking of Sunday as game day.
Most ministers did the same thing, he had discovered, though
without his experience in professional football they probably
didn't think of it as game day.

But you worked toward Sunday. You laid out the plan, which
was the order of worship. Since Good Shepherd was rich enough
to print its order of worship each week the copy for the printers
had to be ready by Wednesday. This meant a consultation, on
Tuesdays, with Tony Agostino, organist and choirmaster, about
the music for Sunday.

Randollph thought of himself as the head coach who spe-
cialized in offense. He looked on Tony Agostino as the defensive
coordinator. Selecting hymns was usually a chore because if you
found one with a text which fit the theme of the service it nearly
always had an unsingable tune. Or if the tune was good the text
expounded a deplorable theology.

Then you had to allow time to fit the other items with the
service. One did not worship the Lord with whatever came to
mind at the moment in a church like Good Shepherd. You put the
service together, like a game plan, in an order that began
somewhere, moved from one point to another, and ended up by
accomplishing your purpose. You selected, or wrote, affirmations
of faith and prayers of confession, and versicles, and offertory
dedications, and benedictions. These were committed to print, so
if you were negligent of syntax or banal in phrasing, your sloppy
performance was permanently recorded. Randollph was amazed
at the time it took to do it right.

The sermon, of course, was the item that took the most time to
prepare. Randollph found he genuinely enjoyed writing and
preaching sermons. If you prepared well during the week things
usually went well on Sunday.

And Sundays came at you awfully fast. In his playing days he'd
had no time to savor a victory or brood over a defeat. On Monday
you had to get up and get ready for next Sunday. A masterpiece
of a sermon, like a winning touchdown pass, was good only for
one Sunday. Sundays pursued a pastor. You had to be ready for

them. You had to be emotionally "up" for them. And only six days separated Sundays.

On Monday morning there was staff meeting. Pastors of small, hard-up congregations didn't have a staff except maybe a wife. If she could run a mimeograph, play the piano, and teach in the Sunday school, she was a staff of sorts. Two employees for the price of one. But Good Shepherd had a bona-fide staff. There were, in addition to Randollph, four other pastors.

Dan Gantry was analogous to the chief assistant to the head coach. He saw to it that the educational program of the church functioned, that the various youth groups kept going, that social activities for young singles and young marrieds were carried on. He was responsible for keeping the scores of commissions, committees, task forces, study groups, and sundry ad-hoc organizations on their toes. He preached occasionally. He did his weekly turn at the hospitals. He did a little of this and a little of that.

The Reverend Mr. O. Bertram Smelser, whose incumbency nearly equaled that of Miss Windfall's, was invisible but hard-working. He was listed as an associate pastor because he was ordained and therefore certified to baptize, marry, and bury. But a more accurate title for the Reverend Mr. Smelser would have been "business manager." He dealt with budget-making, building maintenance, endowment, investments, and purchase of equipment. And he was very good at it. Randollph wondered why a man with Bertie Smelser's business acumen would work for the modest (by business standards) salary he received from Good Shepherd. Perhaps the psychic income from being the Lord's servant made up for the extra hundred thou' he could have made in corporate management.

Then there was the Reverend Ms. Natalie Fisk, a tall, slender brunette just out of seminary and serving her mandatory year as pastor-in-training.

And the Reverend Mr. Henry Sloane, retired. Hank Sloane had spent forty happy years preaching rotten sermons and fouling up, through his administrative ineptitude, the organization of every church he pastored. But when his congregations counted their most beloved pastors, Hank Sloane always led the list. For Hank Sloane had the gift of making people feel better when he visited them. Randollph hadn't quite figured out how Sloane did it, but was grateful that the bishop—when Sloane retired at a healthy sixty-two—had seen to it that Good Shepherd employed him to visit the sick, the afflicted, hospitalized, newcomers, backsliders, the miffed, the mad, the indifferent—anybody who needed a good word from Good Shepherd.

The unordained staff included Miss Windfall and Hattie Carmichael. Hattie was church hostess, who handled receptions and all sorts of meetings which required the allocation of space and some form of refreshment. Then Miss Windfall had two secretaries who worked for her, as did Mr. Smelser. And there were two custodians. But these were troops rather than officers.

Randollph looked on staff meetings as a bore, but necessary. He tried to keep it to an hour, each Monday morning, so that everyone could be clear about what the week would demand of them. After that, he had to find fifteen to twenty hours to write a sermon; spend most afternoons in the office seeing people who wanted to see him; make hospital rounds; and meet with committees almost every evening. Like professional football, or—he supposed—professional anything, the job of pastor combined the exciting, the interesting, the boring; the exhilarating, the depressing, the frustrating; the sense of life rewarded and the feeling of life wasted; the conviction that the Church of the Good Shepherd was witnessing to the faith once delivered to the saints in the midst of a menacing world, and a doubt that all this expensive holy machinery made a damn bit of difference.

But the pastorate was a profession. Randollph had never thought much about it until coming to Good Shepherd, even though he'd been teaching seminary students for several years. He knew that the nomenclature of the ecclesiastical corporation preferred "holy calling" or "divine summons" to "profession"— as if pious enthusiasm were more vital than the skills required by the job. But, Randollph knew, it was a profession. Martin Luther led the Reformation, but he also performed the duties of teacher and pastor. Pope John Paul II was, apparently, a refreshing wind blowing through the musty corridors of Vatican power, but he also had to be a capable executive, and keep St. Peter's roof in good repair. If a pastor forgot that he was, first of all, a professional, he was likely to perform poorly on the job. Randollph was certain of this.

*   *   *

The intercom crackled into life and Miss Windfall's voice said, "Lieutenant Michael Casey to see you." Miss Windfall would have instructed the police commissioner to make an appointment, or forced the mayor to wait. But, she knew Lieutenant Casey rated immediate access to the pastor. Besides, she rather liked Lieutenant Casey.

"Short honeymoon," Casey remarked, settling into one of the comfortable scruffy chairs. "Where'd you go?"

"Nowhere. How can you improve on the accommodations of my parsonage?"

"Cheaper too."

"There's that." Randollph laughed. "And Clarence's cooking."

"He stayed around for the honeymoon?"

"No. He just cooked in advance. Clarence's food, even after freezing, beats anything you can get except in the very finest restaurants."

"My pastor at St. Al's—St. Aloysius—would be envious. The rectory's nice, but he complains all the time about the housekeeper's cooking." Casey reached into the inside pocket of a grayish tweed jacket that Randollph admired and pulled out a pack of Marlboros. "May one smoke in the pastor's study?"

Randollph found an ashtray in a desk drawer. "Half my counselees couldn't make it through a session without a cigarette."

Casey looked at the cigarette he'd extracted, put it back in the pack, and returned the pack to his pocket. "Actually, I'm trying to quit," he explained. "What I came to talk about is the murders of these two priests—well, one priest and one, er, pastor. I think of all clergymen as priests."

"That's natural enough."

"Do you know about them?"

"Horner was a member of my denomination. I didn't know him. I read about the priest, of course. You're in charge of the case, I take it?"

"Yes. You know that Horner and Gropius both got poems in the mail the day they were killed?"

"No."

"It wasn't in the news stories, but Thea Mason had it in her column. Said we had a Holy Terror loose knocking off clergymen with guilty secrets in their personal lives."

"Did they?"

"Seems so. We're checking it out. Horner got mixed up with a stock swindle back in Phoenix. Gropius had a prison record."

"The newspapers will love a story like that," Randolph said.

"Sure they will. Plenty of murders in Chicago. The public is bored with murder. Fourth-rate hoods knocking each other off. Young punks. Rapists. Just part of life in the big city." Casey sounded bitter, Randollph thought. But then, he supposed, a homicide detective was likely to be bitter about the unsavory business of one human being killing another. "But a killer who specializes in the clergy, that's murder with a nice new twist to it. That's a circulation booster for the papers. People go for that kind of crime."

"They like the feeling that they are as good as the clergy," Randollph told him. "Or that the clergy is as bad as they are."

"What a rotten attitude!"

"Human, just human. The public views priests and pastors and rabbis as symbols. It expects them to embody all the virtues they preach about. As a good Catholic you ought to understand that."

"Yeah, I guess so."

"People—parishioners, the public—expect the clergy to be saints. They pay us to be saints. They demand that we exhibit a higher standard of moral conduct than they are willing to impose on themselves." Randollph wondered if he sounded like a professor delivering a stuffy lecture, and decided that he probably did.

But Casey was interested. "You know, I guess that's true. My pastor's a grumpy old Irishman, and I don't think of him as a saint." He chuckled. "The old boy'd ream you out if you called him a saint. But I expect him to lead a celibate life. And I sure as hell don't expect that of myself."

And I sure as hell don't expect it of myself, Randollph thought, and added a devout "Thank God." He thought of Sammy. He wished he were in bed with her right then, her lovely legs locked around him, straining and struggling in a ridiculous-looking wrestle which was the ultimate unity achievable by two human beings.

She was a continuing revelation to him. One evening tender, whispering the words of romance which would have sounded trite and sentimental except that it was Samantha Stack saying them. Another evening sultry and tempting. And yet another time she'd be brassy and bawdy. "Reverend Dr. Cesare Paul Randollph, let's screw," she'd say. Or, "I'm expecting to get laid tonight, and you're the lucky guy." Or some other vulgarity. But lusty. Always lusty. His narrow Protestant upbringing had nailed to his insides a permanent conviction that anything this much fun must be sinful. But that faint perfume of guilt just made the experience more piquant. Was this an example of Divine irony, of Almighty God's wry sense of humor? He decided he'd better get his mind back on the business at hand.

"Did you know that clerical celibacy was inspired, originally, by an economic problem facing the papacy?" He asked Casey.

"Come on!"

"It's true. The Vatican was accustomed to selling bishoprics when they fell vacant. Bishops, on the other hand, liked to pass their see on to a son, thus cutting the Vatican off from a healthy source of revenue. The Vatican didn't mind if a bishop had a family so long as the children were illegitimate and couldn't legally inherit. And that's why they passed the rule that priests had to remain unmarried."

"I always thought—the nuns taught us—that celibacy is a holier way of life, a kind of gift from God to those He chose for a vocation." Casey seemed astounded.

"Well, history is often rewritten for purposes of public relations—even Church history. But I'm sure you didn't pay me a visit to hear me discourse on Church history."

Casey recovered his poise and laughed. "Just remember that I'm not the kind of Catholic who reads nothing but Father O'Malley's devotional pamphlets. I can't think of anything nasty about the Protestants on the spur of the moment, but I'll look it up and give you the business the next time I see you. I'm sure there's plenty of scandalous Protestant history."

"Plenty. Try Oliver Cromwell, or the Church of England in the eighteenth century, or Luther and the peasant wars."

"Thanks, I will. Why do people like it when a saint turns out to be not so saintly?"

"Because no one can stand to be around pure goodness for very long. It accuses us. It spotlights our moral frailty. We feel soiled.

So when a saint—or someone who is supposed to be morally superior to us—slips on an ethical banana peel and falls on his, er—"

"Keester."

"Thanks. Yes. Well, it makes us feel that maybe we aren't so bad after all."

"For a young guy—"

"Youngish."

"Youngish. In good shape, though. You work out? For a youngish guy who's been a pastor only a year you've learned a lot about how people react to the clergy. I'd never thought of it this way."

It was Randollph's turn to laugh. "I learned most of it from the bishop. He gives me these little lectures about the role of pastor, and how to get along with the flock."

"Maybe he can tell me why someone would want to knock off the clergy," Casey said. "But what I really came for was to ask the best way to warn all Chicago priests, ministers, and—I suppose—rabbis about this Holy Terror. You got any ideas?"

"Write them a letter."

Casey looked pained. "I've done that, of course. But you know how everybody treats a form letter. They glance at it and throw it away. Or throw it away first."

"They don't have much impact," Randollph agreed. "Hmmm. You could ask to address the Greater Chicago Association of Priests, Ministers and Rabbis. Ask the association to call a special urgent meeting and let the members know the purpose of the meeting. You won't get everyone. Not too many priests belong. But it'll get the grapevine going."

"Wouldn't it be better to just call the meeting without saying why? We say why and we'll have more reporters than preachers there."

"No."

"Why not?"

"Because the clergy is always busy. Maybe not busy at anything important, but they think it is. They won't cancel a committee or an appointment for an association meeting unless they see it is very much in their interest to be there."

"O.K. How do I go about it?"

"The president of the association is Amory Allen. Get in touch with him."

"What's he like?"

"The kind of chap who becomes president of things. Want me to pave the way for you?"

Casey sighed with relief. "I thought you'd never ask."

Chapter Six

Before coming to the Church of The Good Shepherd Randollph had not really understood who ran a church. He knew a church had a board of trustees, which looked after the property. He knew it had a governing board which adopted policies, established programs, set the budget, determined expenditures, and heard and voted on all sorts of boring reports necessary to the efficient function of a holy corporation. But he had come to discover, during the past year, that it was the strong, the pushy, the politically inclined, who actually ran things.

The bishop had tried to explain to him the ins and outs of managing the governing board of a church.

"First, locate the points of power," he'd said.

"How do I do that, Freddie?"

"Watch. Listen. There are people who by the force of their personality dominate a board. There are people who use a church board as their arena of influence and work hard at being politicians. People like this are often wrong. And they frequently clash with one another. They pretend they are fighting for the good of the church, but they are actually fighting to maintain their own power and influence."

"Sounds awful, Freddie."

"You'll get used to it," the bishop said. "It will take a shifting of your mental gears, though."

"How so?"

"C.P., you've spent your life making your own decisions. You were a quarterback, very successful. Did you ever take a vote in the huddle as to what play to call next?"

"What an appalling idea!"

"Did other players ever try to tell you what to call?"

"Now and then."

"What did you say to them?"

"I wouldn't want to repeat such language to a bishop."

The bishop laughed. "All right. Paraphrase then."

Randollph thought for a moment. "The gist of what I said was that when I wanted their, er, advice, I would ask them for it, and that until I did they were to keep their, ah, mouths shut. I welcomed information about the defense, but I didn't tolerate anyone telling me what to do. A football team isn't supposed to arrive at its decisions by a democratic process."

"Just so. But a church does arrive at its decisions that way. What would have happened if, in the huddle, you would have asked the team what play to call? Would they have made a decision with the good of the team in mind?"

The picture of the team voting on the next play was, to Randollph, so ludicrous that he couldn't help laughing. "No, Freddie. The wide receivers would have insisted that the play be a bomb to them, because that's where they shine. A running back would want a running play with him carrying the ball. The fullback would recommend a play into the line with him carrying the ball. The tight end would probably call for a short pass over the middle to him. Utter chaos!"

"Well, C.P. that's a pretty accurate description of the church's governing board at work—sometimes, at least. With the addition of the one-issue Christian."

"The what?"

"You'll nearly always have one member—maybe more—who is concerned for only one aspect of the faith. I recall that when I was pastor of St. James in Indianapolis there was a fellow on the board who thought the world could be saved by giving every high-school student a New Testament. Had his own organization

to raise money and promote it. He tried to turn every board
meeting into a rally for his cause. One-issue Christians can get
pretty nasty if you don't let them have their way. And you don't
dare let them have their way."

"And just what am I supposed to do about all this?"

"Bring order out of the chaos. Balance one power bloc against
the other. See to it that, in spite of all the irrelevancies and side
issues, the board does what it is supposed to do—which is to
provide for the preaching and teaching of the faith, the due
administration of the sacraments, and the pastoral care of the
flock."

This would be his first meeting with the governing board since
being named permanent pastor, Randollph mused, as he watched
the twenty-five or thirty people straggle into the room prior to
addressing themselves to the nuts-and-bolts problems of carrying
on the work of God's visible kingdom. During his incumbency as
interim pastor he'd managed to skip several of these monthly
meetings. He'd never felt much involved in those he had
attended because he knew his tenure would be brief and he
hadn't expected to pass this way again. Also, nothing very
exciting had happened at any of the board meetings. He'd tried to
give the appearance of being interested, but these meetings—with
Bertie Smelser thrashing through the thickets of cash balances
and investment income, and the meticulous reports of various
committees on how their particular battalions of the Lord's army
were doing in the fight against the world, the flesh, and the
devil—convinced Randollph of what he was already pretty sure,
that he wasn't cut out to be an administrator.

But, watching the little clumps of people break off their
conversations and take places around the large conference table
in response to the chairman's "Let's get this show on the road,"
Randollph realized that he'd better pay attention now to what
happened in these meetings. What happened here would have
much to do with his continuing success as pastor of the Church
of the Good Shepherd. These people had to back him and support
him. If they didn't—well, he could preach brilliant sermons, and
be a good pastor, and direct the day-to-day business of the church
competently, and represent the church in the community with
dignity and grace—he could strike out. He must have the good

will and support of these official Christians gathered around this conference table—a solid majority of them, anyway—or look for another job.

He realized, too, that he didn't know all of them by name, and didn't know any of them very well. He only saw them on Sunday, if then. They lived all over the city, but mostly in North Shore suburbs. There was very little day-to-day contact. He'd have to figure out a way to get acquainted with these people. Maybe a series of dinners in the penthouse. Maybe he could have lunch with some of the men downtown during the week.

There wasn't anything about these people to mark them as disciples. They looked like any other well-dressed upper-middle-class group. Not many here ready to be thrown to the lions for the sake of Christ. But then, he'd never had to brave dungeon, fire, and sword for the faith, either. Randollph, raised on Sunday-school stories of Christian heroes who endured every sort of pain, discomfort, privation and death rather than bow to an Emperor's statue, or claim to believe what they did not believe, or recant some doctrine which officialdom found offensive, had to admit that he was a pallid Christian, a tepid supporter of Christ, a chap who didn't mind serving the Lord if it could be done in bespoke tailoring and from a classy apartment.

Dan Gantry slid into the chair beside Randollph. "Just made it. Ah, the life of a busy pastor—from one meeting to another. This'll be boring, but gotta be here so they can't do some damn-fool thing that'll hurt my programs." Randollph was glad to see that Dan was wearing a comparatively subdued jacket.

"Meeting come to order! You've all got copies th' minutes last meeting. Hear a motion to dispense with readin' minutes? Second? Favor say 'Aye.' Against 'No.' Passed." Tyler Morrison made a good chairman, Randollph supposed, because he had the businessman's impatience with nonproductive use of time, and the jovial optimism of a salesman. Tyler Morrison had made it big with a chain of cut-rate drugstores. Miss Windfall looked on Tyler Morrison as less than top-drawer, Randollph knew, but acceptable for doing scut-work in the temple.

"Reverend Smelser's report—make it short, will you, Bertie, lotsa business tonight, get to the bottom line soon's possible."

The Reverend Mr. Smelser looked hurt. He loved figures and totals and percentages the way some men loved gambling or chasing girls. He did not appreciate having the chairman pour water on his passion. But he peered through gold-rimmed glasses and began reading.

Bertie Smelser's soporific drone sent Randollph's mind drifting. He thought of all the things he might have been doing at this moment had he chosen another of the many roads life had offered him. He might still be quarterback for the Rams. Closing out a career, maybe. But a quarterback, as long as he could think and throw and avoid crippling injuries, could stay around a long time. Or he could be coaching. Or acting in the movies. He'd had offers. Or traded on his name for a comfortable niche in the business world.

Instead, he'd quit football at the peak of his powers, gone to seminary, earned a Ph.D., submitted to the laying on of hands by a bishop, which had transformed him from an ordinary mortal into God's special holy man, and settled into a quiet life of teaching future Abelards and Augustines about the Holy Roman Empire and the Council of Trent and why Luther and Erasmus didn't see eye-to-eye.

Why had he abandoned all the glittering possibilities so available to him for the semi-renunciation of the world, a career surely several blocks off life's main highway? At the time he thought it was a troubling awareness that throwing a football to men in knickers and Buck Rogers helmets was no way for a fellow to spend his best years.

The bishop had an explanation. "You're just the prodigal son coming home, C.P. You were raised in the Church. You were saturated with Jesus' view of life and the world. You were convinced, perhaps more in your heart than in your mind, that it is better to serve than be served. One never quite gets away from that, no matter how long they sojourn in a strange land."

Randollph was diverted from his dreaming self-examination by the conclusion of Bertie Smelser's report. "Hear motion to 'dopt? Second? All favor 'Aye.' 'Posed 'No.' Done. Report from Committee on Social Concerns." Tyler Morrison, duty done, slumped back in his chair, an announcement by body language that they were in for another dull report.

Randollph returned to his reverie, assured that nothing he need note would be said for several minutes. He wasn't sure the bishop was right, but then he had no better explanation of his own motivation. He'd tarried in Sodom and found it unsatisfying. He'd done a moral and spiritual right turn and become a leader in Athletes for Christ. But he'd been disappointed in this muscular Christianity's simplistic theology and uninformed view of the Bible. Something was eluding him. There was something important about life he needed to know but didn't. Thus the hegira to the seminary hoping for a revelation. Well, there'd been no angel visitant or sudden rending of the veil of clay. What he'd found was better. Instead of the instant spiritual gratification and unexamined certainties of Athletes for Christ he'd discovered a trail of truth, open-ended, which, if you kept following it, led to very satisfying places—and then led to more intellectual and spiritual jungles. Thus he'd come to see the life of faith not as a structure of pious acts (which was a relief, because he'd discovered he wasn't made for constant devotional euphoria, or easy affirmations). He had to struggle for faith. But the struggle was the satisfaction.

Dan Gantry nudged him. "Better wake up, boss. Sad Tad Barry's about to make a speech."

Randollph abruptly returned to the world. "Was I that obvious?"

"You had a glazed look," Dan whispered.

"Chair recognizes Mr. Barry," Tyler Morrison intoned.

"Who's he?" Randollph asked Dan.

"Thaddeus Barry, Jr. Family goes back to founders of Good Shepherd. Rich. Bachelor. Lawyer, but doesn't work at it much. Rides his hobby horse most of the time."

"What's that?"

"You'll see."

Randollph saw that Thaddeus Barry was a tall, boney man in his sixties with sparse white hair. His expensive oxford-gray suit was of a style so long passed that it had to be custom-tailored. He wore a high, stiff detachable collar so much like the ones Randollph's grandfather had worn that Randollph wondered where in the world Barry bought them.

"Mr. Morrison." Barry nodded to the chairman, snuffled, and shifted his voice up a notch. "As many of you know, I am active in Citizens for a Moral America. Indeed, I have the honor of being the Midwest regional president of this worthy organization." He paused as if for an ovation. Tyler Morrison slumped lower in his seat. Randollph thought he heard a suppressed groan from somewhere.

Barry continued. "I wish to call your attention to the great crusade the Citizens for a Moral America is mounting—a national crusade—to stamp out pornography once and for all before it ruins, utterly ruins, this fair land of ours, as it ruined Roman civilization, and as it has brought to its knees many a flourishing nation."

"See what I mean?" Dan whispered. "He makes this bullshit speech to the board about once a year. He'll want us to go on record supporting the crusade. They have that about once a year too. Weird people!"

Barry accelerated his pace. "I want you to know that dirty books, magazines, and movies are the root cause of disrespect for the law, drugs, the escalating divorce rate, teenage pregnancies, abortion, prostitution, rape, incest"—he paused—"and the decline in Sunday-school attendance."

"Y' wan' us to do something about this crusade, Mr. Barry? Help finance it or somethin'?" Tyler Morrison had clearly heard this tune before.

"Yes, Mr. Morrison, I do want you to do something about it. Not money. Happily, we're adequately financed—"

"The old boy bankrolls it himself." Dan said behind his hand. "That's why he's always president."

"Whatcha wan' us t' do, Mr. Barry?"

"Give us your moral support."

"How?"

"Go on record with a public statement that the Church of the Good Shepherd—my church"—he paused to let this sink in—"backs the crusade. Invite the national secretary of Citizens for a Moral America to preach at Good Shepherd as part of the kickoff for the crusade."

"Y' wanna put it in form of a motion?"

"Yes."

"Motion is this board put Good Shepherd on public record supportin' Crusade—whatcha call it?"

"Crusade to Stamp Out Pornography Forever."

"Yeah. Support it an' invite secretary your organization t' preach here—that about it?"

"Yes, Mr. Chairman, that covers it."

"Hear a second? Motion seconded. Discussion?"

Randollph felt like Poor Pauline, tied to the tracks with the train bearing down. Thaddeus Barry, Jr., was an example of what the bishop had called a one-issue Christian. And one-issue Christians were seldom charitable to those who opposed them. What a hell of a thing to have come up at my first board meeting as permanent pastor, he thought. He knew he had to gird his loins for battle, but had the gloomy premonition that there was no way to come out of this unscathed.

"Mr. Chairman," he said.

"Chair recognize' Dr. Randollph."

"I wish Mr. Barry had spoken to me about this matter prior to the meeting." He didn't know if this bit of one-upmanship would do any good, but maybe some of the board members would see that Barry had been guilty of discourtesy to the pastor.

"I didn't think it necessary." Barry's voice was hard. "I assumed that a Christian minister would not be in favor of pornography. Although some of them are, I'm sad to say. My sources tell me that the Reverend John Wesley Horner"—now he dropped his voice to a conspiratorial tone—"that chap that was murdered, had copies of *Playboy* in a magazine rack by the, that is, iń his bathroom. I wouldn't be surprised the police will find a connection between his love of pornography and his murder. Are you one of those preachers who favor pornography, Dr. Randollph?"

"No, Mr. Barry, I do not favor pornography." Randollph heard his own voice harden. Watch it, he told himself. Don't let this irritating man provoke you to wrath. "I regret to say"—Randollph tried not to sound at all regretful—"that I am not as familiar as I perhaps should be with the—I'm sorry—the organization you represent."

"The Citizens for a Moral America." Barry snapped it out.

"Yes, of course." Now it was Barry who was uncomfortable, who had gone from being one up to one down. Randollph squashed the satisfaction he felt because he knew it was an example of spiritual pride. "I have two points to make, Mr. Chairman—and Mr. Barry. I think this board should examine carefully the program Mr. Barry's group is proposing. Many organizations advocating the suppression of pornography are not careful to observe freedom of speech and press—"

"Now, just a minute—"

Randollph held up his hand as a stop sign. "I believe I have the floor, Mr. Barry. Do me the courtesy of letting me finish. My second point is that there is no vacancy in the preaching schedule for several months, so it would be disruptive to have your national secretary preach any time soon—"

Barry exploded. "You'll invite him if this board votes to invite him!"

"Not necessarily, Mr. Barry. The tenets of our denomination and the constitution of this church specify that the pastor's control of the pulpit is absolute and unbreachable." It was getting to be fun to best this unpleasant chap.

"You—you—" Barry sputtered, nearly out of control. "It's no wonder some preachers in league with the devil get themselves murdered—"

"Come off it, Tad!" The voice was clear and quiet, but crackled with authority. "I'm ashamed of you! You should have figured out by now that you can't push Dr. Randollph around like you did Artie Hartshorne. And I don't want to hear that gasbag of a secretary you foisted off on us before. He's a dirty old man."

"Now, Susie—"

"Furthermore, you owe Dr. Randollph an apology for that awful thing you said—as if you wanted him murdered if he didn't agree with you—and I suggest you offer him an apology right now."

"Hot dog!" Dan Gantry said to Randollph. "Susie's doing the Lord's work! She sure as hell is!"

"Who is she?" Randollph could see that Susie whatever was mid-fiftyish, exquisitely groomed, and had a face that, were it not softened by expertly styled gray hair falling around it, could have been lifted off a Roman coin.

"Susie—Susan Fosterman. Susan Antonia Fosterman to be exact. Widow. Fosterman Perfumes. Inherited it, but runs it. Fine lady. Grew up with Tad Barry. Same social set. He's scared of her."

Thaddeus Barry, Jr., wilted. He struggled to formulate an apology and retain his dignity. "If I, that is, er, I had no wish to offend Dr. Randollph—"

"You didn't," Randollph lied. "Let's discuss the matter of your crusade at our leisure, Mr. Barry." How pleasant it was to dispense Christian charity when your opponent had just been knocked through the ropes.

"Wish to withdraw th' motion, Mr. Barry?" Tyler Morrison wanted to be done with it. "Second withdraw? Entertain motion t' 'journ. Favor 'Aye.' Meeting 'journed."

Chapter Seven

Franklin Pierce McDougall was gratified by the pile of mail on his desk. Getting larger every day. He knew that radio preaching brought in the bucks—but he was amazed, sometimes, by how much. He loved to slit open the envelopes and take out the money—mostly tens, twenties, and some fifties. Checks too. But the kind of people who listened to him favored cash. So did he. There was something sensuous about a fresh fifty—the look of it, the feel of it.

Frankie also liked cash because there was no good way to trace it. His tabernacle was a tax-exempt religious corporation, of course. He didn't have to report its income to anyone. Wasn't he the sole owner? But he did have to report his personal income to the Internal Revenue Service and pay taxes on it. He reported a very modest salary, paid to him by the tabernacle corporation. The corporation owned his Lincoln Mark V Bill Blass coupe and his white Cadillac sedan. But he liked expensive suits and expensive vacations. He liked high living, and high living took a lot of cash. But he had a lot of cash. Kept several safety-deposit boxes full of it.

Franklin Pierce McDougall reflected that the Lord had blessed him right good. He'd been born in the hills of Appalachia where his father and older brothers scratched out a living from the unfriendly land and mined coal when there was work. Frankie, growing up, didn't know what he wanted to do. What he did know was that he wasn't going to drag through life as a poor dirt farmer and coal miner. He thought of going to Hollywood. He always got the lead in class plays. Everyone agreed that he'd made the greatest Aaron Slick in *Aaron Slick from Punkin' Creek* in the history of the shabby little high school. Being in plays also gave him easy access to the female members of the cast.

Frankie's career was set for him by what, at the time, he thought was a calamity, though later he came to view it as God's providence. Through his careless passion he managed to get two girls pregnant at about the same time. He couldn't marry them both, and he didn't want to marry either one of them. What he wanted was to get the hell out of there. He confided in his mother. He was her favorite child, and she'd always hoped he'd turn out to be a great charismatic evangelist. So she gave him the money she'd been squirreling away and packed him off to the Nazareth School of the Bible in Atlanta, where academic competence was a distant second to evangelical fervor as a credential for admission.

Frankie was intellectually lazy, but he was shrewd. He listened and observed. He soon picked up the tricks of the evangelist's trade. It was mostly a matter of mastering pious nomenclature (though Frankie wouldn't have been able to define "nomenclature"), smart promotion, and sex appeal. If you had sex appeal you couldn't miss on the sawdust circuit. Frankie had sex appeal.

He also learned that a beneficent government, while forcing corporations such as ITT and Texas Instruments to devise accounting tricks for hiding profits, didn't even require financial reports from tax-exempt religious corporations. He learned how the big boys—the really big boys—in the business laundered their millions just like the Mafia and hid them in numbered accounts in Zurich. He learned that a regular radio program for an evangelist pays off good, but that a television program pays off better. He learned that if you own a tax-exempt religious corporation, and the corporation owns a television station devoted solely to religious programming, you have the equivalent of a license to print your own money. Frankie's ambition, after he

decided that evangelizing was a quicker and surer way to fame
and fortune than acting, was to have a syndicated radio program,
then get his own television station. This, he was certain, would
ultimately lead to national television syndication, the pinnacle of
the evangelism business.

Franklin Pierce McDougall hung on at Nazareth School of the
Bible long enough to get his two-year certificate. This was good
enough to get him ordained in a jack-leg Baptist church. Then he
seduced a well-to-do widow thirty years his senior who bought
him a tent and a rather luxurious Dodge motor home with *Full-
Gospel Frankie* and an open bible painted on the sides and hit
the trail. It had been slow going at first, and he'd had to seduce a
few more well-heeled older ladies to keep going. Frankie had
discovered early that postpubescent girls in a state of religious
ecstasy were, as a rule, quite willing to satisfy their spiritual
needs on the fold-down bed in his motor home after the service.
He had learned, out of financial necessity, that middle-aged
ladies, while not offering the firm young flesh of those little
muffets in tight sweaters and no panties, often had something
better—money and experience. They knew how to do things in
bed that made Frankie whoop and groan. And they were so
grateful to Frankie that it was no trick to float loans from them.

He'd chosen the name "Full-Gospel Frankie" because he liked
the sound of it, and because it lent itself to the show-biz side of
the business, so important to the success of a free-lance evangelist who had to fight for attention in an overcrowded field where
the competition for the holy buck was fierce. He was aware that,
in the newspeak of Bible-thumping "evangelistic" Christianity,
what a word or phrase meant was of little significance. Someone
had pointed out to him once that "full-gospel" didn't mean full
gospel in the lexicon of the sawdust trail. It meant just the
opposite—a narrow, distorted view of the gospel that left a large
part of it out entirely. This kind of distinction seemed irrelevant
to Frankie. Often, when preaching, he'd whack the open Bible in
his hand, shout "The Bible says," and then say something that
the Bible didn't say at all. You just yelled "the Bible says" and
people would swallow anything you told them. Actually, Frankie
didn't know much of what the Bible said. He found the Bible
boring. But he knew the verses people liked to hear. He
memorized them. He was a fountain of biblical quotations. He

could gush Bible verses. He considered the verse about being "born again" the greatest verse in the Bible because it was the one that brought in the most dough. Frankie was an apocalyptic preacher, though he couldn't have defined "apocalyptic" to save his own body or soul. What he did know was that if you preached a lot that Christ would return any day, any minute even, to judge all men, to separate the sheep from the goats and cast sinners into a terrible hell, it scared the bejesus out of people and they'd throw extra money in the collection to help buy their salvation. He even subscribed to a magazine devoted to warning an unwary world that the end was at hand because he could cop whole paragraphs from it for his sermons. It never even occurred to him that there was irony in the fact that the magazine solicited five-year subscriptions.

Frankie preached a lot about sin. He preached against sexy female movie stars—he called them Jezebels. He preached against drugs and alcohol (Frankie used neither). Frankie preached against x-rated movies and dirty magazines (He loved x-rated movies and dirty magazines). Full-Gospel Frankie had no developed doctrine of sin at all. Sin was a word that you used as a tool to loosen up the wallet. Anything that hurt him or worked against him he thought of as evil. Anything that gave him pleasure—from his fancy cars to the sexually overheated ladies who frequented his bed—he thought of as blessings from the Lord, and therefore good.

When he tired of traveling, Frankie had tried his luck as a tabernacle evangelist in Charleston. But the competition was too tough. He'd soon pulled up stakes and moved to Chicago. He'd found an old warehouse for sale cheap on the West Side, with plenty of parking space around it. You could have a successful tabernacle operation with a crummy building, but the Christian floaters you hoped to attract would soon drift off to another tabernacle if it had plenty of parking space and you didn't.

But Full-Gospel Frankie's House of Salvation had been an instant hit. Maybe it was the huge revolving sign that portrayed a neon-red Frankie karate-chopping at an open Bible in his hand—two chops per revolution. Maybe it was that feature story the *Trib* had done on the sign. Maybe it was that interview on *Sam Stack's Chicago*. She'd been tough. He'd tried to use his boyish charm on her, but it hadn't worked. But it was good publicity. Everybody in

Chicago watched her program. But whatever the reason, things were going great. He was raising money to start his own television station. Chicago was a seller's market for his kind of Christianity.

Full-Gospel Frankie slit another one of the hundreds of envelopes. When he shook out the contents he was annoyed that it contained no money. Instead, there was a single sheet of cheap paper with a poem on it.

> You did not wear your cleric's coat
> That night you sought her bed,
> You'd been there oft enough before,
> Though you were never wed,
> And when you left before the dawn
> That lovely girl was dead.
>
> She said she was to bear your child,
> And thought you would be glad,
> And you'd be married ere it showed;
> You said that you'd been had,
> That you'd not marry her at all—
> It made her very sad.
>
> She threatened that she'd advertise
> That you her heart had won;
> But that would ruin your career
> So grand, yet just begun;
> And you were powered by the fear
> That you would soon be done.
>
> Some kill their love when they are young,
> And some when they are old;
> Some strangle with the hands of Lust;
> Some with the hands of Gold;
> But you did in that helpless girl
> Because your heart is cold.
>
> They caught you, tried you, let you off,
> The attorney was a goof;
> And from those slanders on your name

You just stood aloof;
Made pious noises, many prayers—
You knew they had no proof.

You did not die a death of shame
On that day of dark disgrace;
But God will send what you deserve,
He will not hide His face;
He'll mete out bullet, fire or sword—
He'll choose the time and place.

The poem reached into the past and hauled out memories he'd hoped he was done with. He'd just gotten started, like the poem said. It was in a red-neck county seat town in Alabama. He'd only been there two weeks, but he'd been asked to speak at the nigger school—the mayor thought a speech about how God intended us to consort with our own kind would be a good idea. She was the music teacher. Skin a creamy tan. Lovely boobs and a twitchy little ass. She'd come around to the motor home to show him an old Bible she'd inherited from her great-grandfather, who was a slave. He could still feel the excitement of bedding her. He didn't want any niggers hanging around his meetings, but when it came to a beauty in his bed he had no social prejudice.

Six weeks later he was holding a meeting a hundred miles up the road and she'd written that she had to see him. He just couldn't resist another tumble in her bed. Then, she told him she was pregnant, and wanted him to marry her, and if he didn't she'd tell the world he'd been screwing her. Well, a nigger wife was out of the question. The kind of folks he preached to might forgive him a little hanky-panky with a nice white girl, but they wouldn't stand for him fooling around with a black dame. He'd lost control. He hadn't meant to hurt her, just to scare her. But she'd started to scream, and he frantically choked her to death.

Some damn pickaninny had seen him leave her place, of course. And they found out she was pregnant. But he'd said she was seeking spiritual counsel and guidance, that he'd been interested only in the salvation of her soul, and that it was against his religion to cohabit with blacks (his lawyer had taught him what "cohabit" meant). The district attorney wasn't exactly a goof, like the poem said, but he hadn't tried very hard for a

conviction. Turned out Amelia—he couldn't even remember her
last name—had been an uppity nigger marching in civil-rights
parades and stuff like that. So the town sort of considered that
he'd done them a favor—if he had killed her—by getting rid of
the girl. Anyway, he was acquitted. The Lord had blessed him
again.

But that had been ten years ago. Who'd even hear about it
today? Who'd know enough about it to write that dumb poem?
Oh, well, why worry. Nobody could pin anything on him.

Had Full-Gospel Frankie heard of the Holy Terror and the
murder of the pastor and the priest he might have been scared.
But Frankie didn't read the papers, except the Saturday church
ads to check out what the opposition was doing, and to see if they
got his quarter-page ad the way he'd specified.

He picked up another envelope—this one lavender and per-
fumed. Oddly, the address was typed. This kind of letter—and
there were plenty of them—usually were in a feminine hand. But
he knew what the note would say. It, too, was typed. But it ran to
form. The sender needed spiritual counsel, but for reasons he
could guess needed to be discreet. She'd like to meet him tonight
at the east end of that little park near the tabernacle. She hoped
he'd drive his Cadillac because it had a bench seat, if he knew
what she meant. She'd be wearing a—Frankie smiled. He hadn't
lined up anything for the evening.

If Full-Gospel Frankie had had a magnifying glass handy, and
if he'd thought to compare the poem with the lavender letter, he
would have discovered that they'd been written with the same
typewriter.

Chapter Eight

An unrelenting December snow, pregnant with moisture, slapped gently at the window wall of the dining room of Good Shepherd's penthouse parsonage, half obscuring the view of the Chicago skyline and the lake. But Randollph wasn't looking out the window anyway. He was looking at his wife. Sam was dressed for business. A beige wool suit, deceptive in its simplicity, its perfect fit proclaiming its quality. Black calfskin boots zippered snugly to the knee. A black scarf bearing a plain silver pin in some modern artist's concept of what a fish, in outline, looked like. Her bright red hair pulled back and tied at the nape of her neck with a black ribbon emphasizing the excellent bone structure of her face. Sam's business was appearing before the harsh eye of the television camera. She was careful to give it no chance to probe for imperfections.

I was coupled with this lovely creature in a lengthy and ecstatic coupling just a few hours ago, Randollph thought, and—the fates willing—I'll couple with her again tonight.

"Why are you looking at me like that, husband dear?" Sam asked.

"Just feasting my eyes and soul on your beauty," he said.

"Oh, nonsense! I'm a good-looking girl, but my nose is a mite short, my hair is too red, and I've got a few freckles."

"I see nothing but perfection."

"Hoo, boy! You see through a glass darkly, as old St. Paul once said." But she was pleased. "I thought I detected a horny glint in your eye."

"You did. Prompted by memory and anticipation."

Sam laughed. Randollph realized that one of the best among many bests about Sam was her laugh. It rippled with joy, the kind of laugh which reflected a healthy and uncomplicated lust for life.

"I might have a headache tonight," she said.

"So take a couple of aspirins."

"Yes, Dr. Randollph. But you know I won't have one. In fact, I'll probably be chasing you."

"I like sexually aggressive women."

"Whoa! You'd better rephrase that. You mean you like me to be sexually aggressive."

"I stand corrected." Randollph grinned at her.

Clarence Higbee rattled the dishes on the serving cart, as he always did, to send before him a diplomatic message that he would momentarily be within hearing and that they should adjust their conversation to topics appropriate to the ears of a domestic.

"Morning, sir, madam," Clarence said in a voice polite enough to be friendly but modified by some tone achievable only by British veterans of household service, Randollph was convinced, that established a clear line between friendliness and familiarity without resorting to servility. He remembered that when Clarence had first come to the penthouse as majordomo, he wondered if he would ever accustom himself to Clarence's proper British ways. The diminutive man, completely bald, skin burned a rich brown by the sun and sea winds of his years as a ship's chef, always dressed in black jacket, gray striped trousers, and batwing collar, was a startling thing to a middle-class American eye. He insisted on an undemocratic recognition of a social hierarchy. Randollph was always addressed as "sir" or "doctor." The bishop was "your lordship" or "m'lord" because Church of England bishops were lords of the realm. Clarence had been raised in a Church of England orphanage, regarded the C of E as the one true church, but felt that all bishops deserved the rank of lord. Randollph had become accustomed to Clarence, of course, and felt an affection for the little bald man which he was careful never to express in words.

"What divine and fattening surprise do you have for us this morning, Clarence?" Sam asked. Randollph had begun by calling Clarence "Mr. Higbee," but Clarence had insisted that he was more comfortable when addressed, as was proper to his station, by his Christian name.

Clarence set out silver bowls on napery whiter than the snow on the window. The bowls held large grapefruit halves, the edges of the fruit serrated, bedded in ice.

"Just a simple dish of eggs baked in tomato shells, madam," he said to Sam. He whisked the cover off a silver chafing dish so that they could see the four ruby cups resting on four golden croûtes on a bed of parsley. "I brown the croûtes in butter. It gives them that nice color, as well as lending a richness to the taste."

"I'll bet it lends to the inches on my waist," Sam said. "What's the brown crust on the eggs?"

"A bit of parmesan cheese baked on at the last minute, madam. I also add a dash of sherry to the eggs. The British are partial to grilled or baked tomatoes for breakfast. I'm sure you'll be, too. I prepared two eggs each, but"—he looked at Randollph—"if either of you wish more it takes only moments to prepare them. This"—he pointed to a flat panlike dish but did not remove the cover—"is that excellent home-cured bacon I obtain from a farmer in Wisconsin, which you have had before. There are croissants and gooseberry jam which Dr. Randollph favors. Also the English marmalade you prefer, madam. And coffee, of course."

"Clarence, you spoil us," Randollph said.

"Not at all, Dr. Randollph. It is my duty—may I say my vocation—to purchase the highest-quality comestibles available, and to prepare them in the most attractive and edible manner my skills can devise. The fathers at the orphanage in which I was brought up taught us to respect God's creation. I do not believe that there is any blasphemy in treating our daily bread, as it were, with reverence. It is more healthful, and surely more pleasant, to eat good food well prepared, than to ingest greasy, badly-done meat or insipid vegetables. If you will permit me to say so, I regard my work as a Christian vocation. Not as important as the work of the bishop—or your work, Doctor. But good and acceptable in the sight of the Lord."

"Amen to that!" Randollph said.

Then Clarence, thinking perhaps he had spoken more than was appreciated from a domestic, excused himself with "If you need anything, you've but to ring."

Sam said, "I wish I felt that way about my job."

"But you like your job."

"I like it. I love it. It's exciting. It's good for my ego. And I do it well—"

"You certainly do!" Randollph pushed his grapefruit dish aside and helped himself to eggs and bacon.

"—but I don't think of it as very important."

"The difference between you and Clarence so far as your attitudes toward your jobs"—Randollph paused to choose his words carefully—"is that Clarence interprets life in terms of a long-held set of Christian values. He thinks of himself a craftsman molding and shaping a part of God's creation. He understands what few Christians understand—that God intended life to be enjoyed. His mission—I really believe he thinks of it as a mission—is to enhance, insofar as he is able, that enjoyment. He finds a spiritual reward in the skillful handling of a part of this material world."

"But, Professor, isn't gluttony a sin? And isn't Clarence encouraging us to gluttony?" Sam whacked her second egg with a fork, bringing a spurt of bright yellow to mingle with the red and white and brown, which Randollph thought was a pretty combination of colors.

"Yes and no," he said, grinning at her.

"Come on! Don't be wishy-washy."

"Yes, gluttony is a sin," Randollph answered her. "And no, Clarence isn't encouraging us to gluttony. I'm sure he believes gluttony is founded in a disregard for the sacredness of this material, this created world. The glutton is contemptuous not only of what is set before him, but of himself. Clarence would consider this an abuse of creation. If we were gluttons he'd quit his job with us. That's why, I suspect, he has quit a number of very nice jobs. Another slice of this superb bacon?"

"Get thee behind me, Randollph. I'll have to skip lunch now."

"Clarence would approve of that."

"Why?"

"Because he serves wholesome food excellently prepared. Better to load up on the good stuff here than supplement it with the miserable offerings of some fry cook."

Sam looked out the window wall, which was now lathered with an opaque and sticky wetness. "Damn this snow! I hate it"— she turned and grinned at Randollph—"even if it is a part of God's creation. You know, love, when I was growing up in a small-town Presbyterian church we had a lot of church suppers and people always pushed the preacher to eat, eat lots of everything. They made jokes about how preachers like to eat. They said preachers were especially fond of fried chicken, stuff like that. Isn't that encouragement to gluttony, encouragement to sin, according to your view?"

"Yes, but they didn't understand what they were doing, those Presbyterians of yours. I grew up in a small-town church, too. It was the same there."

"Why do they do it?"

"Probably because they know—though they couldn't articulate it—they expect the pastor to abjure the excesses of the flesh— even the ones they practice themselves. As compensation, they encourage their pastors to gluttony because they don't think of gluttony as a very serious sin."

"Oh, hell, pass the bacon. All this talk about food makes me hungry, and I don't have to hurry to work today. You haven't told me why my attitude toward my job is different from Clarence's."

"Because you claim you are an agnostic."

"So? Does the fact that I am an agnostic bother my handsome ordained spouse?"

"Not really."

"Amplify that."

Randollph thought a moment before he answered. "I lay claim to being a Christian—not because I think I'm good, and for a certainty not because I'm pious—but because I am convinced that it's the best way of looking at life. There's a lot to be said for honest agnosticism. I'd rather you'd be an honest agnostic than a credulous Christian."

"Will you try to convert me?"

"No. Well, strike that. I won't try to see that you are born again.

I'll probably continue to give you my reasons and explanations for what I believe. That would be trying to convert you, I suppose. But enough theology for one morning. What's in the paper?"

"You preach a good sermon, Reverend," Sammy said. She opened the paper. "Oh, my God! There's been another one."

"Another what?"

"Here, I'll read it to you. The headline is: 'HOLY TERROR DOES IT AGAIN.'" She began to read the story.

"'The body of the Reverend Franklin Pierce McDougall, known professionally as Full-Gospel Frankie, was discovered early this morning by a police patrol checking on a 1979 Cadillac with the motor running, parked not far from McDougall's West Side tabernacle. McDougall had been shot through the head with a small-caliber weapon.

"'Lieutenant Michael Casey, Homicide, who is in charge of the Holy Terror murder investigation, said that this was the third in a series of clergy killings probably by the same person. Lieutenant Casey said a quick check of McDougall's office at the tabernacle had turned up a threatening poem. The Holy Terror, the name by which this unknown assailant has come to be called because he kills only clergymen, also sent warning poems to his other two victims. Lieutenant Casey said the threatening poem to McDougall was being processed by the police laboratory and could not be released as yet. He did say that the style is imitative of Oscar Wilde's "Ballad of Reading Gaol," and that it alleged McDougall had been involved in the killing of a young woman some years ago. The police have not had time to investigate this allegation.'" Sam laid the paper by her plate. "That's awful!"

"Lieutenant Casey certainly made the point that he isn't just a dumb cop, that he knows his English literature," Randollph observed. "Made it rather neatly, too. He's rather sensitive about that. He's always reminding me, in one way or another, that he's a college man."

"Oh, come on, Randollph, is that all you have to say? You're a clergyman. This Holy Terror jerk might pick on you." Sam's eyes showed her concern.

Randollph took her hand. "My dearest, beautiful, red-headed agnostic, I am serious. Of course I weep for—what's his name—Full-Gospel Frankie, no matter how dubious his clerical credentials and in spite of the putative misdeeds in his murky past. I weep for him as I would for any mortal fallen in untimely death."

Sammy drew her hand away impatiently. "That's not what I meant. I interviewed him once on *Sam Stack's Chicago*. He was a long foul ball and probably deserved what he got. He tried to make a pass at me, the moron."

"Can't blame him for that."

"Oh, be serious! I'm worried about you."

"I know," Randollph said gently. "And I'm glad. But you must remember, Samantha, that the three murder victims to date were, apparently, guilty of some scandalous or felonious behavior. That was the excuse for the murderer to do them in. I've never killed anyone. I've never committed a felony. And—since ordination anyway—I've not engaged in anything that could be construed as scandalous behavior."

Sam brightened. "That makes me feel better. You know, Randollph, it just occurred to me that I had all three of these guys—Horner, Gropius, and Frankie—on my show. I've had so many people on it I forget who they all are unless something reminds me. Do you suppose that has any significance—all three being on my show?"

"I can't see how. Read me something cheerful. What does Thea hear today?"

Sam picked up the paper and turned to Thea Mason's column. "'Thea hears,'" she read, "'that her honor the mayor is about to fire one of our better-known political wheeler-dealers from his plush political job because of his "unprofessional conduct,"' whatever that means. . . . 'Thea hears that'—oh, damn!"

"Is that what Thea hears?"

"No, silly. She hears that 'The Reverend Dr. Cesare Paul Randollph, ex-football star and now the pastor of Chicago's prestigious Church of the Good Shepherd, clashed with Thaddeus Barry, Jr., known to all as Chicago's number-one warrior against pornography, at a recent meeting of Good Shepherd's governing board. Mr. Barry, a member of the board, asked the church to go on record as supporting Citizens for a Moral America in its current crusade to stamp out pornography in Chicago, and to invite the Reverend Jack Dan Lancer, national secretary of Citizens, etcetera, to speak in Good Shepherd's pulpit. Dr. Randollph refused both requests, and Mr. Barry accused him of being a pornography-loving preacher. Must have been some church board meeting!'" Sam slammed the paper on the table. "I'd like to kick her ass!"

Randollph chuckled. "Why? She told the truth, if not the whole truth."

Sam laid her head on his shoulder. "Oh, Randollph," she said in a small voice, "because this will hurt you, and I don't want you hurt. And because I told her about it. Do you want to beat me?"

Randollph stroked her hair. "That hardly merits a beating. Barry's going to keep after me anyway. We'll hear more from him. It may get nasty, but that isn't your fault. How did you happen to tell her?"

Sam raised her head. "She was over at the studio yesterday. It's one of her regular stops, we hear lots of gossip. A bunch of us were in the lunchroom, and I got to bragging about how my courageous husband had stood up for freedom of speech and against fuddy-duddyism. Media people are pretty nervous about freedom of speech these days, what with the Burger Supreme Court and all. But I just never thought Thea would put it in her column—at least not the way she did."

"Don't blame her. Were I a columnist I'd write it the way she wrote it. Gossip columnists are supposed to be as sensational as possible. Her admitted animosity toward anything to do with the church might be showing a bit here. She's caught Good Shepherd with its pants down—partway, at least—and she's made the most of it."

Sam was only partly mollified. "I'd still like to kick her ass! What's in the mail?"

Randollph picked several envelopes from the letter tray on which Clarence had placed them. "Bills. A letter from your sister." He tossed it to her. "Something from the alumni secretary of my college—probably soliciting contributions. Here's one without a return address." He slit it open and extracted a single typed sheet. Randollph read:

> Randollph, this is stupid stuff;
> You threw a football hard enough;
> But fame is fleeting, that was clear,
> You studied for a new career.

But oh, good Lord, the way you take,
It gives a chap the belly-ache.
You know your lines, you know your people;
You live beneath a Gothic steeple;
You prate of God, the triune one
The time has come that you're undone.
The dirty show, the dirty book
Ah, will the reverend have a look?
Yes, lustful, concupiscent, bad;
What a God's man you are, lad.

Why, if you're holding out for smut;
And, Lord knows, you're not some nut,
Then time has come that you must fade,
Or why were Mauser pistols made?
A gun does more than Randollph can
To justify God's ways to man.

Randollph, finished, silently handed the poem to Samantha.

Chapter Nine

"Call it off." Lieutenant Casey's voice was hard. "You can have this installation thing after we've nailed this Holy Terror. This guy"—he tapped the threatening poem on the table in front of him—"means business."

Casey didn't look like a cop, Randollph thought. He looked like an up-and-coming executive in a business tolerant enough to permit its executives some small creativity in how they dressed. Randollph admired Casey's subdued gray plaid vested suit. The lieutenant was climbing up the ladder of the police hierarchy, and took care to outfit himself so as to advertise that he would at least look like a credit to the department when he arrived at the higher plateaus of leadership. But today he sounded like a cop. His customary urbane manner had disappeared. He was talking tough.

Captain Manahan had requested a conference with the bishop and Randollph. Ordinarily he would have ordered them to come to his office. But this was Chicago. In Chicago, a Roman Catholic town where the R.C.s ran the police department, public servants always exhibited a proper deference toward the clergy. But you still had to extend to the non-Romans all the courtesy due priests of the one true church or you were in for a hell of a lot of trouble. So Manahan had volunteered to come to the bishop and Randollph. They were now all seated together around a long walnut table in the room where the bishop met with delegations, citizen's groups, or anyone with a godly axe to grind.

"No," Randollph said.

"What you mean, no? You want to be victim number four?" Casey was just short of being unpleasant.

"Of course I don't want to be victim number four. I'm scared stiff. This Holy Terror, whoever he is, has upset the hell out of my life." Randollph realized that he was on edge. He hardly ever used profanity, not even a mild hell or damn. This was a sign, he supposed, of the anxiety which had gripped him like a hostile dog with teeth tearing at his flesh. He'd felt like this ever since he'd received that damned poem. Occasionally, blanketed by the bliss of his new life with Samantha, he'd been nagged by the thought "This can't last. Life is too wonderful! I've done nothing to deserve such great good fortune. This is too perfect. Something nasty is lingering out there, waiting the moment to pounce and shred the fabric of my joy." He put it down to the gloomy theology of his youth which held that life here shouldn't be too much fun, or what's a heaven for? But there had been something lingering out there. It had pounced. Or rather, it had announced it was going to pounce and destroy. And the terror of waiting for that awful moment, the moment when he would pass from the complex combination of work and friends and frustrations and hurdles to be gotten over and all the lovely sensations of life and love and ecstasy which added up to a state called happiness, pass from all this to a state of nothingness until, after the slow march of millenia after millenia, that day when all things are made new—the terror of waiting was worse by far than the moment itself would be. He supposed the Holy Terror knew this. This was the bang he got out of it.

"Then call it off, for God's sake," Casey insisted. "I don't know exactly what an installation ceremony is like, but it's public, there'll be all sorts of people milling around. That's a perfect time for this nut to get at you."

"And what is my alternative?"

"What do you mean?"

"Do I call off Sunday services? Do I cancel all public appearances? Do I hire a bullet-proof car and bodyguards? Do I refuse to set foot out of my penthouse parsonage until you catch this Holy Terror? I'd be safe in the parsonage. Unless he came in a helicopter he couldn't get at me there. But what kind of a life would that be? At the rate you're going I might spend the rest of my life there." Randollph knew this was cruel. He suspected that some of Casey's truculence was generated by a friendly concern. But he'd been pushed as far as he was going to be pushed.

Captain Manahan pushed his fat butt around in the thinly upholstered conference chair seeking a position of maximum comfort. He unpeeled a cigar without asking the bishop's permission to smoke. "Well, now," he said as he lit up, "maybe the best solution would be for me t' order this, wat'cha call it, installation canceled." The bishop started to speak, but Manahan stopped him. "I know, Bishop, you could challenge me. But city inspectors can always find violations of fire codes, stuff like that. No way you're gonna hold a meeting in a church that don't meet safety standards. Egg on your face, somethin' happens."

Randollph thought he saw Casey wince as his boss made this crude threat. But the bishop was all pleasantness and smiles. "I share your concern, of course, for Dr. Randollph," he said. "The decision, though, should be his to make. If he wishes to postpone his installation service, we'll postpone it."

"But I don't wish to postpone it," Randollph said.

"Then we'll have it," the bishop said.

"Din' ya hear what I said?" Captain Manahan was being downright rude now. Randollph wondered if the captain would talk that way to the cardinal archbishop of Chicago.

"I heard what you said, yes," the bishop said to the captain. "I think, though, we should talk it over with my good friend the commissioner. It would be his responsibility to say a final yea or nay, wouldn't it? Perhaps he would have some light to shed on the situation we don't have. I'd urge him, of course, to let Dr. Randollph make the decision. After all, this is an important event in the life of the city. The mayor will take part. Leading clergy from all denominations will participate. The cardinal, unfortunately, will be in Rome at the time, but Bishop O'Manny will deliver the charge to the pastor. If it is a matter of Dr. Randollph's safety we can cancel easily enough. But if he's determined to go ahead with it, I'd hate to disrupt such an, ah, elaborately planned occasion. And I'm sure the commissioner would too."

Manahan knew enough to know that he'd been challenged, rebuked, and insulted. He chomped savagely on his cigar. Randollph was amazed, once more, at Freddie's skill at being a hard-nosed executive yet never saying a hard word. He'd just told Captain Manahan, "Look, buster, if you want to match political weight with me you should understand your power is but a pat on the wrist compared with the muscle I can muster. When it comes to clout, you're not in my class." Strong words, but he'd said them with the kindest expression. Randollph was sure Casey was struggling to suppress a smirk.

Casey sighed in resignation. "I see your point, Bishop. I still don't think it's a good idea, but if I were in Dr. Randollph's place I'd probably want to go ahead with it, too. I mean, a man can't hide from the world forever."

"Perhaps," the bishop suggested, "you could outline precautions that C.P.—Dr. Randollph—could take?"

"Yeah, sure." Captain Manahan reasserted his right to dominate and recover some of the dignity the bishop had stripped from him. "Wadda ya' think, Mike? Police guard?"

"Yes," Casey answered, "a policeman—plainclothes, of course, to accompany Dr. Randollph wherever he goes. Can the elevator that runs to the penthouse be stopped at all floors? I seem to remember that it can."

Another neat thrust at Manahan, Randollph thought. Casey's established that he's been a guest in the penthouse. It's like saying "Captain, I move in wider and better social circles than you do."

"Yes," Randollph told him.

"Then we'll have to take it out of service until"—he groped for a euphemism—"for the duration."

"The hotel that leases from the church won't like that," Randollph said. "The elevators are busy enough as it is. They look on the penthouse as a nuisance, anyway, since it brings the hotel no revenue."

"They'll just have to lump it," Casey said. "Do you mind?"

"No." Randollph permitted himself a smile. "No, I don't mind."

"You'll have to use it, of course. Sam—your wife—and any legitimate guests. But we'll have a police officer in the lobby round the clock. Tell anyone you are expecting to check with the desk clerk. He'll be instructed to phone you. A nuisance, but not too much of one considering the danger. We really don't know how clever this Holy Terror guy is. After all, the first three seem to have been easy kills for him. We'll try to make it tough for him to get at you."

Randollph didn't like the idea of a policeman for constant company, but he yielded gracefully. "The Holy Terror's poems are rather clever. Let's hope his cleverness is limited to his literary efforts. And, Lieutenant, I apologize for my rudeness."

"What rudeness?"

"Twitting you about your failure to apprehend this nut."

"Forget it. Bishop, if I may use a phone I'll set up the protection before I leave the building."

The bishop gestured toward his office. "By all means. We'll all feel more secure when it's done."

Casey and Manahan rose and shook hands with the bishop and Randollph.

"By the way, Doctor, that poem the Holy Terror sent you is an imitation of A. E. Housman, isn't it?"

Randollph knew that Casey hoped he'd say "I haven't the faintest idea."

"Yes," Randollph answered. "More specifically, it takes the epilogue to 'A Shropshire Lad' as its model."

No point in letting Lieutenant Michael Casey leave one up. It might encourage him to the sin of intellectual pride.

After the policemen had gone, Randollph said, "Freddie, just why do we need to have such a showy installation service anyway? I can't recall ever attending a pastoral installation. Why me?"

The bishop sat down, crossed black-trousered legs, and folded his hands across his plump stomach. "For two reasons, C.P."

"And they are?"

"Number one, though the Presbyterians and Congregationalists make a big occasion of a pastoral-installation service, our denomination never has. We scarcely note the coming and going of pastoral incumbents. I think that a mistake. I believe it should be in our tradition, and I'm trying to put it there. I've encouraged all our churches to observe it. So when a pastor is named to our most prominent church in these parts, I'd be remiss were I to let that church omit the ceremony. So," he said genially, "you're stuck with it."

"O.K., Freddie, I see that. What's your other reason?"

"Publicity." The bishop smiled a bland episcopal smile. "Local publicity. You're a most publicizable personality, C.P. We don't often get a chance to blow our denominational trumpet in this city. We're outnumbered. The only time one of our pastors gets his or her name in the headlines is when they are guilty of some variety of scandalous conduct. The press likes that. But, the Lord be praised, that doesn't occur often. We'll never have another chance like this. A nationally known professional football player is installed as pastor of a large, old-line prestigious church located in the bosom of a high-rise office building and hotel smack downtown in the nation's second city. I'd be a poor excuse for a bishop were I not to make the most of this opportunity—an opportunity I choose to look on as offered by a beneficent Providence." The bishop sat back, having made his case.

"I'm not sure I'm as enthusiastic about it as you are, Freddie."

"Tell me, C.P., did you dislike personal publicity when you were playing football?"

"No, of course not," Randollph answered. "I liked it. I liked it very much. I hired a clipping service. I kept scrapbooks. Still have them. Don't look at them often, but still have them. But that's different."

"Why so?"

"It's hard to explain, Freddie."

"Try."

Randollph was thoughtful. "I quit playing football, not because I didn't like it. I did like it. Loved it. I quit because I couldn't escape the feeling that there had to be something more important in life. Call it a conversion, if you like, though there was no Damascus Road experience for me. It was more like a growing awareness of something missing."

"More conversions come about that way than on the Damascus Road," the bishop observed. "What you're trying to say, C.P., is that you don't want your new profession to be like your former profession."

"I guess that's it. I've no objection to publicizing sports. But when you use the same tactics to publicize the church it seems tawdry. Am I making any sense to you?"

"Some," the bishop admitted. "You don't want to be one of those ex-sports heroes who says, 'I'm making touchdowns for Christ' or 'I'm in there punching for the Lord.'"

"Exactly, Freddie. I did some of that in my days with Athletes for Christ, and I'd like to forget it."

"Nonetheless, C.P., the Lord's team"—the bishop smiled—"if you'll forgive the metaphor, needs to let the world know that, how does the cliché go, that it has come to play."

Randollph burst out laughing. "Freddie, Freddie, I never could get around you. You have a plausible reason for everything you want to do."

"All good administrators can find a plausible reason for what they do. Even hard decisions, necessary but unpleasant actions go down better when coated with a plausible reason." The bishop suddenly turned serious. "But, C.P., I don't want you to think that I'm pushing you to go ahead with the installation just for the sake of the publicity. It can be postponed, or canceled."

Randollph got up and walked to the window. A cold winter sun washed the hurrying people in the streets. Impatient traffic was frustrated by what appeared to be a slight accident and a large argument. Was the Holy Terror in that crowd, planning when and how to make the Reverend Dr. Cesare Paul Randollph the next victim of his deadly whimsy? Randollph knew that until the Terror was laid by the heels he'd know no peace.

"Freddie, if I thought that by canceling the ordination or taking a long vacation I could be safe, I would. I'm not foolhardy. But where do I go to escape? There's no place to hide. God alone knows what motivates him—"

"Presumably, the Holy Terror knows."

"Maybe. Maybe not. He may think he's doing this for one reason, whereas the real motive is concealed under layers of his subconscious. But at least I've been warned—"

"So were the others."

"That's true," Randollph said. "But I doubt they took it seriously. Horner wouldn't have known what to make of the warning. Father Gropius, given his notoriety, probably got all kinds of nut letters. And that evangelist chap—"

"'Full-Gospel Frankie' he called himself," the bishop broke in. "A name that would appeal to the devout but ignorant, those poor souls that are the most easily fleeced among the Lord's lambs."

"Full-Gospel Frankie was no doubt a holy shyster," Randollph said. "Which is better than being a Holy Terror. But he wouldn't have known what to make of that warning poem. I'll bet he hardly read the papers. But I do know what to make out of it. You can bet that I'll take every precaution to stay alive. I am going to have a police guard. And I have the good fortune to live in a virtually impregnable fortress in the sky. I'll stay out of dark places. It won't be fun, but I'll be looking over my shoulder all the time. Other than that, it's business as usual. The installation is on."

"So be it," the bishop said. He didn't look very happy.

Chapter Ten

The floor beneath the nave of the Church of the Good Shepherd is a large area planned for the needs of the church choir, and for the Christian education of what—when the church had been built—was a large and growing body of pupils largely disinterested in the simplistic theology dished out to them by untrained volunteer teachers who hadn't a clue as to what the Bible was all about.

Unfortunately, the unanticipated decline of the Sunday school, evident everywhere, but especially disastrous to a church situated in the heart of a city, had left Good Shepherd with a lot of unused space. But tonight, much of it was in use. A number of rooms had been fitted out with mirrors and portable coat racks for the convenience of the visiting clergy who had to shuck topcoats and jackets, then fit themselves into ecclesiastical garments appropriate to their faith. The washrooms were also doing a brisk business. These reverend gentlemen knew from experience that they were in for a long service and availed themselves of this last chance to relieve clerical bladders.

Randollph, sharing a dressing room with the bishop and Amory Allen, president of the Greater Chicago Association of

Priests, Ministers and Rabbis, felt self-conscious. He zipped up his black pulpit robe with the blacker doctor's bars like huge sergeant's stripes decorating the sleeves. He draped a stole around his neck, red, the color for Pentecost Sunday and for important churchly conclaves and occasions. Then he ducked into his long doctor's hood, lined with red and gold silk, the colors of his graduate school alma mater. "Freddie, I look like the NBC peacock," he complained to the bishop.

"So you do." The bishop, unperturbed, zipped up his robe, leaving a swatch of his episcopal purple dickey exposed. "This is supposed to be a colorful occasion. And all this regalia will look very nice on television."

"You look grand, doctor." Amory Allen's Scotch accent stretched the "grand" making it come out as "graannd." Allen, Randolph thought, would be unique in the procession of choir, clergy, and assorted dignitaries. He had a doctorate in theology from the University of Edinburgh, and wore a scarlet robe and European-style mortar board which reminded Randollph of the flat hat that graced the round head of Martin Luther in most of his portraits. Allen surveyed Randollph. "I wish I had your stature, your imposing physical presence. A big, handsome preacher projects more authority from the pulpit than a skinny five-foot-eight like me."

"You make up for it in wit and intelligence," Randollph said. He suspected that Allen liked to be flattered. "I wish I had your Scotch burr."

"They say that a Scotch burr is worth an extra ten thousand dollars in salary to any Presbyterian preacher," Allen replied cheerfully. In my case I'm not so sure." Allen, Randolph knew, had one of the highest salaries of any Chicago clergyman. He was also certain that Allen didn't make any effort to suppress his accent.

The bishop tugged his stole in place. "Actually, we all look impressive," he said. "Hard not to in these gaudy habiliments."

"Don't you think we're overdoing it a little, Freddie?" Randollph thought it was good for the bishop's soul to be challenged once in a while. "We're supposed to proclaim good news to the poor. How can we expect them to listen when we're decked out like emperors?"

The bishop smiled a tolerant smile. "In the first place, C.P., we aren't preaching to the poor. Not tonight, anyway. The people here are all more or less successful—as is your Sunday congregation. Good Shepherd has no members that could be described as poor." He turned to the president of the Greater Chicago Association of Ministers, Priests and Rabbis. "I'll bet Dr. Allen hasn't a member of his flock who has ever missed a meal. Am I correct, Doctor?"

"I expect so," Allen admitted.

"For better or for worse," the bishop went on, "all of our mainline churches preach to the middle and upper middle classes. They may not all be rich, but they all escape the description of 'poor.' A preacher in rags would not impress them."

"That's true." Amory Allen said. "It sometimes troubles me."

"Me too," Randollph chimed in.

"I regret it, I wish our churches attracted more than the middle class," the bishop said. "I've wrestled with this problem throughout my ministry. I've yet to find a solution to the problem. Meanwhile, I'm charged with the responsibility of seeing that the gospel is preached to the kind of people who make up our churches. That is the reality with which I have to deal."

"Sounds a bit self-serving to me, Freddie," Randollph said.

"This regalia"—the bishop patted his pulpit gown—"is not only a symbol of our office but a uniform of leadership."

"Like the military?" Amory Allen asked.

"Yes, like the military. Would General Patton have won his battles wearing white tie and tails? Could Napoleon have conquered Europe in his skivvies?"

Amory Allen laughed. "I'm afraid he's got you, Dr. Randollph."

"I give up." Randollph bowed to the bishop. "I keep trying to best him in an argument, but I never do. Anyway, I rather fancy myself in these duds." He knew that he was carrying on the conversation to quell his nervousness about being the center of attention. He still felt a quivering anxiety, a constant awareness that someone out there was after him.

They went out to what had once been the assembly hall for the Sunday school. The scene, Randollph thought, was from the Middle Ages. The beamed ceiling looked down on figures in gowns as multicolored as a dye chart. The Roman Catholic bishop was wearing a miter, the Byzantine finery of a Greek

Orthodox bishop was fit to clothe a Constantine on his coronation day. Somber black. Cool blue. Hot red. And purple. And orange. And yellow. Freddie would have his colorful occasion.

Dan Gantry and O. Bertram Smelser, associate pastors of Good Shepherd, were marshals. They would organize the procession, lead it in, see that no absent-minded divine missed a turn or wandered to a seat assigned to someone else. Smelser, Randollph knew, was not temperamentally equipped to organize this chaos, but Dan was.

Dan Gantry, wearing a plain black gown, red stole, and master's hood, stepped up on a platform at one end of the hall, pounded his marshal's staff on the floor, and shouted, "Hear ye, hear ye. Quiet!" he paused as the animated chatter faded down, then continued. "Everyone listen. Time's come to get this show on the road. You in the blue robe back there, quit talking and pay attention. You don't listen, you don't know what you're sup-posed to do and you'll screw up. O.K. Now let's line up. Choir first."

Tony Agostino, Good Shepherd's organist and choirmaster, was already upstairs playing the organ voluntary, but he'd organized the mixture of professional (and well-paid) voices and volunteers who just liked to sing into tight formation. The choir marched to the door which led to the stairs which led to the narthex.

"O.K., now I'll read your names. First name I read forms up on the left, next one on the right, then left, right, left, right. Got it? Here we go." Dan read the names rapidly, interspersed with an occasional "Snap it up, snap it up." The reverend gentlemen and ladies, along with civic dignitaries, sorted themselves into pairs and a procession. Randollph winced at Dan's drill-sergeant style, and at the same time admired the quickness and efficiency with which he did his job. A few ecclesiastical feathers might have been ruffled, but this would do them no harm.

"Now," Dan said, "the first three rows of seats on each side of the aisle are reserved for you—except the choir, of course, and those of you who will be in the chancel. They know who they are. We've allowed plenty of room. Mr. Smelser and I will direct you. And we'll lead you out. Watch your spacing. An arm's length and a little more between each pair of you. Questions? None? Good! O.K., bring in the books."

Dan had recruited a squad of ladies from the Women's Guild to distribute hymnals. A janitor wheeled in a dolly piled with red-backed books and the ladies saw to it that each member of the procession had one.

"Everyone got a book? Fine! Now everyone sing the processional hymn as we march in. Anyone who's not singing, got his book under his arm, looks like he's showing off, trying to draw attention to himself. Same thing on the recessional. All set? Our bishop will now address you." Dan stood aside and the bishop stepped up on the platform. He welcomed them. He thanked them for their cooperation in making this occasion possible. He invoked the divine blessing on all of them and on the service to come. Then the marshals and the choir led the procession up the stairs into the narthex.

The Church of the Good Shepherd pretended, outside, to be Gothic insofar as it pretended to be a church at all. The main entrance consisted of heavy doors set in pointed arches chiseled from stone. Forty or so stories above the street a huge multi-storied Gothic steeple trimmed with gargoyles and other medieval monsters ended the upward thrust of the building.

But inside, Gothic was abandoned in favor of a bastard Byzantine. The nave was capped with a pitched roof unlikely to remind anyone of Carthage or Constantinople. But there were columns aplenty crusted with blue and gold mosaics. There was a triptych of gold-leafed saints peering down on the altar. There was a pulpit of blue tile aflame with gold symbols. Randollph's impression, when he had first seen the nave of Good Shepherd, was of spirituality gone to seed. He had told the bishop that it looked vaguely pagan, a house of worship where money was an acceptable substitute for prayer and ritual, a sufficient excuse for trivial living. "But," he told the bishop, "I like it. It's gaudy and it's phony, but I like it. I suppose that's because I like color and am not offended by a little vulgarity."

Tony Agostino put the hammer down on the organ, all its pipes bursting out with "Cwm Rhondda," the sturdy Welsh melody to which the processional hymn was set.

"'God of grace, and God of glory,'" the choir sang with controlled power. The congregation was singing now, and each pair in the procession picked up the hymn at whatever point it had reached as they came through the doors of the narthex into the nave.

Randollph couldn't see any of this, though the singing washed down the stairs where he was standing. He was at the end of the procession, the place of honor, paired with the Roman Catholic auxiliary bishop of Chicago, and it was taking a long time to string the dozens of reverend clergy into the nave. Randollph had expected to march in with Freddie at his side, but Freddie had underlined the ecumenical character of the service by giving way to the prelate of a Christian sect which claimed—but not very loudly anymore—to be the one true church. His Eminence, Bishop Terence Kevin O'Manny, was not at all what Randollph had expected, which was a crusty, aloof servant of Christ who probably regarded all this as the pretensions of an ersatz faith. The bishop was, instead, a sleek and amiable man, no more than a decade older than himself, Randollph estimated, whose black hair and olive complexion could be traced to some sailor or grandee who made it to the shore of Eire after the defeat of the Spanish Armada.

"Good hymn, this," the bishop said pleasantly, thumping his open hymn book with the finger which bore his episcopal ring. "Modern. Good poetry. Says something that needs to be said. Think I'll see if we can't put it in one of our hymn books."

Rabbi Amos Lehman, who ran a large and wealthy reformed temple in a North Shore suburb, said: "This is a hymn of the Church. I don't know if I ought to sing it or not." Freddie had paired him with Amory Allen, just in front of Randollph and Bishop O'Manny. Another bow to the spirit of religious unity, Randollph supposed.

"Why not, Rabbi?" Randollph asked him. "After all, the Church got its start in the synagogue. But I don't have to tell you that."

"I suppose I could substitute 'temple' for 'church' when I sing it." The rabbi, Randollph knew, was just having a little fun. He was known for his liberal views, and his temple held a Sunday morning service, just like the Christians.

"Tell you what, you sing 'church' and I'll sing 'temple.' How's that for a symbol of brotherhood?"

"Splendid!" the rabbi said. "But, Dr. Randollph, you'd be getting the better end of the bargain. You are a Christian, but you're first a Jew. Jesus was a Jew—never anything else. He was educated as a Jew. He was faithful to his Judaism. He thought as a Jew. But as a Jew, I'm not a Christian."

"We Christians conveniently forget that we are Jews first," Bishop O'Manny said, as the procession began to move up the stairs.

"That you do," the rabbi said, holding up the skirt of his black robe so as not to trip over it. "As you know, Bishop, I honor Jesus. I often preach from a text in the gospels. There is no clash between an informed Judaism and the teachings of Jesus—except his claim to messiahship."

"And Jesus himself didn't have much to say about that," Randollph reminded the rabbi.

"That's true. It was your later Christian theologians who propounded the doctrines about Jesus being the son of God. The theologians did you much harm."

"That's what they usually do," Bishop O'Manny observed. The tail end of the procession was at the narthex doors.

When Randollph at last entered the nave he was surprised at the size of the crowd. Freddie had told him the place would be full, but Randollph found it difficult to believe that a lot of people would take the trouble to come out on a snowy evening to see him installed as the permanent pastor of the Church of the Good Shepherd. Some of them were here because they belonged to Good Shepherd and would naturally have an interest. Some of them were here because the Christian soldiers who manned Freddie's publicity department, and whose task it was to tell the world of Godly battles fought and won in this particular corner of the kingdom, had ballyhooed this installation service with all the subtlety of advance men for a circus. And some of them, no doubt, were here because the installee was a Christian curiosity, a well-known figure from the brutal world of professional football now turned to the gentler business of preaching and running a sacred corporation. Whatever their reasons for being here, Randollph mused, twelve hundred people—counting those in the balcony above his   l—when standing, looked like a lot of people.

Randollph knew the words of this hymn by heart, so—while he held his hymnal open and out as per Dan's instructions, he did not have to read from it. He knew he ought to feel lifted up. All this pageantry, the large crowd, the lusty and uplifting singing, the flicker of altar candles shining on the solemn-faced saints in the triptych, the glitter of the blue-and-gold crusted pillars which supported no weight of wall or roof, the sparkle of the costly stained glass windows freed from dependence on the vagaries of sunshine and daylight hours by discreet fluorescent tubes, created an ambience of tradition, mystery, and spiritual truth beyond definition or expression. It was just the right mood for the occasion, and the congregation caught it. But Randollph didn't. His mind kept asking the questions, "Is he here? Has the Holy Terror chosen this occasion to do me in? When will he try it? How will he try it? Is he somewhere in the balcony, ready to plug me when I stand up to respond to Bishop O'Manny's charge to me?"

He knew he was being a nervous old woman about this. What would the world say—the world that perceived him as a brave and fearless knight of a bone-cracking, muscle-tearing sport—if it knew that he saw death and destruction waiting for him in every corner? Would it scorn him as he scorned himself for what he could only call cowardice? He supposed that it would. He hoped that the world would not find him out.

Randollph, glancing to his right, saw the entrance to the chapel, now half-screened from the nave. The chapel, an appendage to the nave, was added many years after the building of the skyscraper church because a Mr. Jeremiah D. Pembroke, who had made a mint in the socially useful business of betting on the commodity market, wanted to give it. He specified that it be named the "Lydia Pembroke Memorial Chapel" in honor of his deceased spouse, a mousy lady devoted to the Church of the Good Shepherd, and whom Mr. Pembroke had neglected for years in favor of chorus girls and the better-class ladies of the evening. The trustees of Good Shepherd knew the old rascal was just putting a poultice on his bad conscience, but what the heck, it was money, wasn't it? Everyone now referred to this gem of fake Gothic architecture as the Lydia Pinkham Chapel. Dark and unoccupied now because no one could meditate and pray there with all the holy racket going on outside it, it reminded Randollph of the day, so short a time ago, when it was lit up by artfully concealed neon fixtures and Samantha Stack's presence. He wondered if he would be as frightened of this Holy Terror as he was if he had not married Sam. He had thought of himself as a reasonably happy man before he had met her. But his life was different now. He'd changed. His new status had brought a fulfillment that he had not imagined possible until he had met Sam. It had also made him vulnerable to the fear of losing what he had gained. This bliss which so intensified his sense of being alive; the joyful anticipation of seeing her at dinner; the small talk comparing the events of their day which wove their separate lives together; the tender and sensual lovemaking of the night. Randollph believed he had learned to like himself better just by loving Sammy. Now an unknown idiot with a gun wanted to stop his life when it had just begun, shoot him down in the name of some nameless delusion. It made him mad; it made him sad; and it made him very, very skittish.

As they came to the front of the church Randollph noticed, on his right, a pewful of burly young men, some black, some wearing beards, and was startled to recognize a number of his former teammates. Sticky Henderson, very black and very fast, had been Randollph's favorite receiver and best friend when they were with the Rams. Sticky, whose Christian name was Lamarr, and who had maybe lost a step or two of speed, was now with the Chicago Bears. Randollph guessed that Sticky had taken it upon himself to round up all the ex-Rams—retired, or now with Chicago, Green Bay, St. Louis, or Cleveland—for his installation. Sticky grinned at him as the procession swept by and made a thumbs-up sign. Randollph felt a lump in his throat. He was moved by this unexpected presence of a group of men whose interest in the Church of the Good Shepherd or in standard middle-class Christianity on display was minimal to nonexistent. They had come out of respect for him. Who wouldn't be moved?

As the last of the clergy not scheduled for participation in the formalities peeled off into their reserved pews, the members of the procession who would have something to pray or something to say during the evening proceeded into the chancel area. Bishop O'Manny split off to the left and followed Rabbi Lehman. Randollph split to the right after Dr. Amory Allen. The hymn coasted to an "Amen." Then, Rabbi Lehman went to the lectern and said a short prayer in Hebrew, which Randollph—who had forgotten most of his Hebrew—supposed invoked the blessing of the God of Abraham, Isaac, and Jacob on these doings. The choir answered with a musical plea that the Lord hear their prayer, and everyone sat down with many sighs and much rustling.

Freddie stood up, welcomed the congregation to "this great and solemn occasion," made brief remarks about what was happening, and introduced the mayor.

Her honor, the mayor, was a peppy blonde lady who looked sweet and feminine but was reputed to be a tough baby not at all unwilling to dump the hard and corrupt City Hall politicians of her own party when it suited her purposes. She made a sprightly little speech which did not neglect to mention the hopes and plans her administration had for turning Chicago into a better place. She tied it all up with a tribute to the Church of the Good Shepherd, its strategic location in the heart of the secular city, a bastion of moral values, a light to help guide us. She polished it all off by saying that she hoped every cleric moving to Chicago would be as handsome as Dr. Randollph, whose imposing appearance was exceeded only by the beauty of his wife and her good friend, Sam. Randollph looked for Sam, found her in the first pew behind the robed clergy, and saw that she was looking radiant. She had invited Lieutenant Casey and his wife, Liz, to sit with her. Casey, Randollph thought, looked worried.

Dr. Amory Allen spoke for all the ecclesiastics and ecclesiastical traditions represented by the Greater Chicago Association of Ministers, Priests and Rabbis. He took a text from the Gospel of John: "A new commandment I give to you, that you love one another; even as I have loved you, that you also love one another. By this all men will know that you are my disciples, if you have love for one another."

The words of Jesus, he said, were a description of the unity that held all people of good will and who loved God—held them together. He was sure that his good friend Rabbi Amos Lehman would forgive the reference to those who loved one another being disciples of Jesus, because there was nothing narrow or sectarian about it. All could confess this creedless creed. He said nice things about the Church of the Good Shepherd and its long history of religious leadership in Chicago. He said nice things about his good friend, Dr. Cesare Paul Randollph, making a little joke about the name Cesare being unusual, but appropriate because Randollph was an unusual man with an out-of-the-ordinary personal history of excellence in a vigorous professional sport, and eminence in the more passive task of teaching seminarians. But the name Paul, he said, was a constant reminder that Randollph stood in the tradition of that doughty old warrior for the Faith who was deterred neither by shipwreck, imprisonment, nor the lash from preaching the gospel of a God who loves and redeems us, and he hoped that the memory of Paul would be a beacon ever to guide this good man to be installed as pastor of this great church.

A polished, witty, and sophisticated performance, Randollph thought. Worthy of a preacher drawing down forty thousand a year in salary plus housing allowance and generous fringe benefits.

Then the choir shot a musical petition heavenward asking God to pay attention to the prayer He was about to hear. Bishop Freddie, in beautifully wrought prose, extolled Randollph's merits to the Almighty, and sought divine guidance for him as he went about the grave and vital task of leading this great church. The choir punctuated this orison by banging out a harmonious triple amen.

The choir then did an arrangement of Chesterton's hymn "O God of Earth and Altar" as the anthem of the evening. The Reverend Mr. O. Bertram Smelser, who kept a beady eye on all monies subtracted from Good Shepherd's treasury, had suggested that the evening's ritual include an offering "to defray the considerable expense" of this unbudgeted service. But the bishop vetoed the suggestion on the grounds that everyone knew Good Shepherd could afford these festivities and it would be a pious form of blackmail.

So when the choir had blasted out the last line of the anthem and subsided, the bishop called on His Eminence, Bishop Terence Kevin O'Manny, to deliver the charge to the Reverend Dr. Cesare Paul Randollph.

Bishop O'Manny dispensed with any ecumenical pleasantries. He figured, Randollph supposed, that his presence was testimony enough that the church of Peter, St. Francis, Ignatius Loyola, and not a few popes and high muckety-mucks of dubious character and best forgotten was at least now willing to say a prayer with the separated brethren. Randollph honored him for it.

His eminence took a text from Paul's (or somebody's) first letter to the young missionary Timothy. "'Let no one despise your youth,'" he read, "'but set the believers an example in speech and conduct, in love, in faith, in purity. . . . attend to the public reading of Scripture, to preaching, to teaching. Do not neglect the gift you have, which was given you when the elders laid their hands upon you. Take heed to yourself and to your teaching; hold to that, for by so doing you will save both yourself and your hearers.'"

Bishop O'Manny shut the Scriptures and—in terse and well-trimmed English—explained why this was about all the advice a preacher needed.

Randollph was not exactly a youth, the bishop said, but he was a young man. He was a youth in the sense that he was like Timothy, assuming his first pastoral responsibility. Good Shepherd was his first venture into the complicated and sometimes frustrating world of the parish ministry; a rookie, learning the ropes.

He wasn't entirely certain, his eminence said, that Paul should have exhorted Timothy to think of himself as an example. All the faithful ought to set good examples, lay or clergy. But laymen too often expected their pastors to lead personal lives which would strain a saint, and which the laymen had no intention whatever of emulating. Thus, the laity—quite unconsciously, he was sure—isolated the clergy from the stream of ordinary humanness. His own church, it was true, had a celibate clergy. But the vow of celibacy was taken voluntarily, and it had to do with vocation, not with a self-conscious moral superiority. The worst thing about looking on the clergy as example-setters, he said, was that the clergy came to think of themselves as professional example-setters, and ended up as moral prigs full of spiritual pride.

Be a gentleman, he advised Randollph. Be kind, courteous, well spoken. Conduct yourself so as to be a credit to your congregation. That's all anyone had a right to expect of a pastor. Be human. A good human, but human. He was rather sure St. Paul would settle for this, and he was quite sure he would.

As to the rest of Paul's counsel, Bishop O'Manny advised Randollph to stress preaching and teaching. These days, he said, you often have to combine the two. About the only time most laymen heard anything about the Bible was from a sermon. It takes skill, he warned, to get sound information about the Bible across "in a fifteen- or twenty-minute sermon, especially when

your listeners haven't the foggiest notion where the Bible came
from, why the various books were written, or what the Bible
really has to say. But the modern preacher has to do it if he is to
live up to Paul's instructions to Timothy."

But preaching isn't the same thing as teaching, he told
Randollph. Preaching is supposed to move people from one
spiritual and moral state to another. It is supposed to show them
what they had not seen before. At its best, he said, Christian
preaching offers a new outlook on life, mankind, and the world,
and what is important in life and what isn't—all of which we find
in the teaching of Jesus, teachings based on the insights of the
Judaism which nurtured him. This is what we mean by prophetic
preaching, the bishop said—which he knew that Randollph
already knew, but which the bishop wanted the congregation to
hear. Randollph, he said, had a God-given platform—the pulpit
of this great metropolitan church—for prophetic preaching.
Thousands would hear him. God knew, the bishop said, that this
great, wicked, beautiful, ugly city needed a thundering gospel of
righteousness and love. If he preached it, if his sermons always
rang with his own inner convictions, his sense of what was right,
a sense of rightness informed by his knowledge of the Bible and
Christian tradition, he'd be criticized, he might even be reviled.
But that just went with the job of being a prophetic preacher.
And, the bishop said, as St. Paul had pointed out, this kind of
faithfulness would bring salvation not only to his hearers, but to
himself as well.

Then the bishop made the sign of the cross, said, "In the name
of the Father, Son, and Holy Ghost," and sat down.

Randollph stood up to respond. He wasn't sure this was
customary in an installation service, but Freddie had insisted.
Randollph had told him that it was like being on display, like
trotting out the guest of honor for the mandatory "I'm overwhelmed by this honor" kind of talk.

"Nonsense, C.P.," the bishop had replied. "This is a major
transition not only in your life, but the life of this church. The
Christian church has always marked life's transitions with
ceremonies. Baptism, confirmation, marriage, death, ordination,
investiture of bishops, and the installation of pastors. Of course I
want to display you. The Church of the Good Shepherd has
survived a quarter century of your predecessor Art Hartshorne

preaching pleasant little homilies which charmed everyone but neither challenged nor offended anyone. Good Shepherd has been a Kiwanis club at prayer. I want the city to know that things have changed, that a different drummer is now beating the time. That's why you have to be on display. You'll see. This isn't just a religious circus. You'll feel the importance, the gravity of the moment. You'll be inspired by it. You'll be moved."

And inspired and moved he was, Randollph had to admit. Gone, for the moment at least, was anxiety about the Holy Terror and what that nameless nut might do to him.

He told the crowd that he felt what he understood every pope felt at his election—a crushing sense of his unworthiness for the task to which he had been assigned to lay his hand. He wanted to be a preacher in the tradition of Amos and Jeremiah and Isaiah as Bishop O'Manny had instructed him. He thought, he said, that any modern preacher who failed to tell the world what God expected in the way of justice and mercy and compassion from His people, from society, was simply copping out. He hoped he could say these things with a clear note of "Thus saith the Lord," for this was what he believed. As yet he had no credentials which would assure them that he could do it, but he intended to do it.

He intended also, he said, to stress the helping and healing ministry of Jesus. He would do this, insofar as he was able, on a one-to-one basis as a pastor. But he'd also try to structure the program of the church to stress it too.

He wanted to avoid any false humility, but he knew and they knew that this was an awesome responsibility he'd assumed, and he wasn't sure he was up to it. But it was a worthy task, one that not many people had the privilege of addressing. And he was heartened by the support manifested by this gathering. He was touched by the presence of his old comrades-in-arms from his football days. He named them. And he was inspired by these new comrades-in-arms, representing a variety of churches, faiths, and theologies who had graciously taken part in this service. They reminded him that he was not alone in this task, but was surrounded by a cloud of other witnesses. The Kingdom of God, he said, will come when it will come, and at God's good pleasure. But, meanwhile, all those who believed in it were under the injunction to work as if it were up to them to build it. He couldn't think of a nobler activity, and he was glad to be engaged in it.

Whenever he felt flawed and inadequate, as he often did, and as he felt tonight—only tonight it was writ large—he turned to a piece of Tennyson's poem "Ulysses" which always helped to nerve him up. He'd like to read it, not for them, but for himself. Then he quoted:

> " 'Tis not too late to seek a newer world.
> Push off, and sitting well in order smite
> The sounding furrows; for my purpose holds
> To sail beyond the sunset and the baths
> Of all the western stars until I die.
> . . .
> We are not now that strength which in old days
> Moved earth and heaven; that which we are, we are;
> One equal temper of heroic hearts,
> Made weak by time and fate, but strong in will
> To strive, to seek, to find, and not to yield."

Then he sat down.

There was a collective sigh from the congregation, an exhalation of breath that also exhaled tension. He looked for Samantha. She was blowing her nose. Liz Casey was dabbing at her eyes with a Kleenex. Randollph had that empty feeling he always had after he preached, and a nagging worry as to whether he had said the right thing or not, or whether he had overdone it. But he hadn't been putting on a performance. He'd said what he felt, what he believed, and if it wasn't good enough, so be it.

There was a brief ritual of installation. A bishop of the African Methodist Episcopal Church pronounced a fervent and lengthy benediction. Then Tony Agostino whipped the organ into "A Mighty Fortress Is Our God," the recessional hymn. A few years ago, Randollph knew, the Roman Catholics present would have taken this as a direct insult because Martin Luther had written the words and the music, and it was the battle hymn of the Protestant Reformation. Now, Randollph had heard, the hymn was much admired in at least the more progressive sections of the Roman Church and often used in their services.

> "A mighty fortress is our God,
> A bulwark never failing;"

the choir and congregation bellowed. Dan and Mr. Smelser saw to it that the reverend clergy and honorable dignitaries moved out of their pews on time, formed up correctly, and began the exit with dignity.

> "We will not fear, for God hath willed
> His truth to triumph through us,"

the people sang. They'd have to sing the hymn through four or five times to get everyone out, Randollph estimated. The choir and congregation had gotten to the last verse for the second time when the marshals signaled the chancel party to form up.

> "The spirit and the gifts are ours
> Through him who with us sideth."

They were, Randollph thought, making a joyful noise unto the Lord. What with twelve hundred people singing and Tony blasting away on the organ, you wouldn't be able to hear a bomb go off if it were dropped on the street in front of the church. It was exhilarating. It lifted you up.

The last of the chancel party was down now, and on the last lap up the center aisle. As he came abreast of the pew filled with football players Randollph leaned down to grasp the hand Sticky Henderson, with a wide and warm grin, was offering him.

> "And though this world, with devils filled
> Should threaten to undo us,"

the people sang. And suddenly Bishop Terence Kevin O'Manny, Randollph's partner, and on his right, collapsed to the floor.

"Hey, man," Sticky Henderson said to Randollph, "That dude's fainted. He needs help."

Several of the football players piled out of the pew and surrounded the fallen bishop. Tony Agostino, from his organ bench hidden from the congregation, couldn't see that something was happening and went on playing. The recessing clergy, backs to the event, marched right on like a snake with its tail cut off. But the congregation could see that something was happening. Voices died. There was a babble of oohs and ahs and what's going on.

Hedrick Drake, a big black tight end for the Bears and a student in medical school, bent over the bishop, then looked up at the huddle peering down at him.

"Can't help him none," he said. "He's dead. Somebody shot him through the head."

Chapter Eleven

By the time Hedrick Drake had pronounced Bishop O'Manny dead, Sergeant Garboski, who had this shift as Randollph's bodyguard, arrived at the huddle around the fallen prelate.

"Let's get you out of here," he ordered Randollph. "Here, you"—motioning to Sticky Henderson—"help me clear the way. We'll get the doc out the back door. That guy might try another shot."

They hustled Randollph out, then through a growing crowd outside the church, and into the hotel.

"We're goin' up to the penthouse," he told the plainclothesman sitting near the penthouse elevator. "Don't you let nobody on this elevator till I get back down, and I mean nobody."

"What happened, Sarg?"

"Tell you when I get back." He pushed Randollph and Henderson into the elevator and stabbed the penthouse button with a thick forefinger. When they arrived at the small anteroom where the elevator emptied its passengers, Garboski said, "Give me your keys. I'm going to go through this place before you can come in."

"Why, in heaven's name?" Randollph asked.

"Precaution."

"Mr. Higbee will be in there."

"Who's he?"

"Our majordomo."

"Your what?"

"He's our cook," Randollph, exasperated, explained. He wasn't sure Garboski would be able to understand if he referred to Clarence as a chef. "He won't know what has happened. If you go crashing in there, Sergeant, you'll only upset him."

"Well, O.K.," the sergeant conceded. "You"—he nodded toward Henderson—"stay out here."

"No, Sergeant," Randollph insisted, "he'll come in with us."

"I don't know him."

"He's one of my best friends," Randollph said. "Think of him as an extra bodyguard. He'd be a good one."

Garboski looked puzzled. White people, by his lights, shouldn't mix with the colored. But he knew better than to insult someone like Randollph.

They walked up the three steps (three for the Holy Trinity, Dan Gantry had once suggested). Randollph unlocked the door. They passed through a foyer that also served as a cloakroom and into the penthouse living room. Randollph remembered the first time he had stepped into the penthouse living room. It was night, and Dan Gantry was showing him around.

"It's the damndest place you ever saw," Dan had said. "This thing is an octagon. It's in the base of the tower. They just knocked out some masonry and put in glass—so that it would be light and cheerful, I guess. Or maybe glass is cheaper than bricks. Anyway, it's nifty."

Randollph agreed that it was nifty. The octagon had been bisected by a wall, leaving half the floor as a large living room. It was carpeted wall to wall in deep-pile grassy green. The furniture had looked to Randollph to be the kind you see in display windows of expensive stores. It had the correct look, suggesting the work of a professional interior decorator. There was a real fireplace in the middle of the bisecting wall. When it was night, as it had been when Randollph had first seen the room, and as it was now, the lights of Chicago's Loop flooded through the walls of glass, providing a sight that was as spectacular as it was unexpected. He heard Sticky Henderson say, soft-voiced and to himself: "Oh boy! Some digs!"

Clarence Higbee came out of the kitchen. He was dressed, as always when on duty, in striped trousers, white shirt, bat-wing collar, and gray-and-black-striped tie. He was not wearing his customary black jacket, but instead a long chef's apron covering most of his shirt front and ending well below his knees.

Clarence said: "Good evening, Dr. Randollph. I hadn't expected you to return so soon." Quickly appraising the sergeant and the black man, he added: "Is something wrong?"

"Clarence, this is Mr. Henderson, an old friend, and Sergeant Garboski of the Chicago police. Yes, something's wrong, and I'll tell you about it in a minute. Meanwhile, Sergeant Garboski wishes to go through the apartment."

"Of course, sir, everything is in order. Sergeant, if you'll follow me." Randollph blessed Clarence Higbee's professionalism. He did what he was supposed to do without fuss or unnecessary questions.

Sticky Henderson sank into a huge blue chair and stretched out his long legs. "Who'd want to kill that mackerel-snapper in the pointed hat?"

"He wasn't shooting at Bishop O'Manny," Randollph said, "he was shooting at me."

Sticky Henderson sat up straight. "Come on, Con, nobody wants to do you any harm. You the best." He grinned suddenly. "Come to think of it, couple times after you chew my ass for droppin' a pass I thought of killin' you." He shut down the grin and was serious again. "How you know he was shootin' at you?"

"Have you been reading the stories about the Holy Terror?"

"You mean that screwed-up weirdo jus' pops preachers?"

"That's the one."

"Yeah, but the way I read it, those psalm shouters he hit all had somethin' nasty in their past. You ain't got nothin' to hide. I know you for a lotta years now. Maybe you din' fight off all the dames chasin' you. You give out a few autographs I bet." He grinned again. "Nobody goin' hold that against you. I give out a few myself, 'fore I married and settled down. Goes with the game. Nobody gonna shoot you for that."

"He was shooting at me."

"Why didn't he hit you?"

"Because I bent over to shake the hand you were sticking out at me. I bent over just as he pulled the trigger. That's the only way I can figure it. You saved my life, Sticky."

"Jus' bein' friendly," Sticky Henderson said. "That service, that was somethin'! More dignified than my Baptist church, but movin'. They sing that hymn "A Mighty Fortress Is Our God" an' my hair stood on end! I could feel the power! An' all for my old ass-chewin' quarterback friend, Con Randollph. I mighty proud I know you. I feel warm and happy and glad I'm there, bein' a part of it, and I just thought I'll give Con some skin as he passes by, bet he'll appreciate it." Sticky was sober now, his voice trembled. "Never knew that I'd be savin' you. Mighty glad I did it." He paused to get hold of himself. "Still don' know why this Holy Terror after you."

Randollph explained to him about Thaddeus Barry, and Citizens for a Moral America, and people confusing his convictions about freedom of expression with a liking for pornography, and the poem.

"You mean this Terror dude got it in for you because he thinks you like to look at all the beaver in *Playboy*, somethin' like that?" Sticky Henderson clearly could not connect an appreciation of the unclad female form with the idea of sin and evil. "Boy, he gonna hafta shoot a lotta people. Ain't enough bullets in the whole world to shoot every guy likes t' look at pussy pictures." He shook his head in wonderment at such thinking. "This Terror asshole, I can understand him gettin' hot and righteous over some Bible-thumper knockin' up a girl then killin' her instead of marryin' her. Makes a dopey kind of sense. He's got to have some planks missing in his building, else he wouldn't be playin' God's holy avenger. But I can understand that. But bein' pissed off about a preacher looking at nude pictures—not sayin' that you do, Con, but he say you do—that I can't understand. Sounds more like he's pretendin', like he's cooked up a reason."

Sergeant Garboski and Clarence Higbee returned from their tour of inspection.

"Everything's O.K.," he told Randollph. "I'll get back to the lobby, check out anyone wants to come up. You know who you're expectin'?"

"My wife," Randollph said. "Probably Liz—Mrs. Casey, she was sitting with my wife. The bishop and his wife perhaps. Mr. Gantry. No doubt Lieutenant Casey will be along as soon as his duties permit."

"I know all them," Garboski said. "Anyone I don't know tries to come up I phone first for an O.K. from you. Don't let anyone in without checking with me."

"Someone could get on the elevator at another floor," Randollph pointed out.

"Yeah? Well, I'll just run the elevator for a while. And just to cover all possibilities don't answer your doorbell unless you know who it is. I mean that. Got it?"

Randollph got it.

After Garboski had gone, Clarence said: "I'm preparing a collation for your guests, Dr. Randollph. If you'll give me a few minutes' notice . . ."

"I doubt that anyone will be hungry," Randollph broke in. "I know I'm not."

"I am," Sticky Henderson said.

"I'll be prepared in any case," Clarence said. "Now, if you'll excuse me . . ."

"You got any whiskey?" Sticky Henderson asked.

"Of course, sir. What would you like?"

"Bourbon. Wild Turkey if you got it. Powerful stuff. 'Bout three fingers. No ice. This not for sippin', for my nerves. Ain't every day I see someone shot before my eyes."

"I'll join him," Randollph said. He knew he was shaking from tension, and he wanted to keep hold of himself.

Clarence returned promptly with the whiskey.

"Here's to catchin' that son-of-a-bitch real quick," Sticky said and tossed down the whiskey, and said, "ahhh." Randollph did the same, feeling the alcohol burn all the way down, and hit with a pleasant fiery sensation.

"Ain't much of a drinkin' man," Sticky commented. "Stuff's so good, makes you feel so good, a man could get to dependin' on it. Don't like to lean on crutches to get through life. But there are times when a snort's the best medicine."

"There are times," Randollph agreed, then added, "I think this is one of them."

They heard the telephone ring. Then Clarence came in to announce that Mrs. Randollph, Mrs. Casey, the bishop, and his wife were on the way up, along with Mr. Gantry and the Reverend Ms. Fisk.

Randollph went to the door to greet them. Sammy was the first one in, and she threw herself into Randollph's arms with an "Oh,

Randollph, I'm so scared for you!" She sobbed on his shoulder, her whole body shaking. The rest of the party discreetly departed for the living room.

When Randollph had comforted his wife, they joined the others. Dan Gantry was talking to Sticky Henderson. Randollph was so accustomed to seeing Dan dressed in a variety of flamboyant haberdasheries that he looked almost strange in a black suit and clericals. He and Sticky were standing, and though Dan was above-average tall, Sticky had to look down at him.

"They kid you some about that name of yours, Gantry?" Sticky was asking.

"Ha!" Dan replied.

"That mean yes? Elmer Gantry," Sticky said. "Had to read that book for English Lit class. I'm a college man—don' talk like it. I can, but I don't," Sticky said. "Went to college to play football. Only way I could get there. Played football more 'n I studied, I guess. Won a shot at the pro's instead of a Phi Beta Kappa key. But I learned some things. Learned likin' to read. That Elmer Gantry, he some crooked cat. Chasin' women, an' him a soul-saver. You anything like him?"

Dan grinned at the big black man. "I like girls. But I'm a bachelor. I don't go around jumping into bed with every pretty little filly I meet, though."

This kind of talk, Randollph recognized, was an attempt at lightheartedness to stave off the gloom and sadness that was bound to settle over them.

"We're about to turn on the ten o'clock news, C.P.—that is, if you think you can bear it." The bishop was solicitous.

"Turn it on," Randollph said.

"I'll get my station," Sam said. "They have the whole service on tape. I had them do it, because it was going to be my Christmas present to Randollph. Now . . ." She blinked back tears and turned to the television.

The black face of the big TV set suddenly erupted into color. Johnnie DeBeers's friendly boyish face was sitting there, flanked by Marva Luscome, looking like a pretty little angel.

"Bishop Terence Kevin O'Manny was shot to death during a church service tonight," Marva trilled, as if announcing the winner of the weekly state lottery or a cut in the prime rate.

"President to visit Israel again," Johnnie DeBeers said. "Details after this."

They sat silently through a cheerful friendly banker blathering about his bank's interest on savings being the highest allowed by law; a Ford dealer who said he was Low-Price Larry inviting them to inspect his acres of new cars and "absolutely dependable reconditioned pre-owned beauties"; and an actor gotten up as a gangster growling about the superiority of his brand of pizza and saying he was going to make an offer you couldn't refuse. Then the news desk faded in.

"Bishop Terence Kevin O'Manny, auxiliary bishop of the Chicago Roman Catholic archdiocese, was murdered tonight in the Loop's Church of the Good Shepherd." Johnnie DeBeers was probably reading from an idiot board, Randollph thought, although he appeared to be looking right at them. Johnnie continued: "Bishop O'Manny had taken part in a service installing the Reverend Doctor C. P. Randollph as permanent pastor of the historic church, and was marching down the aisle in the recessional when he suddenly crumpled to the floor. At first it was thought that he had fainted, but examination by a doctor revealed that he had been shot through the head. Our cameras, which were filming the service, got the entire incident."

Johnnie and Marva faded out and were replaced by a picture of the nave of the Church of the Good Shepherd. They saw what, but for the dress of the congregation, could have been a scene from the Middle Ages. Candles flickered. Gold mosaics glittered. The recessional, moving slowly down the aisle, clothed in robes, cassocks, miters, university hoods, stoles, and various other species of academic ecclesiastical frippery, spoke of ancient and musty traditions. The organ's lusty throat sounded over the singing of a hymn written out of the awful struggle between a dying but still powerful way of looking at people, society, life, and the world, and an upstart but vigorous challenger which sought to replace the old order with one it believed would be lots better. On the tube the service looked like a clipping from a movie, an act in a play. It cast a spell.

Randollph sensed that everyone in the room was holding his or her breath as they watched him come to the center of the chancel, join with Bishop O'Manny, then the two of them walk down the

chancel steps. They passed the empty front pews, just vacated by
reverend clergy who were, by this moment, nearly to the narthex.
Then he and Bishop O'Manny came even with the pew with
Randollph's football buddies in it. He saw Sticky Henderson, a
wide grin on his face, hold out a big black hand that had caught
many a ball Randollph had thrown not quite on target. He saw
himself bend over to grasp that hand, and at almost the same time
Bishop O'Manny sink to the floor. The camera had a good shot of
the bishop's face as the bullet hit him. His last expression in this
life was a look of surprise.

The scene at the church ended abruptly. Johnnie DeBeers said,
"We now go to Chuck Mendoza at the Church of the Good
Shepherd."

Chuck Mendoza, a chunky, handsome Mexican American with
a thick black mustache, had established himself in a corner of the
narthex.

"Johnnie, I have here Lieutenant Michael Casey of Homicide.
He was attending the service this evening. Lieutenant Casey,
could you tell us how you happened to be at the service?"

"Dr. Randollph is a friend of mine," Casey said.

"You were best man at his recent wedding, were you not?"

"I was." Casey didn't waste any words. He looked pretty grim,
Randollph thought, though—as usual—he looked as well turned
out as a junior partner in a prestigious law firm. Randollph
admired his hard-finish worsted three-piece suit with a blue-and-
white polka-dot tie on a white shirt.

"Was there any other reason you were here tonight—other than
your personal relationship with Dr. Randollph?"

"Yes."

"Could you tell us what it was?"

"Dr. Randollph is under police protection," Casey stated flatly.

"You were on duty?"

"No, but I was nervous about this service and the possibilities
it presented someone who wanted to harm him."

"Why was Dr. Randollph under police protection?"

"Because," Casey said, "he had received a warning from what
you people in the media call the 'Holy Terror.'"

"Wait a minute, let me get this straight," Chuck Mendoza said,
a puzzled expression on his face. Randollph was sure he had
extracted all this information from Casey before the cameras

started turning, but was milking this scene for all the drama in it. Your death, dear, departed Bishop O'Manny, Randollph thought, is being used to boost a TV station's ratings, which in turn will enable it to charge higher prices for hawking detergents and fast-food chain restaurants.

"Are you saying," Mendoza continued, "that the bullet that killed Bishop O'Manny was actually meant for Randollph?"

"That's what I'm saying."

"Why would he want to kill Dr. Randollph? Doesn't this Holy Terror only kill clergymen with a shady past? Did the warning say why he had it in for Randollph?"

"That bastard, that stinkin' bastard," Randollph heard Dan Gantry mutter. And Sticky Henderson nodded. "Yeah, sure is."

"I wouldn't be at liberty to divulge that," Casey replied to Mendoza, looking grimmer than ever.

"That just makes it worse!" Sam wailed. She was near to tears again.

"Mike didn't mean to make it worse," Liz Casey soothed her. "He had to answer, and that's the best answer he could have given." Mrs. Michael Casey was a bouncy blonde, usually talkative. Randollph noticed tears trickling from the corners of her eyes. He supposed they were tears shed for a popular and much-respected church leader.

"I know, Liz, I know." Sam patted Liz Casey's hand.

"Can you tell us, Lieutenant, if you have made any progress toward identifying this Holy Terror? This would be—the bishop would be his fourth victim," Mendoza was saying to Lieutenant Casey.

"That's right. And, no, we haven't any idea as to who he is. Like Jack the Ripper and Son of Sam, he's obsessed. When you can't pin down a motive for a murder it's very difficult to get a lead. They're the toughest kind to solve. We'll get him, of course, but it won't be easy. We have the gun he used this time, but it's unlikely to have any fingerprints on it, or be traceable. This killer's too clever to do anything stupid like that."

"Where did you find the gun?"

"I think we'll have to end the interview now," Casey said.

"Back to you, Johnnie," Mendoza said. He knew he wasn't going to get any more out of Casey.

The picture changed to the news desk. "The President's press

secretary announced today," Marva Luscome prattled, "that—"
Sam shut off the TV.

Clarence Higbee announced that he was ready to serve them.
Some of Randollph's guests protested that they weren't hungry,
but Dan Gantry and Sticky Henderson said they were starved,
and Randollph discovered that he was ravenous—whether because of a light and hasty dinner before the service, or from a
need to do something to dampen the nervous tension of the
recent hours, he didn't know.

Clarence had arranged a buffet on a sideboard and a portable
hot table down one side of the large dining room.

"This is a simple buffet supper," he explained to Randollph's
guests, now seated around the dining table. "Let me explain the
dishes. There are two hot entrees. This—" he lifted the cover
from a long platter heating over a chafing dish, "is breast-of-
turkey fillets in a hot sour-cream sauce."

"Look like deep-fry fish to me," Sticky Henderson commented.

"That's because they're dipped in egg, then bread crumbs, then
browned in a heavy skillet before baking," Clarence said, smiling.
"They're baked in a sour cream and butter sauce until they form a
crisp crust. Then the sauce is poured over the fillets."

"Sounds better 'n fried fish," Sticky said.

"And the other dish?" the bishop asked. "Would you tell us
about it? Your descriptions, Clarence, always heighten my
anticipation, and thus my pleasure."

"Certainly, m'lord," Clarence replied. "I'll describe it as I
finish it. This is Scallops Bordeaux." He took the cover off a very
large skillet cooking over a low flame. "I've simmered finely
chopped carrot, onion, shallots, and parsley in butter, and added
a bit of thyme and bay leaf, and browned the scallops in the
sauce. Then I added a cup of white wine and chopped tomatoes,
simmering the dish a few minutes more. Now I'll pour in a fourth
cup of heated brandy"—as he poured in the brandy blue flame
shot out of the pan. "I'll now put the scallops in another pan and
keep them warm while I reduce the pan juices and add a bit of
butter. That makes a most savory sauce to pour over the scallops.
If you'll be patient a moment the dish will be ready."

The phone rang. "I'll get it," Dan said. "Wouldn't want to
interrupt you, Clarence." He left the room and was back almost

immediately. "Your husband's coming up, Liz," he told Mrs. Casey.

"I had anticipated that the lieutenant would be here, and have set a place for him," Clarence said. Randollph wondered if Clarence ever missed a trick connected with his duties.

When Casey arrived he kissed his wife, nodded to the others, and sat down. He looked tired and out of sorts. He gazed briefly at the wine glass beside his place and announced, "I'd like a beer. I'm thirsty."

"Certainly sir. Domestic or imported?"

"Imported."

"I have Urquel, a vigorous Czechoslovakian product."

"Fine."

"I know where it is." Sam got up. "You go on with your preparations, Clarence."

There was an expectant hush, everyone looking at Casey as if he were possessed of vital information and was about to divulge it. Casey didn't say anything, though, until he had poured a glass of beer and taken a big swig. "Ah," he said, patting his lips with a napkin.

"We saw you on television," Liz Casey said to her husband.

"You said you have the gun." The bishop put it as a question.

"Yes," Casey answered. "In the chapel. Don't know how he got in there, but it wouldn't be hard to do. That front entrance to the chapel—the one where you come in off the street instead of through the church—it's open all day. Open tonight, too. Fire laws." He paused for another draft of beer. "He could have taken his time strolling out that way, too, what with all the confusion. Nobody realized what had happened for a while."

"He shoot from the chapel?" Dan asked.

"Yeah, easy as anything. That screen butts up against the back pews. It's got little openings across the top, like the top of a castle wall, what do you call them—"

"Fenestrations," Randollph said.

Casey gave Randollph a look which Randollph read as "I told you so."

"That's right," Casey said. "All he had to do was stand on that back pew, put the gun through one of those fenestrations, and wait to pull the trigger. Nobody was looking that way. Anyway, it's kind of dark where that screen is, and it would have taken good eyes to spot the tip of a gun barrel. He probably leveled it about five seconds before he expected to shoot."

"You have no doubt, Lieutenant, that he was aiming for Dr. Randollph?" The bishop spoke as if he hoped someone just might have had it in for the Roman prelate.

"None at all. Bishop O'Manny had no known enemies. He had received no threats from the Holy Terror or anyone else. I know. I checked with Father Duffy, his personal secretary. We'd be foolish to go on the assumption that he was the target with all the evidence telling us that he was after Dr. Randollph."

"The buffet is ready," Clarence announced. "M'lord, would you lead the way? Please don't neglect the watercress and orange salad. It accompanies this menu very nicely. And the sautéed tomatoes. Now if you'll excuse me, I'll bring the wine."

"Why he call you m'lord?" Sticky Henderson asked the bishop.

"Because Church of England bishops are members of the House of Lords," the bishop explained. "Mr. Higbee—Clarence—believes that all bishops deserve the title, even though they are from a nonconformist sect."

"You like him to do that?"

"I confess that I find it gratifying to my ego."

"But a temptation to spiritual pride." Randollph entered into the conversational game Sticky Henderson had started, a signal for a truce on talking of dismal things until they had enjoyed the meal.

"I'm glad to risk it," the bishop countered.

Randollph found it difficult to reconcile this scene of elegant dining with the events of the last few hours. But, he told himself, life goes on no matter what. Just as in the midst of life we are in death, so in the presence of death we are in life. City Hall won't close tomorrow. The traffic is still running in the streets below. Sticky Henderson will be, tomorrow, preparing for Sunday's game. He couldn't take time out to brood about the tragedy of Bishop O'Manny's death, or let the guilt of knowing that he was the cause of the murder wash over him. Had there been no shooting, this same group, minus Sticky Henderson, would be dining at this same table on this very food. Randollph knew that going through the motions of normality generated a sense of normality. It would take a mighty act of will for him to do it, but he was determined to follow the established routines of his life.

"Good eatin'," Sticky Henderson commented, as he dug into a second helping of Scallops Bordeaux.

"Better than soul food?" Dan Gantry asked him.

"Soul food's overrated. A fad. One reason I wanted to better myself was to get away from stuff like that. Me and Louise—that's my lady—when we go out we head for a French beanery. They the best cooks. Learned to cook French myself—a few things. Beef Bourguignonne, Ris de Veau—that's sweetbreads, love sweetbreads. I can even make a soufflé—sometimes it falls too quick, though. 'Spose this Clarence fellow'd give me a few tips?" He turned to Natalie Fisk. "You really a preacher?"

"Yes," she said, "halfway."

"What that mean?"

"I'm an ordained deacon," Natalie told him. "After my year here—I'm called a pastor-in-training—I'll get my seminary degree and be ordained an elder."

"I see. You preach a good sermon?"

"I haven't done much preaching. I hope so."

"Don't Con let you preach none?"

"Well—" Natalie looked embarrassed.

"I'll have a word with him," Sticky assured her. "Playin' football, he bossed me around pretty good. Quarterback's always the boss. But I got influence with him."

"Put in a word for me, too, will you?" Dan said.

Sticky grinned at Randollph. "Reckon you need a little help with interstaff relations, Con. You and me better have a little talk."

Randollph appreciated this light talk acting out the concept that life was normal even though it wasn't. But Mike Casey wasn't acting normally. Casey usually enjoyed arguing theology with Randollph. But there was none of this tonight.

"We're going to increase your protection," he announced abruptly, looking at Randollph. "You'll have a policeman—plainclothes of course—go with you wherever you go. There'll be one in the office during office hours. He'll screen your visitors. We'll continue round-the-clock protection in the hotel lobby. Anybody wants to visit you in the penthouse has to clear with the man on duty and call ahead for your O.K. Don't let anyone in unless you know who it is. I'll instruct Clarence."

"I've already sent condolences to the chancery," the bishop

said. "I'll attend Bishop O'Manny's funeral, of course. I'm sure that C.P. will want to attend also."

"Of course," Randollph said.

"No," Casey said.

"But—"

Casey interrupted Randollph. "I can't order you, Doctor, but I'm asking you, please don't. This nut might think the funeral would be an ideal time to—"

"Oh, God!" Sam moaned.

"I see your point," Randollph said.

"I'll speak to Father Duffy," the bishop said. "He'll understand why C.P. can't attend."

"I'll speak to him, too," Casey said. "This business tonight is going to keep the Holy Terror on the front pages until we catch him. The commissioner of police is going to have every important politician in town waiting for him tomorrow morning. They're going to demand a massive police effort to clear this up fast. This is a Roman Catholic town, and when a Catholic bishop gets shot there'll be no peace for the police until we find the guy that did it. I won't be getting much sleep for awhile. Meanwhile, Dr. Randollph, you're going to be having a problem in public relations."

"I'd thought of that," Randollph said. "It isn't a pleasant thought."

"What problem?" Sticky Henderson asked.

"People will have to know why the Holy Terror was after Dr. Randollph," Casey answered. "We'll have to give the poem to the media. Then they'll make a big deal out of this pornography business. They'll make you out to be a defender of dirty movies and magazines."

"But I'm not," Randollph protested. "Though I know that's the way the story will come out. 'Loop Preacher Likes Pornography'—that's how the stories will be started."

"Oh, dear," the bishop said. "We'd better do something about this. Just what, I don't know. Our publicity director could issue a statement, but that would just lend credence to the accusation."

"If you issue a statement that Dr. Randollph doesn't really like smut people will form a mental picture of him staring bug-eyed at a girlie magazine. If I might make a suggestion—" Natalie Fisk seemed to feel that it was presumptuous of a young lady divine not yet fully ordained to speak up in the presence of a bishop.

"Please do," Randollph said.

"Well, Dr. Randollph, your wife has the most popular television talk show in Chicago. If she would put you on to discuss it, people could see you, and see how silly it is to accuse you of such a thing." She looked at Sam.

Sam said, "It wouldn't look good for us to have Randollph on as my only guest. People know he's my husband."

"Sam, love," Dan Gantry said, "why don't you invite Sad Tad Barry and that old gasbag of a secretary of his kook organization to discuss pornography and free speech—"

"And you might include a lawyer and someone from the A.C.L.U., and a psychologist," Liz Casey suggested.

"Make a helluva show," Dan said.

"Now that idea I could sell to John—DeBeers, that is," Sam said. "But I'm not sure I want to sell it."

"Why not?" Dan asked.

"I think I understand." The bishop was peering into his coffee cup as if seeking some divine revelation in its muddy bottom. "It would serve to publicize a situation best not publicized. It's one of those positions one sometimes gets into where you're damned if you do and damned if you don't. And Barry would do his best to exploit Samantha's relationship to C.P."

"I guess that's why I don't like it," Sam said. "I appreciate the suggestion, though. Nat." She smiled at the pastor-in-training. "I'll think about it."

Chapter Twelve

There is something about the routines of daily life which acts as an analgesic for a spirit under stress. The British people, in World War II, endured the nightly terror of German bombs in the sure knowledge that, come the next night, there would be more of the same. Yet they got up every morning, went to the bathroom, ate breakfast, and went out to their work. This daily routine somehow assured them that the world was still fundamentally sound and would keep going for a while yet. Martin Luther, in hiding at the Wartburg from the malevolence of the Holy Roman Empire, chafed and fretted that he couldn't get back to Wittenberg and get on with the Reformation. But he kept his restless soul on a leash by daily toil which, in two years or so, produced a dozen books and the translation of the entire New Testament into the German language—aided, no doubt, by the daily routine of a good dinner and plenty of German beer.

Randollph knew that going about his business was the only way to hold himself together. The daily life of a pastor, even of a small congregation, is made up of the various small tasks laid upon him every week—sermon preparation, selecting hymns, creeds and prayers for the Sunday worship bulletin, attending committee meetings, imploring the Almighty to bless the Kiwanis Club or a P.T.A. meeting. But the routine is always interrupted here and there. Perhaps by an unexpected trip to the hospital to make a call. Maybe by someone in the parish in real need of pastoral counsel. Often by people who "just dropped by for a chat." These unanticipated interruptions actually become a part of the routine.

In a large ecclesiastical corporation such as the Church of the Good Shepherd the routines as well as the interruptions are writ in larger script. Randollph dealt every day with staff members, administrative decisions which would not wait, Miss Windfall hovering over him with her ever voluminous paper work that demanded—or so she was convinced—his prompt attention. Plus a sermon to write. And people who "just had to see him right now." Plus invitations to speak to every kind of civic and religious organization in the city—"we don't have any budget for a fee, Dr. Randollph, but we know you realize how important our cause is . . ." Plus, plus, plus.

Sometimes Randollph wondered why he had ever left the cool and measured pace of teaching future John Wesleys and Harry Emerson Fosdicks how Savonarola created the Kingdom of God in Firenze or why Torquemáda burned Jews alive for the good of their souls, for the overheated and hectic pace of a big pious business. He guessed that he did what he did because he liked it, taken as a whole. There was the daily shot of something new turning up. There was the lift of playing a role on a large stage. And now, with the threat of the Holy Terror hanging over him, it was a blessing to be so busy. He had no time to tell sad stories of the death of kings or brood on the machinations, often malignant, of the fates.

Today he welcomed the press of the familiar. He'd started the day by seeing his own face staring out beneath screaming headlines. This was a sensational story, and the media were not disposed to make it any less so. What had been a series of murders of no great interest to the city had been transformed, by the killing of the Catholic bishop, into front-page material.

Randollph was very much aware that people now looked at him differently. As he walked through the hotel lobby with his police bodyguard people whispered behind their hands to their companions. The two office secretaries greeted him with a subdued, "Good morning, Dr. Randollph," and turned quickly to their work. Miss Windfall, never cheerful, looked grim. Randollph supposed this was how a leper must feel as he walks among disease-free people.

He explained to Miss Windfall that there would be a policeman in the office at all times, and that any visitor unknown to her would have to pass the policeman's inspection. She understood the necessity of this, but, without uttering a disapproving word, made it clear that she was being asked to endure the well-nigh unendurable. Randollph said, "Please don't disturb me for three hours. I have sermons to prepare," and fled to the quiet of his study.

The note at the top of his calendar for the day said "Plan advent and Christmas sermons." Sermons for the high seasons of the Christian year were especially difficult. Was there anything new to say about a holy child born in a manger? Did the idea of the incarnation mean anything to people today? Who was in the market for a savior? How did a preacher go about rescuing this lovely and timeless story from the ennui of overfamiliarity? How did you tell people that this story wasn't a historical account of what actually happened? Anyone at all familiar with Church history knew that the early Christians weren't interested in the birth of Jesus until long after his death, when the facts were no longer recoverable. Mark, the original gospel, had no nativity story at all. How did you get it across to people who thought poets were sissies and weirdos that Luke's incomparable nativity account is the poetry of faith? How did you make them see that poetry doesn't deal with facts but with truth?

Randollph reread the nativity stories in Matthew and Luke. He made notes as he read. He had to come up with four advent sermons, a Christmas Eve service, and a sermon for Christmastide. Ideas began to form themselves. Perhaps he could do a series on some of the lesser-known players in the Christmas drama. Let's see—how about a sermon based on Simeon, the righteous man who only got on stage long enough to bless the baby Jesus in the temple? That might have possibilities. Or the men that Herod sent out to slay the young children, committing mass murder to be sure of one death? No one knows their names, but they are always with us, the men who justify doing the politicians' bloody work because they are just obeying orders.

Maybe the hotelkeeper at Bethlehem would make sermon material.

Randollph was writing rapidly now, jotting ideas and references, possible sermon titles, and sketchy outlines. The Holy Terror did not exist for him.

The buzzer on the office intercom summoned him to snap a switch and hear what Miss Windfall had to say. He was momentarily irritated by the interruption. But he knew that Miss Windfall was not frivolous or capricious with her interruptions.

"Yes, Miss Windfall?"

"There are three newspaper reporters out here who insist on seeing you," she said. Her tone carried the clear message that newspaper reporters are unworthy but inescapable. Randollph was surprised that she hadn't sent them packing. Then he surmised that Miss Windfall's affectionless concern that the pastor of Good Shepherd come off well when entangled with the press prompted her to grant these reporters access to Randollph. Miss Windfall knew that people who treat the press rudely do not come off well in the papers.

"I'll see them," Randollph said. He was irritated that, just as he was getting up to speed with his sermonizing, he had to put on the brakes. But, having staked out a position affirming his belief in freedom of speech and press, he could hardly turn away these reporters just because it was inconvenient for him to see them now. He knew they would attempt to extract the sensational quote, the unguarded statement. They might be rude. They might badger him. Their stories, when printed, might be—and probably would be—garbled. What they wrote might make him look bad. No matter. He'd see them.

They were all young. The *Sun-Times* reporter was a plump blonde girl named Debbie Green. The *Tribune* had sent a black who introduced himself as Harold Fleming and who looked more like a showcase junior executive than a cub reporter. The reporter for a large suburban paper said he was Dexter Young. He wore a beard and hadn't combed his hair.

Randollph seated them on a long and deep old brown leather sofa and took a matching chair. He didn't like to sit behind a desk when talking with people who came to him for pastoral counseling. He saw the desk as a barrier to communication. It emphasized the superior position of the person who sat behind it. He had learned, in his brief tenure, that people who came to a pastor with a serious problem often had difficulty articulating the problem. Admitting a moral indiscretion or a fouled-up marriage wasn't easy for anyone. People assumed that a pastor would censure them for their weaknesses of the flesh or spirit. They hated to "look bad" in his eyes. The human ego struggles to preserve itself even when it is fragile at best. "I have this problem with my marriage, Dr. Randollph. It's my husband. It really isn't my fault . . ." Randollph thought a man behind a big, impressive desk had the look of a judge, especially to people who were carrying guilt feelings, real or imagined, that they were trying to hide from him and from themselves. He was convinced that it made for better rapport between counselor and counselee if they just sat down together around a coffee table as if for a friendly chat. This was the sort of thing they ought to have taught him in seminary, but hadn't. You had to learn it on the job.

The reporters didn't waste any time.

"Do you believe that you were the intended target of the bullet that killed Bishop O'Manny?" Dexter Young asked.

"Yes."

"Because you had received a warning from the Holy Terror?"

"Yes."

Debbie Green: "The Terror accused you of being a porno-freak?"

Randollph: "Substantially."

Green: "Is that a yes or no?"

Randollph: "It's a yes."

Green: "Are you?"

Randollph: "No."

Harold Fleming: "Then why the accusation?"

Randollph knew that Fleming, as well as the others, knew why. They wanted to quote him. He'd have to be careful.

Randollph: "Because, when urged to support an antipornography campaign sponsored by Citizens for a Moral America, I refused—refused on the grounds that the tactics and methods proposed by this organization infringe on the right to freedom of speech and freedom of information—some people attributed my refusal to a predilection for smut."

Fleming: "Sad Tad Barry?"

Randollph (smiling): "Yes. You know him?"

Fleming: "We know him. Always after us to publicize his Citizens for a Moral America. He's a member of your church, isn't he? And of your, whatever you call it, the board of something or other?"

Randollph: "Governing board. And yes, he's a member."

Debbie Green (aggressively): "You think women ought to be looked on as sex objects? You talk elegantly, Doc, but you are an ex-jock. Jocks are notorious for treating women as servants to their sexual appetites. Are you different from other jocks? Were you more holy than your teammates?"

Randollph couldn't tell whether Debbie Green was a truculent feminist or if she was just pushing provocative questions at him in hope of evoking an off-guard answer that would make a good headline. He selected his words carefully.

Randollph: "You've asked me several questions, Miss Green. You have categorized all athletes as looking on women as sexual objects. That is guilt by classification. Some athletes no doubt do look on women as sexual objects. As do some bankers and truck drivers and insurance salesmen, and, I suppose, some clergymen. No, I don't look on women as sexual objects. And I hope all of you understand that because I object to censorship of the press, even the pornographic press, it does not follow that I favor smutty magazines or movies. That is the mistake Mr. Barry is making." That ought to get them on his side, he thought. Freedom of the press was under the guns of the Supreme Court, and many politicians, and all sorts of organizations such as Citizens for a Moral America. These reporters knew they were vulnerable to police search and seizure of their files. They knew the courts were making it increasingly difficult for them to protect their confidential sources. They ought to welcome any partner in their battle. They ought to give him a good press. Then he hated himself for this kind of thinking.

Harold Fleming: "Mr. Barry has called for your resignation as pastor of Good Shepherd. He says you aren't fit to be a minister. Will you resign?"

Randollph was startled. "I didn't know."

Fleming (smiling): "I interviewed him an hour ago. I'll run it as a sidebar to the piece on you."

Randollph: "No, I won't resign."

Fleming: "Will you call for his resignation from your governing board?"

"No, of course not. He's served long and honorably on our board. We don't demand that our board members like, or agree with, or approve of the pastor." Randollph wondered if he were stretching the truth a bit here. Thaddeus Barry had certainly served long on the governing board of the church. How honorably he had served was open to some debate. Apparently he had been a big fat pain in the neck to pastors, the other board members, and the church in general for countless years. He thought maybe he ought to ask God to forgive him for this "stretcher," but decided that the Almighty approved of minor lies in a good cause.

Young: "Are you scared?"

Randollph: "Of course I am."

Young: "What are you going to do?"

Randollph: "What I always do. Write and preach sermons. Call on people in the hospital. Attend committee meetings. See people who want to see me. Meet with the church staff. Take care of the desk work—write for the church paper, any number of things."

Debbie Green: "Sounds boring."

Randollph: "Some of it is. Some of every job is boring. Taken as a whole, though, it's an exciting and satisfying job." He wondered if every pastor could say that about his job. What about the men (and women—there were nearly as many women being ordained now as men, or so the bishop had told him) slogging along in small churches, always beset by the problems of too few people in the congregation, and too little money to run the church properly or pay the preacher a decent wage. How did they feel about their jobs? How did they feel, trying to preach an informed gospel and watching their congregations decline and seeing a commensurate increase in the fast-food Christian franchises promising a quick fix for the hungers of the soul? Peddlers of God's word, St. Paul called this kind of religion. Didn't ministers working under these burdens sometimes feel that they had a rotten job? Randollph suspected that they did.

Dexter Young: "Do you think the Holy Terror will try again—to get you, that is?"

Randollph: "I assume so. I have no reason to think that he won't. I'm his first failure, and that's bound to bother him."

Harold Fleming: "Do you have any thoughts on what kind of guy this Holy Terror might be? I mean, he has it in for the clergy. Can you think why?"

Randollph: "No. Only what the police psychiatrist thinks. His profile says he's compulsive, for some reason hates the clergy. Perhaps he has a personal reason for hating the clergy. Or perhaps he hates authority, so when he kills a clergyman he kills an authority. You have to know something about any suspect's psychological history in order to find a motive. And Lieutenant Casey—that's Lieutenant Michael Casey of Homicide who's in charge of the case—says that until you find a motive you aren't going to get far in solving a mystery like the Holy Terror."

Fleming: "That can't be very reassuring for you, Doctor."

Randollph: "Not very."

Debbie Green: "Thank you, Dr. Randollph, for your time." The three reporters headed for the door. Dexter Young was the last one out. As he left he turned to Randollph and said: "I sure wouldn't want to be you, Doc."

After the reporters left Randollph tried to get back to his sermonizing, but couldn't. He'd lost his momentum. You never understood until you did creative writing—for that was in part what a sermon was—the necessity of doing it in uninterrupted time. You could allot so many hours to the task, but they needed to be consecutive hours. A couple of hours here, an hour tomorrow, etc., wouldn't get the job done, at least not done well. The muses were fickle mistresses. Once they had fled they were not always easily summoned again.

He decided he'd get some desk work out of the way, then make hospital calls. That would keep him busy. He asked Miss Windfall to come in with anything that needed his immediate attention.

Miss Windfall, he reflected as she came steaming into his study with an armload of paper, was a formidable woman. The very bulk of her, too generous to be labeled "stout," made her appear formidable even before you looked at her face or heard her speak. Add to her impressive dimensions the air of one who had for long years acted as chancellor of her kingdom and you had a person

who could not be intimidated by captains or kings. Randollph
didn't know whether he liked her or disliked her, because Miss
Windfall didn't fit into any category which required feelings of
affection or offense. But he admired her loyalty to Good Shepherd. He wondered if she were devoted to God, or considered
herself a follower of Christ. She never said. He speculated on the
possibility that she had ever clasped a man to that copious
bosom, and then put the thought out of his mind as unthinkable.
Did she have a life of her own, apart from Good Shepherd? Did
she, home from the office, get tiddly on gin or sherry? Did she do
crossword puzzles? Did she bet on the ponies? If he knew that
she read Gothic romances or belonged to the John Birch Society it
would make her more human.

Randollph permitted himself to be directed to answer mounds
of correspondence, attend to reports, clean up this and that
detail, make piddling administrative decisions, and take care of
other boring tasks.

When Miss Windfall had sailed out triumphant, Randollph
looked at the neat stack of cards she had left him listing everyone
in the hospital on whom he should make a pastoral call. Hank
Sloane did the bulk of the hospital work. But the other pastors,
with the exception of Bertie Smelser, did some of it. Even Natalie
Fisk, as a part of her training program, did her weekly turn in the
hospitals. Bertie Smelser continued to serve God by managing the
property and investments acquired over the years by Good
Shepherd. Anyway, he wouldn't have been any good at hospital
calling. He probably would have bored the patients into a
relapse, leaving their last state worse than their first.

Randollph went to the coat closet where he kept a supply of
clerical shirts and collars. The bishop had told him that a pastor
calling in large city hospitals ought to wear clerical garb. It saved
a lot of time. No one questioned the presence of someone in
clerical garb, even out of visiting hours. And you didn't have to
explain to patients who never came to church and didn't know
you that you were their pastor and not a doctor or a malpractice
lawyer looking for business. The clerical collar, the bishop said,
was a universally respected uniform. Even if the wearer was a
mountebank or a fool the collar proclaimed to an indifferent
public that, at the very least, here was someone under holy
orders.

Randollph shucked his jacket and took the shirt and collar into the small bathroom that had been built into the study for the convenience of Dr. Arthur Hartshorne's weak kidneys. He took off the pale gray button-down shirt and black tie splashed with red polka dots that he had matched with his gray flannel suit. Then he shrugged into the black collarless shirt and attached the stiff white reversed collar. As usual, one of the little gold-wash collar buttons escaped his grasp and flipped into the wash basin with a clink-clink-clink.

"Damn!" Randollph said, as he retrieved it before it went down the drain. He supposed he ought to lay in a supply of those new-type clerical shirts with the collars slotted for a band of plastic which you just slipped in and looked like you were wearing a clerical collar even though you weren't. The shirts were available in blue and brown and cerise and heaven knew what other colors so that you could match them to whatever suit you were wearing. But to Randollph's eye they had a cheap and frivolous look to them.

Randollph rather fancied the way he looked in clerical garb. The severe black and white emphasized the premature specks of gray in his dark hair, and brought out the angular planes in his face. Clericals made him look older, more mature. He knew he looked impressive in this holy uniform and had even thought of adopting clericals as his everyday garb. But this would have meant neglecting his extensive wardrobe, of which he was very fond. Besides, the stiff plastic collar chafed his neck.

He picked up the cards Miss Windfall had left him and noted that he would be calling in Wesley Memorial Hospital. No need to order up the Ford LTD the church leased for the use of the pastors, and which hardly anyone but Dan Gantry ever drove. He'd be chauffeured in a police car.

His policeman bodyguard for this shift was a huge, taciturn black man named Roosevelt Jones. He silently preceded Randollph into the elevator and preceded him out of it, then fell into step with him as they walked to the curb where a blue police Pontiac was waiting in a no-parking zone.

At the hospital Roosevelt Jones nosed the Pontiac into a space marked "Reserved for Administrative Staff." He told Randollph to stay in the car until he took a look around. Satisfied that no snipers were crouching behind parked cars, he escorted his charge into the hospital.

"I go with you everywhere," he announced. "Orders."

"Even to the bathroom?"

Jones grinned. "Well, maybe I'll stand outside, guard the door. Check it out first, though."

Randollph wanted to comb his hair which, he was sure, didn't need combing. He doubted that St. Peter worried about his grooming before preaching to the three thousand, or that John Calvin fussed about the set of his cap when making pastoral rounds in Geneva. But he couldn't help it. He knew he was guilty of narcissism or at least unnecessary pride in his appearance. But he felt certain the Almighty had too much on His mind to concern Himself with a minor vanity.

Roosevelt Jones checked out the gentlemen's comfort station for visitors, then said, "O.K., Doc." As Randollph was about to enter, a black man, old, shabbily dressed, came to the rest-room door. Jones put his huge arm across the door.

"Hey, brother, let me in," the man said. "I gotta piss, bad."

"Sorry, brother," Jones said. "Just hold it for a couple of minutes until the doc is finished."

"Who's he, the Pope?" The man eyed Randollph's collar resentfully. Then his eyes widened. "You, you the guy I see on television, the Holy Terror—"

"I'm the guy," Randollph said. "Mr. Jones, this gentleman's need has a higher priority than combing my hair. I'll just skip it."

"Thanks, Reverend," the man mumbled. As he hurried in he was saying to himself, "Oh, you pore bastid, you pore bastid."

Randollph reflected ruefully that he was now an object of public pity. He could be stern with himself, and fight off attacks of self-pity. But what could you do when people looked on you as a "pore bastid"?

Roosevelt Jones accompanied Randollph to each patient's room, first checking it before permitting Randollph to enter. Randollph wondered if Officer Jones looked under bed sheets to see if they hid a weapon. Then the policeman stationed himself outside the door while Randollph made his calls.

Most of the calls were routine, if there is such a thing as a routine pastoral call on a hospital patient. No one recovering from a severe operation. No strokes, heart attacks, cancer. No one just a step ahead of the grim reaper.

Randollph never looked forward to making hospital calls, but, once done, he was always glad he had made them. He still fidgeted about whether to say a prayer over a hospital patient or not. If he did say a prayer, his just-barely-religious parishioners were uncomfortable with it, and the very ill were afraid that, all other hope gone, prayer was the last resort. On the other hand, if he didn't pray some people said, "What kind of preacher is he that doesn't even pray with us when we're sick?"

The last card in the stack Miss Windfall had prepared was Susan A. Fosterman. Randollph had to think a minute, then remembered her as the patrician-looking lady who had scolded Sad Tad Barry at the meeting of the church's governing board. Miss Windfall had noted on her card that Susan Fosterman was a widow, wealthy, and was a member of the church's governing board.

Mrs. Fosterman was sitting in a chair, a best-selling novel in her lap. She was wearing an expensive-looking blue-and-gold brocade dressing gown. Her gray hair fell in soft, perfect waves around her face.

"Why, Dr. Randollph," she said, "how nice of you to come. Who in the world was that black man who came charging in, said "Sorry, ma'm," looked around, then charged out?"

"My bodyguard," Randollph explained. "Did he startle you?"

"Not really. Nothing much startles me anymore. I'm so sorry for all this trouble, this killing, and the threat to your life. It must be awful to live with that hanging over you."

"I'm not enjoying it. But I came to see how you are."

Susan Fosterman said: "Oh, I'm just in for my semiannual physical. Nothing wrong with me, apparently. They do have to commit indignities to your person to find out, though. I'm apparently blessed with good health, but I don't want something sneaking up on me before I know it. Is Tad Barry still pestering you?"

"I've been told that he has given a newspaper interview demanding my resignation as pastor of Good Shepherd. Says I'm unfit to be a minister—or so the reporter told me. You'll probably read it in tomorrow's paper."

Susan Fosterman sighed. "Tad is a nuisance. Always has been. He's all mixed up about sex. It fascinates him and repels him. He was orphaned when his parents died in the flu epidemic of 'eighteen. Raised by two fussy, Victorian maiden aunts, so I suppose it isn't his fault, really. But that doesn't make him less obnoxious, does it?"

"No," Randollph said. "I confess to feelings about Mr. Barry that fall short of Christian charity—way short."

Mrs. Fosterman laughed. It was the laugh of a woman who enjoyed life. "It's nice to know you're human. You're so big, and masterful, and learned that one could take you as a different order of creation."

"Please don't." Randollph, always uncomfortable when he was the subject of the conversation, changed the subject. "You're a business executive I understand?"

"Yes, I run a perfume-marketing business. I inherited it, but I'm quite good at running it. We make spectacular profits. I've put Good Shepherd in my will. Partly because I grew up in the church, was baptized there, married there, and—God willing, many years hence—will be buried from it. And partly, it's conscience money."

"Why conscience money?" Randollph was intrigued.

Mrs. Fosterman fiddled with the fat novel on her lap. "It's not easy to explain. I'm not very pious."

"I'm not either."

"No, you aren't. That's one of the things I like best about you. I believe you are pious in the best sense of that rather abused word. But you don't come on as pious. Is that a terrible thing to say to your pastor?"

"Not to me. Except that it might encourage me to pride in my nonpiety."

"Spiritual pride is a tricky business, isn't it?" Mrs. Fosterman said with a smile. Randollph noted how pleasant she looked when she smiled. "But to get on. I can't escape my religious training. I was brought up to believe that a Christian does something useful with the life he's been given. I have frequent doubts that selling perfume at outrageous markups fits the definition of a useful life." She paused a moment, then said, "I'll bet you can guess my favorite passage of Scripture."

"I'll bet I can. It's the story of the woman who anointed Jesus with expensive ointment."

"Right. It's in Matthew's gospel, isn't it?"

"All four gospels tell the story. They differ a bit in the details, but it's the same story."

Mrs. Fosterman looked as if she were annoyed at herself. "Now why didn't I know that? Could you give me the references?"

"Not from memory. I'll look them up and let you know."

"Would you?" she asked him. "Do all the stories make the point that Jesus was pleased, and that he commended the woman, and rebuked those who said it was a waste?"

"Yes, all of them."

"That's reassuring to my conscience. You've been a good pastor to me. Now let me help you."

"How?"

"By fighting your battle with Tad Barry for you. I know him so well. He'll be at the next board meeting screaming for your resignation. Don't you say a word. Don't defend yourself. He'd like that. But he's afraid of me. I have a sharp tongue. He isn't afraid of making a fool of himself, but he just hates it when I make a fool of him. I've got his number, and he knows it." She looked pleased at the prospect of making a fool of Tad Barry.

"I accept, gladly accept, your kind offer," Randollph said.

"But, Dr. Randollph, don't underestimate Tad Barry," Susan Fosterman warned him. "He's an old fuddy-duddy, but he's a fanatic. He'll go to any ends to have his way. He can't get at you through the church—I'll see to that. But he'll use the newspapers, that ridiculous organization of his, and heaven knows what else to bring you down. Fanatics are hard to handle because they are so irrational."

"I know," Randollph said. "The history of the Church is my field, and that's a story filled with fanatics. I don't claim to understand them, but I know enough to be afraid of them." Randollph decided a prayer wasn't called for in the case of Susan Antonia Fosterman, and left.

When Randollph returned to the church he was still aglow from the pleasant and stimulating conversation with Susan Fosterman and the sense of having performed good works. He decided the euphoria would brace him to face reading Bertie Smelser's financial reports, and asked Miss Windfall to bring them in.

She placed the stack of photocopied sheets on his desk, and also a letter.

"This came for you special delivery while you were out," Miss Windfall said.

Randollph glanced at the envelope and knew immediately

from whence it came. The dime-store envelope, the typed
address, no return address.

He tore it open. One sheet of paper with a poem typed on it.

> A wise man wrote in accents pure
> "Luck's a chance, but trouble's sure."
> I missed you once I'm frank to say
> But there will come another day.
> And mark it well (I do not rave)
> That day will see you in your grave.

Chapter Thirteen

Randollph was dressing for a party he wished he didn't have to attend. Struggling with a recalcitrant over-the-calf hose he ripped a seam in the toe.

"Oh, hell," he muttered.

"My, did I hear the good doctor use bad language?" Sam asked as she stepped into very brief, very flimsy panties.

"There may be worse to come," he said. "Why do we have to go to this confounded party anyway? Why can't we just stay home and—"

Sam put two fingers across his lips. "Don't be naughty, Reverend. We have to go for the sake of appearances."

"Why? What does that mean?"

Sam looked as if she were collecting her thoughts. "It means that I haven't been entirely honest with you, Doctor dear. I'd better do a little confessing." Then, demurely, "I hope you won't hate me."

"Samantha," Randollph said, "no matter what you confessed to, it would not diminish my love for you."

Sam lunged into his arms. "Oh, Randollph, I wish you

wouldn't say a lovely thing like that when we have to go out. It makes me so horny."

"We could be late," he suggested.

She pulled away. "We're already late," she said. "And I haven't confessed yet." Noticing his disappointment, she said, "Don't worry. I'll still be horny when we get home."

"So confess," he said.

"It's about Johnnie DeBeers. This party to kiss him good-bye before he leaves for his new job in California, well, it's all my fault, or my doing—his leaving, I mean."

"You had an affair with him, then discarded him and married me, is that what you are trying to tell me?"

"For a clergyman you have a dirty mind," she replied.

"That's what Tad Barry says."

"Oh, Randollph, I'm sorry. I didn't mean it like that."

"I know," he said gently.

"Would it make any difference if I'd had an affair with Johnnie?"

"No," he said thoughtfully. "No. It wouldn't thrill me to know that you'd had that kind of relationship with him. But I could swallow it. I repeat, I wouldn't feel differently about you."

"That's beautiful, really beautiful," she said. "But rest your mind. Johnnie DeBeers had it bad. He tried to get me into bed, and when that didn't work he asked me to marry him. He begged. He pleaded. He crawled. He was angry. He was kind. I'm used to the boys who are out for a quick lay," she added. "They figure there's no harm in trying. You learn to brush them off like flies. But Johnnie, well, he started out just trying his luck, but ended up bat-eyed in love with me. He never gave up until we announced our wedding. Then he went out looking for another job far, far away."

"Like joining the Foreign Legion?"

"Something like that. I never told you because I thought you might want me to quit working there with a man who still had the hots for me."

"Samantha, let's get one thing straight." Randollph knew he was using his classroom voice but couldn't help it. "You are not my chattel. You have a career, and how you conduct it is up to you. Consult with me if you wish. But the decision is yours. I'll not interfere. Anyway, how could I order you not to work around men who have the hots for you? You'd be unemployed."

She gave him a quick kiss. "Professor, you do put things beautifully. Now hurry up and get dressed."

The party was being held at the television station so that Johnnie DeBeers could take time out to do the ten o'clock news with minimal interruption to the farewells and best-wishes. A studio the size of a small airplane hangar had been decorated for the occasion. Cables and cameras and props were pushed to the side, and a long buffet table set up in the center. In one corner a bar was catering to a constant line of customers. The room, though large, was full of people. To Randollph's eye it seemed like a sea. Little clots of people in conversation formed islands through which those headed for a table or the bar had to navigate with some care. A strip down one side of the studio was in use as a dance floor.

"Johnnie DeBeers must have many friends," Randollph observed to Sam.

"He's very popular around town. Then, his father has friends. And his mother, I suppose, but probably not many. Some of these people are from other stations. Some are newspaper people. Politicians too. They like to stay close to the media. Some gate crashers. Kup's column will have a story about the party. Thea Mason's, too. People like to see their names in the paper."

"Then this crowd isn't entirely due to a spontaneous outpouring of affection for Johnnie DeBeers?"

"The beautiful people—I guess these are the beautiful people—sometimes have less than beautiful motives for what they do," Sam replied. "Some of them may just be looking for a free lunch."

"Dance with the guest of honor, Sam? With the reverend doctor's permission, of course." Johnnie DeBeers had approached from their blind side. Randollph wondered how much of their conversation he had overheard.

Sam looked quickly at Randollph. "How could I say no to the guest of honor?" Randollph answered him. "Trot along, children."

Randollph, to suppress a tweak or two of jealousy, was

meditating on the bizarre events of the last few weeks. He speculated about the identity of the Holy Terror. Did he, like the Son of Sam, hear voices telling him to kill? What kind of personal history had forged and fashioned his hatred of clergymen whose holiness—if any—was spattered with moral ugliness? Why was he, Randollph, selected for a target? Even if Sad Tad Barry's charge against him were true, how could anyone class a liking for pornography with greed, manslaughter, and murder? How soon would Lieutenant Casey catch him? Would it take a lucky break such as the one that had nabbed Son of Sam? How long would he have to endure the companionship of a police guard? Would the Holy Terror win, after all, and see Randollph in his grave?

"Is that Seven-up you're drinking, preacher man?" Thea Mason slid into the chair vacated by Sam. Her dark, hard beauty was accentuated, Randollph thought, by very tight-fitting sand-colored gabardine slacks, black silk shirt unbuttoned halfway to her navel, and heavy gold-and-ruby earrings. She looked like a well-tailored gypsy.

"No, Thea," he said, looking at his glass of colorless liquid now tepid, "it's a little white wine and seltzer water. Good for the stomach and it doesn't inebriate."

"God, I thought you were one Bible-thumper who's a swingin' guy. 'It doesn't inebriate,'" she mocked him. "You sound like my holy-holy old man."

Randollph could see that the gossip columnist was half drunk. He hoped she wouldn't be trying to get some kind of quote out of him for her column.

She drank from a highball glass whose contents were dark enough to be almost straight whiskey. "However, my offer to rent you for a week still stands. You game?"

Randollph tried a pleasant smile on her. "You'd have to work that out with my wife. She arranges for all my female companionship. She tells me, though, that she has me booked up for the foreseeable future."

"I'll bet she does." Thea took another drink. "Perpetual honeymoon, huh? Well, I can wait. The old magic, it wears off. I ought to know. Been through plenty of husbands, lovers myself. Sooner or later everyone needs a little variety. I'll wait. Know why I drink?"

"Because you enjoy it, I suppose." It was all Randollph could think to say.

"No. Don' enjoy it. Stuff doesn't taste good. Feel lousy next morning. Drink to forget. Lot to forget."

"Most of us have a lot we'd like to forget." Randollph thought this might placate her. He didn't want to hear a recital of what Thea Mason was trying to forget.

Thea Mason snagged a fresh highball from the tray of a passing waiter, tasted it, and made a face. "Ugh! Too weak. Have to drink too much mixer to get enough th' real stuff. Have to keep trotting to the ladies' room, drink many of these. Know why I've got a lot to forget?"

"No." The less he said, the better, Randollph decided.

"'Cause I'm a gossip columnist. I know everything about everybody. I keep files on anybody that is anybody, an'"—she coughed as she swallowed more of her drink—"an' on plenty people aren't much of anybody. Thea hears. Thea knows. Jus' pick out someone out there in that mob, anyone you know, an' I'll tell you 'bout 'em. Go on."

Randollph didn't think this was a good idea, but getting into an argument with the drunken columnist was even a worse idea. He looked at the dance floor. The only people he saw immediately that he could identify were the tall news director who was dancing with a petite female reporter. He decided it was safer to choose the man. He couldn't remember his name.

"The tall fellow, the news director or whatever he's called."

"Adrian Holder. Yes. Well. Studied to be an actor. Loves Shakespeare. Married a sweet little Polish Catholic girl. Chicago's got more sweet little Polish girls than Warsaw. But Adrian, dear boy that he is, he's got a violent streak in him. Got a little drunk, beat up the sweet little wife. Spent time in jail once. Got out. Got drunk. Went lookin' for sweet lil' wife. Found out she was stayin' at church rectory for protection. He bangs around, tryin' get in. Priest, a big Pole, comes out and beats him up so good puts him in hospital. Exit sweet lil' wife. Hates Pollacks. Hates Cath-Catholics." Thea stopped to burp. "Hates Catholic priests. Spe-cially big ones."

Thea's speech was becoming progressively slurred. Randollph hoped she would be unable to unload any more information on other people's sins.

"Now take dear little Marva Luscome—she's the one dancing with Adrian. Let me tell you about her."

Randollph wanted to say, "Excuse me, but there is someone I have to see," but that would be cowardly. He thought of saying, "Shut up." But that would be rude. Anyway, he didn't have a chance to say or do anything. Thea went right on.

"Marva, she's a witch. She's pretty. Good at her job. Looks like a saint. But she got a wicked soul. A nympho, nympho—what am I tryin' to say, guess I'm a little drunk."

"I expect you are trying to say 'nymphomaniac.'"

"Yeah. Someone screws anybody comes along. Marva's had it on with half the men here and plenty of the women. The lil' darling's a switch hitter. You should see her naked." Thea's eyes glittered. "Lovely, ab-abshlutly exshquisite! She's cap, capble— ah hell, she'd do anything. Wicked lil' girl. Likes t' see people suffer. Shud see her naked! An angel. Why—"

Randollph hastily diverted the conversation the only way he could think of.

"Tell me—ah—" He searched for a name and noticed John DeBeers at the bar. "Tell me about John DeBeers, Mr. DeBeers senior, that is."

Thea immediately warmed to the idea. "Good man. Sad life." She fumbled for a tissue and wiped her eyes. "Marriage turned sour. Wife should be in a convent. Lives for prayin' an' Johnnie junior. Wan' him to be a priest—prob'y though' he'd make pope. Nice lady once. Then got more 'n more religious. Mass every day. An'—what Catholics do, confess, say rosary, 'tend spirishal retreats all the time? That's our Lucia. Her husband wants to love her but she's too busy lovin' Jesus an' Johnnie junior. Drives him to other women's arms when rather be in hers. I ought to know. I ought to know." She wiped her eyes again. "Then, when Johnnie junior flunks out priest school, an' husband seeks sol, shol, what 'm I tryin' say?"

"Solace."

"Yeah. Seeks solace with other dames, she turns sullen an' takes up drinkin'. Can you beat that? She has to drink 'cause she's so religious." Thea started to giggle, then laugh, then cry. Randollph felt as helpless as if someone had instructed him to diaper a messy baby.

He was rescued by John DeBeers.

"Doctor, help me get her out of here," he instructed Randollph. They half carried, half walked a limp and unprotesting Thea Mason to an office that had a couch in it. They deposited her on the couch and DeBeers found a light blanket in a closet to throw over her.

"A troubled lady," he said. "Lots of hostility under that sophisticated, woman-of-the-world pose. She does this every now and then when she's under too many pressures. Let her sleep awhile, and then I'll see that she gets to her apartment."

"Will she be able to go to her office tomorrow?" Randollph asked, more to make conversation than elicit information.

"Her apartment is her office. She has a large penthouse over on the drive. Most of her work is by telephone, anyway," DeBeers explained. He seemed to be quite familiar with Thea Mason, her apartment, and her habits, Randollph thought.

"Sit down, Doctor. This is my office. Your policeman, by the way, is just outside. He followed us here. I suppose he's a comfort, under the circumstances, but it must be a nuisance all the same. I'm awfully sorry you're in this fix."

"Thank you," Randollph said. "And may I say I'm sorry your son is leaving these parts."

"We'll miss him," DeBeers said. "His mother is crushed by it." He looked thoughtful. Also, Randollph thought, a little sad. "I sometimes think it's a mistake to have only one child."

"One is better than none." Randollph knew that sounded inane, but what do you say to a man who, too late, says he should have had more children?

John DeBeers abruptly switched subjects. "Doctor, do you think, how shall I say it, a person can be too religious?"

"Yes," Randollph answered. "Yes, of course."

"My father would be turning in his grave if he knew I even asked such a question. And"—a grin spread across DeBeers's broad, handsome face—"he'd pronounce you a heretic for answering as you just did.

"You see," he continued, "I was raised in a strict Dutch Reformed home. My father was a schoolteacher, but, like most people in our community, he was obsessed with religion. Dutch Reformed Christians, at least the kind where I grew up, loved, simply loved, the doctrine of man's total depravity. My father, I'm sure, thought of Jesus as a disciple of John Calvin. The trouble with the world was too little religion. There could never be too much."

"You've rejected all that, I take it?" Randollph asked.

"Yes. Yes, if you can ever cleanse your mind of what was rubbed, beaten, and riveted into it when you were young. My father wanted me to marry a nice religious Dutch girl—he picked her out—and become a clergyman. So I went into journalism, rejected the Church, and married an Italian Catholic girl. So you see I'm not the one bothered by too much religion. It's my wife."

Randollph didn't say anything. This, apparently, was his night to listen to people inclined to talk about the devious and uneven roads they had traveled.

"Lucia was a lovely girl when I met her," DeBeers's monologue continued. "She was an English teacher, and I taught journalism at the same high school. This was in northern Michigan, and we both enjoyed the outdoor life. Skiing. Camping. Fishing. Hunting. She looks frail, but she could shoot a deer and skin it out faster than I could. Those were marvelous days!" DeBeers ran a hand through his thick blond hair. "Marvelous days! Do all marriages run down, people just grow apart with the years?"

"I should hope not," Randollph said. He was unable to imagine that time could eat at his love for Sam, or chill the burning need to be near her, to know that their lives were one. Yet already this evening two people had testified that the flame of love does flicker and burn low.

"Sorry. I shouldn't have asked that of a bridegroom. But what I'm trying to say is that religion—too much religion—is hurting my wife. As reality becomes increasingly difficult for her she retreats into the peasant Catholicism of her youth. As a pastor, don't you think that's bad?"

Randollph had learned, in his year or so at Good Shepherd, that people with problems—especially marital problems—nearly always try to enlist the counselor on their side. It was easy for a pleasant, well-spoken man like John DeBeers to phrase his account of a situation so as to exonerate himself. Religion, too much "peasant Catholicism," was the culprit. This was a neat way of saying that it was, after all, his wife who was at fault. Randollph hadn't heard Lucia DeBeers's side of the story. The best thing to do was to give a straightforward answer to John

DeBeers's question, a general statement that might or might not apply to this situation.

"I am convinced," Randollph spoke slowly, "that religion— Christianity or any other worthy faith—serves best by presenting us with a picture of reality and showing us how to respond to it, deal with it, cope with it. Religion, healthy religion, provides us with the values by which to live in the real world. Do I sound too much like a professor teaching a class?"

DeBeers laughed. "My father and his friends sat around the kitchen stove debating the doctrine of predestination. I feel right at home. Please go on."

"You asked for it," Randollph said. "Well, take Christianity. It tells us how the godly person should handle life's plain, disappointments, frustrations. But some people can't manage it, or won't try. So they use religion as a shield against reality. They find—in acts of piety and rigid adherence to what they imagine are God's demands—they find an alternative to the real world, a better world, a world they can live in. That kind of religion is bad for people because, in distorting reality, they also distort their own personalities."

"You're against acts of piety, as you call them?"

"Not at all. Worship, meditation, prayer—when performed in the context of reality—enlighten the mind and strengthen the spirit for living by faith in the world. I must admit, though," Randollph added, "that I'm personally not given to lengthy pieties. I am unable to pray for hours on end—or even minutes on end. I'm impatient with sermons that go much over twenty minutes, and worship services that last more than an hour. Symptoms of my imperfect faith, no doubt."

"Lucia goes to mass and confession every day. She has a prie-dieu in her room and wears out her knees on it. And now she says she has daily conversations with various saints. That's just too much religion! She's nervous and snappish and unhappy, and I think all that religion is making her that way. At least, it's a contributing factor." He sounded angry.

"Jung says somewhere in his writings that"—Randollph scratched his head—"I can't quote him exactly, but what he said was that the exceedingly virtuous are often irritable, and given to moodiness and frequent flashes of temper. Religion and virtue are not synonymous, but I've observed that these symptoms are common to the very virtuous and the overly religious."

"Is there any cure?" DeBeers sounded hopeless.

"Not unless the patient wants to be cured. That, or a miracle."

DeBeers sighed in resignation. "I was afraid of that." He looked at Thea Mason, who was snoring softly. "I appreciate your listening to me. Not many people I can talk to. I have no priest or pastor. Well, let's get back to Johnnie's party."

Johnnie's party was galloping along. People were crowding around the long buffet table. Sam was still dancing with Johnnie DeBeers, but broke off when she saw Randollph and came to him, Johnnie following.

"Wherever have you been, C.P.?" There was a note of reprimand in her voice.

"I led him away," John DeBeers, Sr., said. "That is, we had to help Thea, ah, to a place she could, ah, rest. We took her to my office, and the doctor and I remained to talk a bit. Sorry."

Sam brightened. "Marva said he'd gone off somewhere with Thea. She didn't say anything about you, John. She just said I'd better watch out because Thea had a passion for my husband—"

"That's the way Marva would tell it," Johnnie, Sr., interrupted. "She loves to make trouble."

Randollph chuckled. "Thea Mason was in no condition to exercise her charms."

"Oh." Sam said. "One of Thea's nights to get a snootful."

"Why don't we have something to eat?" John DeBeers suggested. "May I fix you a plate, my dear?" he asked his wife, who had quietly joined them. She was sober, Randollph noticed, but looking very depressed.

"Randollph, there's steak tartare," Sam said, pointing to a large platter. "Eat your fill. Ugh! Raw meatballs."

"You like that stuff?" Johnnie DeBeers asked.

"An exotic taste, perhaps," Randollph answered. "One I'm seldom able to indulge. Samantha detests it. Clarence refuses to prepare it for me."

"Why?"

"On the grounds that raw, scraped beef combined with raw eggs, no matter if it is flavored with onions and anchovies and capers, is proper food only for dogs. God intended meat to be cooked, he claims."

"In other words, you're a savage?" Johnnie DeBeers persisted. He was just short of being downright nasty.

"Dance with me, C.P. You can eat that cannibal food later." Sam led him away.

The next morning, at breakfast, Sam was reading to Randollph from Thea Mason's column.

"Thea hears," she read, "that the Reverend Doctor C. P. Randollph, target of the Holy Terror and of Thaddeus Barry and his antiporno organization, didn't drink any inebriating beverages at Johnnie DeBeers's farewell bash, but filled up on steak tartare instead. . . . Loves the stuff, he says, but since his wife (TV's Sam Stack) hates it, he can't get it at home. . . ."

"How did Thea hear all that while sleeping it off in John DeBeers's office?" Randollph asked.

"Thea has plenty of spies," Sam informed him. "She knows everything about everybody. Makes her a little kinky, I think."

Chapter Fourteen

"I don't like it, I don't like it, I don't like it!" Sam Stack was almost yelling at Adrian Holder.

The news director was patient. "What don't you like about it, Sam?"

"I don't like anything about it, Adrian, not anything. And don't hand me any of that 'You're lovely when you're angry' bull."

Holder smiled gently. "But you are, you know." He paused. "Now, Sam, we agreed that we would change the format of *Sam Stack's Chicago* to an audience-participation show—sort of make you into a female Phil Donahue. You said you'd like that."

"I like that, sure. Who wouldn't? But—"

Holder interrupted. "Now let's take it step by step. Hear me out, O.K.?" He got a curt nod from Sam and went on. "This antipornography racket Tad Barry and that reverend sidekick of his are making—is it or isn't it the hottest public issue in Chicago at the moment?"

Samantha awarded him a reluctant nod of agreement.

"Now," he said, "can you think of a better, more provocative topic, a topic that would produce higher ratings for our first show under the new format than this porno thing?"

"No, Adrian, I can't. But why in hell does my husband have to be on the show?"

"Because, dear Samantha, he's at the very center of the antismut storm. He's a big name. Famous pro quarterback turned to calling the plays for God's team—"

"Oh, cut it out, Adrian!"

"Sorry, Sam. I'm just painting the picture the public sees. The average schmuck thinks in those terms, you know that. The slob in the street feels all warm and nice inside when one of these big boobs turns in his shoulder pads for a Bible—"

"Now damn it, Adrian, I won't—"

Holder stopped her. "Let me finish, Sam. I don't mean your husband is one of those spiritual Neanderthals who grunts about how good old God helped him slap the other guy senseless. That's part of the angle. The jackasses staring at the tube can understand the brain-damaged hulk who says he's joined up with Jesus—he's a stock character on the American scene. What will intrigue them—and give your new format a hell of a kick-off program—is a big-name athlete-turned-preacher who isn't at all what they expect. He's educated. Theologically informed. And—to their amazement—doesn't come on with the standard I-hate-dirty-books-and-movies stuff they expect from a preacher."

"You make it sound like he's all for T and A, maybe worse." Sam spoke like a prosecuting attorney.

"I know he isn't, you know he isn't. But the public doesn't understand that he isn't. That's the beauty of the show. He's got a big television platform. It's up to him—and to you—to convince the public that he's not proporn but anticensorship."

Sam rolled this around in her mind. "People know he's my husband. They'll think I'm giving him the best of it."

"No," Holder contradicted her. "No, period. You play the devil's advocate. Just like Donahue does. You're a pro, Sam. Your husband can take care of himself. Surely you've had some practice in disagreeing with him?"

Sam laughed at him. "Come on, Adrian, you sound like Thea trying to get a scandal started. Sure, we disagree. He's a Christian preacher. I'm an agnostic. How's that for a disagreement?"

"Wow! That would make a smash program—you versus your husband—"

"Knock it off, Adrian."

"O.K. O.K. No harm in dreaming."

"And I suppose that it doesn't make this porno debate any less attractive because my husband is also being chased by the Holy Terror?"

"Look, Sam, I'm sorry about that. But that's the way it is. No, it sure won't hurt the program's ratings."

"All right, Adrian, I'll do it. I don't like it, but I'll do it. C.P. won't want to do it, and I won't coax. But he knows he needs to explain himself publicly on his stand against Tad Barry, so he'll probably do it. Will you have other guests?"

"Sure. Sad Tad and that preacher he tows around—the Reverend Jack Dan something—the national secretary for Citizens for a Moral America." He looked pleased with himself. "That ought to blow out a few picture tubes!"

Randollph dressed carefully for his guest appearance on his wife's television show. Adrian Holder had wanted him to wear clerical garb, but he'd refused. He wasn't appearing as a representative of a holy calling. People looked on a man in clericals as a stereotype, and expected him to talk and act as they thought a clergyman should. Randollph had learned that people wanted their preachers to be human enough to eat a sixteen-ounce steak, snicker at a scatalogical joke, while presenting a straightlaced I'm-against-sin demeanor in public. They'd know he was a pastor, of course, but he didn't want them reminded of it every time they looked at him. He wanted to get across to them that he was speaking, tonight, as a citizen. Sam had explained to him that, in television, what people see makes more of an impression than what they hear. This, Randollph supposed, was a measure of the growing indifference to precise verbal expression. The image, not the substance, was what got across on the screen.

He'd try to look like a well-turned-out concerned citizen, he decided. He should have gone for a blue or gray suit, white shirt, and dark tie. But that was just too much. He selected, instead, an olive vested suit, blue oxford-cloth button-down shirt, and a blue-and-olive tie in regimental stripes. Too stylish for IBM or a Boston investment house catering to the Cabots and Lowells, but acceptable in Chicago as conservative enough for bright young executives.

He wasn't looking forward to the evening. At the same time he was anxious for the opportunity to explain himself, defend himself against Sad Tad Barry's charge that he was a pornography lover. Sad Tad Barry was an idiot. But, Sam had told him, you have to be wary of idiots when they confront you on a TV talk show. No matter how sincere and well spoken you are, they can make you look bad.

The bishop had also urged care and caution.

"It's a golden gift, this opportunity to explain yourself on a popular television program, C.P. I don't mind saying that I've been more than a bit worried about your Mr. Barry and his charges." The bishop, Randollph saw, looked worried. Usually he reminded you of a grown-up kewpie doll. His round face, topped with sparse graying hair, normally reflected a placid amiability. The weight of office, the exasperating problems of dealing with clerics whose professional ambitions substantially exceeded their abilities, placating congregations demanding pastors combining the best qualities of Francis of Assisi, St. John Chrysostom, and Henry Ward Beecher (and at a minimum salary), plus the pesterings of special interest groups wanting episcopal blessing and money for their righteous causes—all this had failed to cut any lines of care into his chubby face. But now he frowned with concern.

"Barry's a fool, Freddie. It's ungracious of me to speak of one of my parishioners that way, I know, but it's a fact. I'm worried about it, naturally. But people know him for what he is. And I know how important it is that I state my case. That's why I'm willing to go on this confounded television program. Samantha, by the way, is reluctant to do the show and urged me to refuse if I didn't want to do it. But I'll be careful. Aren't you making too much of it?"

"No, C.P., I'm not making too much of it. It's more complicated than you seem to grasp."

"How so?"

"It's not Barry I'm worried about."

"What, or whom, are you worried about?"

The bishop took a moment to answer. "I'm worried about the situation getting out of hand. Through no fault of your own you could get plastered with the image of a free-wheeling—that's a dated figure of speech, isn't it? But let it suffice—a free-wheeling, sex-oriented, swinging pastor. And this damnable Holy Terror and his poetic charges only serve to reinforce that image."

"I know that, Freddie."

"No, C.P., you don't know. Or—in the confidence of one who knows his heart is pure—you refuse to believe that you might lose this battle."

"I don't intend to lose it."

"I know you don't. But, as one who has great affection for you and"—he emphasized the "and"—"as the one who has the responsibility for whatever problems this mess causes the church, I have to consider the possibility that you might lose."

"You mean I might have to resign my pastorate?" Randollph was amazed that this thought chilled him more than the specter of the Holy Terror. That threat, dreadful as it was, could be lived with. He had learned to live with it, however uncomfortably. Constant danger dulled fear. But he didn't know if he could live with a forced resignation from Good Shepherd. He suddenly realized what he had not comprehended before—that his marriage, his sense of his place and significance in life, his feeling that he was doing what a benign Providence had laid out for him to do before the foundations of the world were hammered into place, were all structured on his pastorate at Good Shepherd. He felt that his whole life would come apart if this were to happen. He could put his life back together. He knew this. But he didn't want to have to do it.

"C.P.," the bishop answered, "I'd fight for you. I'd gladly be bloodied in the fray if it would save you. But a bishop isn't God, even if some of my episcopal brethren fail to understand this distinction. If a minister, however innocently, gets himself stuck with an image unacceptable to the public and to his congregation, there's nothing a bishop can do to help. I know you aren't addicted to lecherous art. You know it. You can state that you aren't. But if Barry and his gang can persuade the public that you are, or even raise substantial doubt in the public mind, you can't live it down."

"That bad, Freddie?"

"Yes. That bad. The public will forgive a preacher who is a glutton." The bishop patted his plump belly. "It will even overlook pecuniary shenanigans. Just look at all the big-name television evangelists and their irregular financial affairs. But the public simply will not accept a clergyman it suspects of even thinking a lot about sex."

"All right, Freddie, I'll keep that in mind, even though it's hard for me to understand."

"And another thing to keep in mind," the bishop continued, "is that no one is more vicious and hateful than a religious extremist. I understand this is to be a show where the audience is allowed to ask questions or make comments."

"That's right."

"Then, repeat after me, C.P. 'I will refuse to argue theology or the Bible with anyone in the audience.'"

"Oh, now, Freddie—" Randollph protested.

"No, I mean it, C.P. That's a game you can't win."

"Would you kindly explain that?" Randollph was beginning to feel irritated.

"It's this way," the bishop said blandly. "You will be better informed on these subjects than anyone else—guests or audience—on the show. But the viewing public knows nothing of theology, and less than nothing about the Bible. Meaning that what they do know, or think they know, or the vague notions they have about it are almost invariably wrong."

Randollph started to speak, but the bishop stopped him. "I know I sound as if I suffer from intellectual pride. But I state what is a regrettable fact."

"So?"

"So, when some zealous but ignorant Christian flings Bible verses at you, you—with your teacher's instincts—will be tempted to set him straight."

"I fail to see what is wrong with correcting error, Freddie."

"I know, and that's why I'm warning you. In the first place, people who misuse the Scriptures are not vulnerable to logic. They are devoid of the irenic spirit. They see themselves as embattled defenders of the faith. You will not change their minds."

"So I won't change their minds. I ought to say where I stand." Randollph wasn't feeling much of the irenic spirit himself.

"If you do that, you'll win your point but convince the viewing public that you are a smart-aleck professor who thinks he knows it all," the bishop said. "Once convinced of that, the viewers will have little difficulty believing that you are guilty of Thaddeus Barry's charges against you."

Randollph suddenly felt weary. "Am I permitted to say anything at all?"

"Don't be testy, C.P. Say as little as possible. Stay away from any discussion of pornography—at least, as much as you possibly can. Stick to the freedom-of-speech-and-information issue. You're on solid ground there."

Randollph sighed. "All right, Freddie, I'll try my best."

"And remember, C.P.," the bishop admonished him, "that St. Augustine said the three great Christian virtues are humility, humility, and humility."

Randollph knew the bishop was right. He disliked admitting to himself that if he ended up in hell or even was sentenced to a long stretch in purgatory it would be for the sin of intellectual pride. He knew he wasn't a drunk or a thief, didn't covet other men's property or wives, and—even though tempted daily by Clarence Higbee's table—had not fallen to gluttony. But his spirit of Christian charity was always strained by militant ignorance. He couldn't abide the greedy Christian businessman who testified at prayer breakfasts that God had shown him how to knock out his competitors and become top dog in his particular field of commerce. That was terrible theology. Nor could he stand the Bible-thumpers who knew a lot of scriptures but knew nothing about the Scripture. Worst of all, he was unable to quash the conviction that, because of his superior knowledge, he was superior to such people. He was ashamed of himself. But he enjoyed the smug feeling that his knowledge saved him from being like these self-righteous ignoramuses. He had to admit that he was not burdened with an excess of Christian humility.

"All right, Freddie," he said. "I'll do my best to curb my tongue. Maybe I'd better take a Valium just before the program."

Adrian Holder assembled the participants for *Sam Stack's Chicago* show and gave them a preprogram pep talk.

"This is our first program with an audience and with telephone call-ins," he said. "Now, we believe in Murphy's law around here—"

"What's that?" Thaddeus Barry asked suspiciously. Randollph noted that Barry was wearing the same old-fashioned oxford-gray suit he had worn at the Good Shepherd board meeting. Or maybe it was a duplicate. Maybe Sad Tad had an entire wardrobe of these suits. With his Herbert Hoover–style high attached collar and narrow dark tie he reminded Randollph of a Norman Rockwell painting. Except that Rockwell's characters always had a kindly look about them. Barry looked hostile.

"Murphy's law states that if anything can go wrong it probably will." Adrian Holder spoke with a practiced patience. He was accustomed to dealing with difficult guests.

"Such as?" Barry persisted.

"Well, your microphone might become disconnected, or the telephone switchboard malfunction, or someone in the audience might make an obscene remark. We're live, you know. We do have an eight-second delay which gives us a chance to cut off obscenity and other unacceptable speech. My point is, don't get flustered if something does go wrong. You don't have to handle it—we will."

"Now," he continued, "this is Sam Stack." He nodded to Sam, sitting in the corner of the room. "Isn't she pretty?" Indeed she is, Randollph wanted to say. She was dressed in a plain chocolate-brown suit over a beige cowl-neck sweater. With knees together and brown pumps planted on the floor, she looked both the demure beauty and the self-possessed career woman. But for all her modest dress she was radiantly feminine. He watched the Reverend Dr. Jack Dan Lancer look her over from ankle to bright red hair and wondered if the stalwart battler against dirty pictures was mentally undressing her.

"She's the hostess on the program, which means she's the boss," Holder went on. "She has the right and duty to prevent any guest from monopolizing the conversation. She can cut you off for commerical breaks. She will, at times, play the part of devil's advocate. She will indicate which guest is to answer questions from the audience unless the question is specifically directed to one of you. It is our custom for her guests to address her as Sam."

"Why not call her Mrs. C. P. Randollph—that's her name, isn't it?" Tad Barry sounded mean.

"Yes, I agree," Lancer said. "Dr. Randollph does seem to have an unfair advantage with his wife acting as hostess and asking the questions. I've been on many television shows"—he paused to let this fact sink in—"and I know from experience that the host can make a guest look good or bad just in the questions they ask and the manner and tone of voice in which they ask them. It is only natural that Mrs. Randollph will want her husband to look good, which means she might well do that by making some of us look bad—"

"Dr. Lancer, let me explain—" Adrian Holder sought to pacify Barry and Lancer, but Sam interrupted him.

"Let me answer the gentleman, Adrian," she said. She turned a sweet smile on the complainers. "Gentlemen, I am here tonight not as Mrs. Randollph, but as Sam Stack. As Sam Stack I'm a professional television interviewer. Whatever my personal opinion of a guest or an issue, I am always fair with them. I may challenge you. I may challenge my husband. Mr. Holder told you I'd play devil's advocate. But I'll be fair."

"I think the public ought to know that you're Mrs. Randollph. If you won't tell them, I will."

"Why, you go ahead and do that, Dr. Lancer." Sam's smile was still sweet. "But let me tell you another rule I have. When a guest tries to get crafty or pull a cheap trick like that on me, all rules go out the window. I can be ruthless, and I will be. You said a host could make a guest look bad. You're right. And you can bet your next big fat speaker's fee I will make you look bad. I told you I'm a pro at this. I know more dirty tricks than you ever thought of."

Thaddeus Barry stood up. "Come, Doctor," he said angrily, "let us withdraw from the program."

"Maybe that's a good idea," Sam shot back at him. "We have Mr. Edward Cromartie here from the American Civil Liberties Union, and Mr. Julius Brad from the City Council—and, of course, Dr. Randollph. We'll have a lively program, which will include a discussion of why you two gentlemen chose to chicken out at the last minute. One possibility we must discuss is that your complaint is just a device to let you escape a debate for which you have no stomach."

"You wouldn't!" Barry said.

"Try me, Mr. Barry, try me." Sam was all sweetness again.

"Uh, Thaddeus, let's not be hasty," Lancer muttered. "We committed ourselves to this program. We'd better see it through."

Lancer was a professional, too, Randollph thought. He knew that to stay in business he had to fight, scratch for and demand publicity. He even bought it when necessary, but his organization couldn't afford the kind of money this television exposure was giving him. If he couldn't get publicity for his cause he'd be out of a job. Randollph guessed that Dr. Lancer had no taste for giving up his national platform to preach the joys of a pornography-free society in some obscure parish. Obscure parishes seldom furnished their pastor with fat expense accounts.

Adrian Holder, appearing a bit shaken, said, "I think that now that we understand each other, we'll have a lively show. Let's find our places."

The large studio was jammed with folding chairs, and every chair was taken. Randollph knew that at the end of every row of chairs sat a policeman or policewoman in plain clothes. He saw Lieutenant Casey in the back of the room. Casey did not appear to be enjoying the occasion.

The five guests sat on a low platform, high enough to be visible to the entire audience, but not so high as to establish a marked separation between them and the people. Councilman Brad and Jack Dan Lancer both made for the center chair, with Lancer winning. Thaddeus Barry sat himself to the right of Lancer, with the A.C.L.U. lawyer, a self-possessed bulky man of about fifty, on the end. Randollph was glad to take the chair at the opposite end. Let Lancer have center stage. He didn't want it.

The TV monitor, having utilized the last possible second for advertising, suddenly flashed a mélange of city scenes accompanied by a brassy arrangement of "Chicago, Chicago, That Toddlin' Town." Then an archepiscopal voice intoned, as if announcing the second coming, "*Sam Stack's Chicago!*"

The camera switched to Sam.

With a bright smile she spoke into her hand microphone. "Chicago's talking about the campaign to suppress pornographic books, magazines, and movies here in our city. That campaign is sponsored by the Citizens for a Moral America. Mr. Thaddeus Barry, Jr."—she indicated Sad Tad sitting stiffly on his uncomfortable chair—"is president of the Midwest Regional Chapter of the C.M.A." Barry favored the audience with a minuscule nod. "We also have the Reverend Doctor Jack Dan Lancer, national executive secretary of the C.M.A. That's a nice name, Dr. Lancer."

The Reverend Doctor broke into an amiable grin. "Thank you,

Sam. I often say I'm just a Lancer for the Lord." Randollph winced.

"Mr. Walter Cromartie represents the American Civil Liberties Union, and has been a guest on our program before," Sam continued, "as has Councilman Julius Brad." Cromartie and Brad nodded pleasantly. Randollph thought Brad looked like a used-car salesman.

"Our last guest is the Reverend Doctor C. P. Randollph, pastor of the Church of the Good Shepherd. He was invited because he declined to open his prominent pulpit to Dr. Lancer, on the grounds that the 'Citizens for a Moral America' campaign is a threat to freedom of speech as guaranteed in the First Amendment to the Constitution.

"The question is, then, does pornography pose such a serious danger to our morals and our society that, in this one instance, the guarantees of freedom of speech should be set aside? We'll let the gentlemen speak briefly to the issue, then with questions from the audience, and from our viewers at home. The telephone number is on your screen." Sam paused, turned to the guests and said, "Mr. Barry, as the local leader of C.M.A., would you state the position of your organization?"

Thaddeus Barry extracted from the inside pocket of his jacket what appeared to be several folded sheets of typescript. Handling the papers as reverently as a priest elevating the host, he placed them on his knee and smoothed out the fold. "I have here," he said, "a statement which will prove beyond doubt that dirty books and pictures are at the root of every problem which is ruining this great country. If I may—"

Sam interrupted him gently. "Mr. Barry, could you summarize your statement?" She eyed the sheaf of pages on Barry's knee. "We have so many voices to be heard that brevity is essential."

"But that's not fair," he protested. "It is essential that we be given the opportunity to present our message fully—"

"I know it's not fair," Sam said. "Television isn't fair. It insists that we cram too much into too little time. But we have to obey its command, don't we?"

"I still say—"

"Perhaps I could summarize for Mr. Barry." Jack Dan Lancer smoothly swiped the camera from Tad Barry. Lancer was no dummy, at least when it came to television talk shows, Randollph decided. He looked like he could be a younger brother of the bishop. He was short, nearly fat, and bald. Like Thaddeus Barry, he was dressed in a dark suit, white shirt, and dark tie. But the suit was well cut, and selected from the three-to-four-hundred-dollar rack, Randollph estimated. His tie was a tapestry of small geometric patterns in various shades of blue. He could be taken for a vice-president of an insurance company except that he wore ankle-length black socks which left off too soon, revealing a section of plump milky calf when he crossed one leg over the other—a sartorial transgression not tolerated in bank or boardroom. But whatever his incongruities of attire, Lancer knew how to conduct himself on a talk show. He rapidly mounted an attack on "this vicious and degrading traffic in the obscene which is contrary to Christian morality and corrupts our children." He received long and loud applause from the studio audience. Randollph, clearly, was a prisoner in the enemy's camp.

When the applause died, Sam said, "I can't see why Christian ministers would disagree about the issue of pornography. Dr. Lancer has made a strong and lucid case against the dangers of exposing the public, especially our children, to written and pictorial filth. Do you challenge this, Dr. Randollph?"

"No," Randollph said.

"You mean you believe, like Dr. Lancer, that pornography is a danger to society?" Sam had assumed a puzzled expression.

"Yes," Randollph said.

Sam puckered her brow. "Then why do you refuse to support C.M.A.'s campaign to suppress it?"

Bless your pretty little red head, Randollph thought. "Because I see no way to do it without destroying, at the same time, freedom to say, or write, or draw what we wish. If we have to choose between the dissemination of material which offends us, or suppressing freedom of information, then we'd best tolerate the offensive material. Our society would survive that—at least, it has survived it up to now. But there is absolutely no doubt that we could not survive the suppression of freedom of speech, of free access to information." You sound like a professor lecturing students, he told himself. But he got a hand. Not so boisterous as the cheers awarded Dr. Lancer, but sturdy applause.

Sam had her microphone stuck under the nose of a woman in the audience. Randollph's appraising eye put together a picture

of a stylish brown tweed suit, expensive coiffure, lightly painted
sixty-year-old lips, and eyes that glittered with hostility. He was
pretty sure that he was about to catch it.

"My father was a preacher man," the lady said. "The first thing
he did when he took a church was to lead the community in a
campaign to clean up the news stands. Clean, that is, ah, get rid
of the dirty magazines. Then he'd, he, ah, got the citizens to
examine the books in the libraries—he always went after, ah,
went first to the school libraries, and, that is, what he got the
people to do was make them, I mean the school board, get rid of
books that had sex and anti-American ideas—"

The A.C.L.U. lawyer interrupted her. "And books that presented the theory of evolution, did he get rid of them also?" Mr.
Cromartie's voice was genial, and he asked the question with a
friendly smile.

"Yes, them too. He wouldn't allow a modern novel in our
house. I just want to say that, you know, if Dr. Randollph had the
same high Christian ideals my father had—that is, what I mean,
how can a Christian minister approve of pornography? I loved my
father." She sat down, put her hands over her face, and shook
with sobbing. The audience applauded.

She's like a character out of a Harold Pinter play, Randollph
thought. She says one thing and means something else. She says
"I loved my father," but her hard and loveless voice is saying, "I
hated my father." Randollph felt compassion for her. What a grim
childhood and adolescence she must have had in a house ruled
by a stern patriarch rigid with the righteousness of the uninformed. How awful it must be, years after her father was dust and
a memory, to force herself to proclaim that she loved and revered
him. She probably believed with her mind that she did love him,
but her spirit knew differently. She had constructed an iron-
bound personality, probably similar to her father's, which stood
guard against the world, and fulfilled her duty as faithful
daughter. But inside her soul was seething. Had the lady's
preacher-man father also had a rigid and domineering father? Or
mother? Had she inherited an acquired characteristic? That
didn't hold water biologically, Randollph knew. But maybe it
was valid psychology. A person could go on pretending and
proclaiming to believe what, in the murky depths of his soul, he
rejected. Or one could rebel and kick over the traces. Or could

he? Could rebellion—total rebellion, or what one thought to be total rebellion—ever chase away these demons that lurked in the spirit? One could be broken by the conflict, Randollph supposed. One could try, through violent and irrational behavior, to exorcise the evil spirits. Or one could have a nervous breakdown. He'd be willing to make an even bet, he decided, that this lady would end up in the funny farm. And, he told himself, best he should take some courses in psychology if he intended to carry on as a pastor—though God knew when he'd find the time.

But suddenly a cloudlet of insight was forming up in his brain. It had something to do with the identity of the Holy Terror, but was too amorphous as yet to yield any information. Anyway, he'd better keep his mind on the business at hand lest he make a fool of himself before this audience, thousands of viewers at home, his wife, and God.

"I'm sure this lady's father acted according to his best conscience," Randollph said. He guessed that the old tyrant acted not from conscience but from a reinforced concrete will to make others behave as he thought best for them. But such gracious prevarications as he had just uttered were lightly punished in the hereafter, Randollph believed, if at all. "But," he continued, "the lady asked how could I, a Christian minister, approve of pornography? Again, I do not approve of pornography. I approve of free expression." Moderate clapping punctuated his words, but the lady who had started the dialogue, he noticed, still had her face in her hands. He doubted that she had even heard him. He was learning, he thought ruefully, what the politicians and the Jack Dan Lancers had mastered early on—that people hear what they want to hear.

Sam pushed the microphone at a tall man with a beautiful mop of white hair.

"Eric Svensen from Rockford," he said. "Why can't we get rid of this filth on the magazine racks, and the dirty movies too, without giving up freedom of speech?"

"Why, we can, Mr. Svensen," Walter Cromartie was quick to reply.

"Then what's the argument all about?"

"The method used to get rid of pornography, that's what the argument is about."

"I don't get you."

Walter Cromartie was patient. "It is legitimate, it is American, if you will, for a community to persuade booksellers and movie houses to refuse any traffic in pornography." Cromartie paused, then asked, "Did you ever buy a copy of *Playboy* magazine, Mr. Svensen?"

"Well, ah, hmm, yes. You see, hmm, well, *Playboy* has some good articles. . . ."

The audience roared! Mr. Svensen sat down abruptly, and wished, Randollph imagined, that his chair would sink right through the floor.

"It's a dirty, nasty magazine!" Thaddeus Barry spit it out in a voice worthy of Elijah denouncing Jezebel.

"How do you know that it is a dirty, nasty magazine, Mr. Barry?" Cromartie was all innocence. "Do you read it?"

It took a second for this to sink in on the audience. There were a few snickers, then giggles, then laughter, then hilarious abandon. Thaddeus Barry writhed in fury. Randollph was afraid the old man, for whom he felt a little sorry, would have a stroke, or at least wet his old-fashioned gray trousers.

"I'm just illustrating my point," Cromartie said when the audience quieted down. "Mr. Svensen, who opposes pornography but sees literary merit in *Playboy*, wants to buy it for its editorial content. And he's right. It does carry good stories and informative articles."

"But Mr. Barry is right, too." He turned in his chair and smiled agreeably at Barry. "It does have art and written material that is pretty raw."

"It ought to be banned!" Barry shouted. Randollph wondered if the eccentric old man was quite sane. At any rate, he was grateful to Cromartie for taking the camera away, thus sparing him the wrath of Sad Tad Barry. Barry was a university graduate, presumably tutored in the arts and sciences. He held a law degree and a license to practice, never exercised. He must have enough self-awareness to know that he was making a fool of himself, that he regularly made a fool of himself. He was just one great bottle of anger and hostility. At what? The world that laughed at him, and had always laughed at him? At the maiden aunts who had raised him, turning him into a "little gentleman" and painting for him a world in which goodness meant to loathe sex? Were those boiling hatreds inside him directed at the parents who abandoned him by dying from influenza? Randollph didn't know. He was surer than ever, though, that he'd better take some courses in psychology.

"*Playboy* ought to be banned, Mr. Barry?" Cromartie's tone carried the assurance he was not trying to bait or ridicule Sad Tad, that the lawyer sought only information. "But how shall we go about banning it?"

The Lord's Lancer decided it was time to ride to the rescue. "Why, Mr. Cromartie," he said gently, "Citizens for a Moral America believes that, following the Supreme Court decision that community standards should prevail in the decision of what and what not to ban—porno material, that is—a county or municipal government should provide for the appointment of a committee of responsible citizens to decide what is permissible and what is not. That's simple enough, isn't it, Mr. Cromartie?"

"No, Dr. Lancer, it isn't."

"Why not?"

"For one thing, how do you define 'responsible citizen'?"

"Is the caller there?" Sam asked, getting Lancer off the hook. "Go ahead, you're on."

It was a harsh male voice that came out of the public-address system. "I just want to say that you ought to be ashamed of yourselves for inviting a commie from the American Civil Liberties Union on your program."

"Oh," Sam answered. "You have definite, documented information that Mr. Cromartie is a member of the Communist Party?"

"They all are, that outfit, com-symps anyway. They defend communists in the courts, don't they?"

"Yes, we do." Cromartie answered the voice in a genial tone. He'd fielded this one many times, Randollph figured. "We defend the civil rights of communists, the Ku Klux Klan, organizations of the left, political groups on the right, anyone whose civil rights are threatened."

"Commies don't have any civil rights," the public-address system said.

"Oh, yes they do," Cromartie answered. "Every American citizen enjoys all the rights provided by the Constitution. And thank you, sir, for helping me make my point. Freedom of speech has no real meaning unless it means the freedom for someone to say or write or advocate what may be repugnant to us."

Sam walked up the aisle to her husband. "Surely, Dr. Randollph, there must be limits, there must be material so utterly vile that you would not want to see it in print. Isn't there anything, anywhere you would draw the line?" She sounded accusatory. "Doesn't the Christian Church look on sex as something sacred and beautiful?"

"Yes and yes," Randollph said.

"Why two yeses?"

"Because you asked me two questions. That requires two answers."

"Oh, so I did." Sam looked just a bit put off. "Let's take the first question. You say you would draw the line at certain kinds of pornographic material. Where would you draw it?"

"At material that gratuitously portrayed sex as degrading or dehumanizing. As a Christian theologian, a theologian of sorts anyway, I start with God's gift of creation—which includes our sexual natures—as a good gift. I draw the line at material which denies this concept of sex. Do I sound like a preacher?"

"You sure do, Reverend." Sammy favored him with a malicious smile. "Good sermon, though." The audience laughed. Randollph supposed a fair portion of the people numbing their rumps on the studio's hard chairs knew that he and the pert hostess who was giving him the business were bound in holy wedlock.

"And why, Dr. Randollph, did you say 'gratuitously'? That's a big word." She got another laugh from the crowd.

"So it is," Randollph agreed, hoping that he sounded amiable. "One of the meanings of 'gratuitous' is 'uncalled for' or 'apparently unwarranted'—"

"I know that," Sam said.

Randollph grinned at her. "I was rather certain that you did know," he said. The audience tittered and giggled, seemingly enjoying this duel between husband and wife.

"We'd like to hear what you meant by it."

"I meant," Randollph explained, "that I object to the lewd and lascivious when it is portrayed for its own sake."

"That's how it's always used," Thaddeus Barry blurted out. "There's never any excuse for it. You, a Christian preacher, and, I'm ashamed to admit, my pastor—for the time being anyway—you ought to know this!"

Take it easy, Randollph warned himself. Be kind. Be gracious. Remember that he is a child of God, even if you wonder just what God had in mind when He created Sad Tad Barry.

"I understand Mr. Barry's feelings," he said in the gentlest tone he could muster. "He's seriously—and I believe sincerely—committed to his cause. Perhaps it will help make my point, though, if I remind him that the Old Testament could never have been written had it not included some characters who were guilty of rather ugly sexual behavior. When the Bible, or a novel, or a movie wants to show us an ugly character—or the ugly side of a character—they cannot do it without reference to their behavior."

"I don't believe it!" Tad Barry shouted. "There aren't any dirty words in the Bible! You're a preacher, God help us. You just show me where there's a dirty word in the Bible." He sat back, smiling the smile of one who has hurled an unanswerable challenge.

"What is a dirty word, Mr. Barry?" Randollph asked.

"Why you—" Barry struggled to control himself. "I wouldn't utter one anytime, much less on a television program. I won't say it—"

"We might have to bleep it if you did," Sam said.

"I won't say a dirty word," Barry continued, looking at Sam darkly. "You know that comedian that did that show about the seven words you can't say on radio or television?"

"George Carlin," Sam said.

"Yes. Well, those are dirty words. You won't find them in the Bible. You know what those words are, Dr. Randollph?"

"Yes. I'm not sure I could recite all seven, but I know some of them," Randollph answered.

"Well?"

"At least one of them appears in the Old Testament, perhaps more. That's in the King James translation. Later translations generally substitute euphemisms for that kind of word."

"I don't believe it. Where?"

"I think you'll find it in both books of Kings, though I can't cite chapter and verse."

Jack Dan Lancer, who, Randollph guessed, could cite chapter and verse, thought it time to get Tad Barry out of the camera's eye and himself into it. "It seems to me," he said, "that Dr.

Randollph's statement that he would draw the line puts him close to our position—"

"We have to break for a commercial," Sam said. "Back in a minute."

The studio screen flashed three commercials at them. One showed the glories of a brand of pantyhose by a generous and seductive display of female legs. It was followed by an ad touting the benefits of a shaving lotion, illustrated with several bikini-clad nymphets clustered around a chap who exuded this particular odor. The third was a promo for a daytime soap opera, luring potential viewers with a scene of a man kissing a woman as if he were munching on her.

"We're back," Sam announced. "Dr. Randollph, are you close to the position of the C.M.A., as Dr. Lancer suggested before the break? Do you want to draw the line too?"

"For myself, yes," Randollph said, a little wary now of his wife's questions. "And I'd try to persuade others to adopt my position. What I wouldn't do is petition for laws that would force other people to observe my standards."

"Why not?" the Lord's Lancer pressed him. "You agree that raw, rotten sex in books or pictures is contrary to the Christian faith. You agree that you would draw the line. But you can't draw a line without laws to keep people from stepping over it." Jack Dan Lancer leaned forward, adjusted his voice upward a few decibels to an impassioned plea with all the smoothness of a well-maintained automatic transmission. "Why won't you take the logical step, the one step that can free this great country of this filth?" The audience cheered heartily. Randollph wearily summoned his wits to say again what he had already said, when the American Civil Liberties Union lawyer said, "I'd be willing to take that step, Dr. Lancer. I'd agree to censorship, to draw that line by law."

Jack Dan Lancer was startled. Having jousted with many a Walter Cromartie he knew there was a trap somewhere—but he didn't know just where.

"You would?" he asked cautiously.

"Yes. Provided we can agree on exactly what is pornographic, and what isn't—you'll have to draw the line exactly, Dr. Lancer."

"Why, that's easy—"

"For example, Dr. Lancer, were those advertisements we just

saw on the screen there, were they pornographic? I found them to be, well, stimulating. This country sells its products—many of them—through advertising with a lot of sexual content. Would you ban that kind of advertising?"

"Well—"

"Have you been to the beach lately, Dr. Lancer? If you have, you know that many of the girls wear next to nothing. Would you establish regulations by which bathing suits could be judged modest or provocative?"

"That, uh, seems to me an—well, you see, you are, I think, getting into another area here, Mr. Cromartie." Randollph guessed that Jack Dan Lancer was hastily reviewing the size and number of contributions to his organization which came from businesses that advertised their products with the help of inadequately clad females. It took money to be the Lord's Lancer, and you had to hustle a buck wherever you could.

"No, Dr. Lancer, we're still talking about sexually suggestive material. You'll have to define precisely what is and what isn't acceptable. Have you done that? Do you have it spelled out?"

"That doesn't seem to me to be necessary—"

"Oh yes it is. Without a standard by which we are to judge, how can we pass judgment? And there's one more condition you must meet. You will agree that the censor must be fair, wise, competent to judge, and unbiased?"

Lancer, Randollph saw, was in a box. A wise and impartial censor wasn't what he had in mind. But he knew he'd better say it was what he had in mind.

"Why, yes," he said, "I agree to that."

"Then where are we to find him, Dr. Lancer? I've thought about it a lot and I've concluded that I am the only person I know who is acceptable to me as a censor. But I won't last forever. Then who can you get for the job?"

"Is the caller there?" Sam asked.

"Hello, yes, am I on?"

"You're on. Go ahead." Sam's tone was a pleasant invitation to join this clambake.

"I have a question for Dr. Randollph," the voice said. The voice painted a picture, for Randollph, of a middle-aged lady, gray hair in curlers, and wearing a tatty bathrobe.

"Ask your question," Sam urged gently. Apparently people

who phoned in to a talk show couldn't quite believe they were being heard.

"Dr. Randollph, are you a born-again Christian?"

Randollph was startled. He hadn't expected a question like that. And he didn't know how to answer it honestly. He knew what the voice meant was "Have you been to the altar in a revival-type meeting and had the emotional experience of Christ coming into your heart?" To that he would have to answer no. On the other hand, he knew that being "born again" was a metaphor for being a changed person through one's faith. Certainly he was a much different person than he would have been, than he had been, before he had consciously decided to follow the Christian faith and see where it led. Maybe he wasn't a wiser person. Maybe he wasn't even a better person—although he hoped that he was. But he knew he was a different person. Religion had been good for him, of that he was sure. It had squared him away to life in a way that nothing else could have done. It had shown him how to take an unwieldy mess of a life made up of fame, fortune, good luck, tenuous romances, and no direction or purpose, and sculpt it into if not a work of art and beauty at least a shape and a design of usefulness and inner satisfaction. The sureties of the saint he had not achieved, and probably never would. The hot ecstasies of the mystic were a mystery to him. No voice from the infinite had ever fallen on his ears. He could not summon up the peace that passes understanding by the use of recommended devotional tricks. But religion had knit up the straggling threads and rips and tears in the fabric of his life into something resembling a whole cloth. This—as he understood the meaning of the word in the New Testament—was at least the beginning of salvation.

"Yes," he answered the voice that had asked if he had been born again. He remembered the bishop's order not to debate theology or the Bible, but decided he had to add something if he were to be even in the same ballpark with honesty. "Anyone who chooses a religious faith and makes any serious attempt to follow it is, in some sense, a different person, a new person."

"Thank you for calling," Sam said. Plainly, she wanted no more of this debate—whether because she wished to rescue her husband from a fruitless and possibly damaging discussion, or because she wanted to avoid the boring pieties of the born-again crowd. Whatever her reason, Randollph thought, I am profoundly grateful to her.

The show moved away from him. Tad Barry called Walter Cromartie "a dirty-minded pagan," which didn't seem to bother the American Civil Liberties Union lawyer at all. The Lord's Lancer made several speeches in response to questions from the audience. Cromartie genially nailed Lancer's hide to the wall. Tad Barry shouted and sputtered.

Randollph tried to retrieve that glimmer of enlightenment that, earlier in the program, had kissed him briefly and then danced beyond the grasp of his mind. He had a feeling that it was important to retrieve it. If he could only get hold of it, turn it over, upside-down and right-side-up, he was sure he would know something about the Holy Terror that he needed to know. But the glimmer was gone. If not forever, at least for now.

Sam was closing the show.

"We'll give each of our guests the opportunity to sum up his position in one sentence," she said. "Mr. Cromartie?"

"Our civil rights, our freedoms are our most precious possessions."

"Dr. Lancer?"

"Pornography, smut, filthy magazines, books and movies will do more than anything else to ruin our country."

"Mr. Barry?"

"I want to say that the disgraceful stand of Dr. Randollph on this great moral issue is a—a, well, a shame and a disgrace, and if we can't turn to our pastors to help us stamp out sin and evil who can we turn to? Furthermore, I want to make it clear that—"

"Thank you, Mr. Barry. Dr. Randollph?"

"I'm not in favor of pornography. I only oppose any method of suppressing it which erodes freedom of press or speech."

"That's two sentences, Dr. Randollph." Sam was grinning at him as if to say you did O.K., kid.

"They were short sentences," Randollph said.

"So they were. Mr. Brad?"

"Thank you for having me."

Randollph suddenly realized that the councilman had nodded and smiled and even applauded every speaker, every point of view. He had been seen by thousands, his face printed on their minds, committing himself to nothing, voicing no opinion, but—

in the process—gathering up the good will which accrues to a politician who does not offend you by embracing an ideology with which you disagree. "Thank you for having me," were the only words he had uttered the entire evening. Randollph wasn't sure who had won the debate, but it was certain that Councilman Brad hadn't lost.

Chapter Fifteen

Through the window wall of his penthouse parsonage dining room Randollph could see that it was going to be a marvelously clear and cheery December day. Early-morning sunlight probed for patches of darkness it could erase. The air, rich in noxious effluvia, according to the Environmental Protection Agency, looked pure as a saint's life style. The prairie supporting oversized shafts of brick and steel and stone which stretched toward the lake and north along the shore reminded him of a vast and jagged Stonehenge. These cathedrals of commerce, he supposed, were erected, quite appropriately, to the deity served by those who inhabited them. Icons of a secular devotion though they were, the sight of the powerful buildings, of this skyline, always lifted Randollph's spirits. He was glad again to be alive, to be starting a new day in this beautiful, ugly, miserable, glorious, cruel, and good, and bad, and inspiring city.

The bishop reamed the last segment of ruby flesh from his half grapefruit, patted his lips with a fine linen napkin, and said, "It is good to be doing the Lord's business at one of Clarence's splendid breakfasts. Though the Scriptures enjoin us to take no thought of what we shall eat and what we shall drink, I wonder what's next?"

"Truffled omelet," Dan Gantry said, working away at his second grapefruit. "I already asked Clarence. What Lord's business we here to discuss, bishop?"

"Perhaps we should let business wait the end of the meal," the bishop said. "However, I'll give you a hint. In my considered judgment—reached, I might add, after thorough research by our City Mission Society—we should initiate a program, and I hope a vigorous one, to establish a number of new churches in areas of promising population growth. I also hope that Good Shepherd, as our leading church, will undertake a leadership role in this program."

"You mean money?" Dan asked.

"We'll get around to that." The bishop smiled complacently. "We usually do."

"Let's eat first, then I can beat it. Church finance is not one of my specialties." Sam's winter-white wool slacks clung to her like the skin of a peach. She wore a man-style white shirt open at the neck and a kelly-green cardigan. She looked to Randollph like an elegant college girl.

Clarence Higbee came in silently and placed a large mixing bowl on a portable hot table with two spirit lamps in the center surrounded by bottles, skillets, and covered dishes. He quickly cleared the grapefruit rinds from the table, lit the spirit lamps, and said, "May I assume that you all like omelets?" Being reassured, he put a chunk of butter in one skillet, poured from two bottles, and dumped in something from a small dish.

"Enlighten me, Clarence," the bishop said. "What are those ingredients?"

"Butter, m'lord. Then sauterne wine and a bit of brandy. And finely diced truffles. As soon as the liquid is reduced I'll proceed with the omelets."

Clarence really is something of a showoff, Randollph thought. No, that wasn't fair. He saw himself as a craftsman and an artist. He presumed that bishops and ordinary clergy were above him in status, significance, and in the eyes of God. But he was confident that he practiced a respected craft, fulfilled a minor but useful purpose in life, and occupied a deserved niche in the scheme of things.

Clarence had stirred the contents of the mixing bowl, put butter in a long-handled iron skillet, then followed with a measure of viscous liquid from the mixing bowl. He jerked the skillet vigorously a few times, dipped sauce from the other skillet onto the omelet, folded it over, and transferred it to a heated plate. He then rubbed butter across the top. From the oven of the cart he pulled out a dish of baked tomatoes, put one on the plate, then added a sprig of parsley and set the plate in front of Sam, saying, "Madam." The whole operation, Randollph estimated, had taken less than a minute.

Clarence repeated the operation three times, then indicated a basket covered with a napkin. "I've baked cornsticks, my own recipe. There are several kinds of jam, including the gooseberry which Dr. Randollph favors."

"Ah," sighed the bishop, "gooseberry jam. I never see it in the markets. Where do you find it, Clarence?"

"It is a matter of knowing the purveyors, m'lord. A competent majordomo must be familiar with the best sources."

"Clarence, I'm going to need another one of these," Dan said. "They're damn good!"

Clarence smiled. "I anticipated that you would need more than one, Mr. Gantry, and prepared accordingly. May I ask if anyone prefers tea to coffee?"

"I do," the bishop replied. "I acquired a liking for tea during my years at Oxford. Do you mean, Clarence, that you know where to find any kind or description of food?"

"If it is edible, m'lord, and obtainable, I would know where to go for it. Since Mrs. Randollph's friend, Miss Mason, has written in her column about Dr. Randollph's table, I find the purveyors are eager for our custom. She wrote one about his liking for gooseberry jam and several merchants sent complimentary samples of their brands. They hope for a favorable appraisal."

"From you or Randollph?" Sam asked.

"Either, or both, madam. Because of Dr. Randollph's prominence, and of yours, it is to a merchant's advantage to say that he is supplier to this house."

"You're the one deserves the credit," Dan said. "The boss here—well, he's like me, he knows if it tastes good, but he doesn't know why."

Clarence was enjoying this, Randollph saw. "Dr. and Mrs. Randollph's prestige has enhanced my reputation, of course," he said modestly. "But you must be fair, Mr. Gantry. Dr. Randollph's palate has grown more sophisticated. Now, if you'll excuse me, I have duties to attend. If you need anything, you've but to ring."

"I don't know if your palate's become more sophisticated or not, Danny boy, but your wardrobe surely has. What's with the vested-suit and narrow-tie bit? Where are those glorious way-out togs and long hair that said, 'Here's a free spirit'?"

Dan ate the last of his second omelet, leaned back, lighted a cigarette, and said, "Sam, dear girl, this is the new me."

"What was wrong with the old you?" Sam pressed him. "Aside, that is, from being opinionated, too many girlfriends, and practically no humility."

"Oh, the new me hasn't changed any of that," Dan assured her. "I'm still the same bright, handsome, charming, sought-after bachelor I've always been. But a mature man approaching thirty has to review his image from time to time. Dress for success, that's the big deal now. The cute little birds nowadays flock around a guy that looks like he's a yes-man in some corrupt corporation."

"How could you, Danny boy?" Sam put on a face of mock consternation. "How could you sell out? You, the champion of the downtrodden, the enemy of special interests, the foe of lobbyists, the disciple of Ralph Nader—how could you sell out all that for the favors of a few fickle females, sell out to the bastards, as you used to call them?"

"Oh, they're still bastards. And I haven't sold out. I've just changed my image. The girls like it, but they soon come to love me for myself, not my clothes. Anyway, I got tired of being mistaken for a rock musician."

"I must say, Dan, that I have had mixed feelings about the new you," the bishop said as he smeared a cornstick with gooseberry jam. "Even allowing for my approval of the improvement in your appearance—a natural prejudice in a man of my generation—I've wondered if it signaled a retreat from your bold stand on significant social issues."

"That would bother you, Freddie?" Randollph seemed surprised.

"Again, I have mixed feelings, C.P. I get plenty of complaints about Dan from members of Good Shepherd and other sources too because he's prominent as a spokesman for such causes as the

Equal Rights Amendment, minority movements, and consumer groups. He's tagged with that dirty word "liberal."

"I don't think it's a dirty word," Dan said.

"Many people do, though," the bishop said. "And every complaint is one more administrative problem for me."

"You mean some people want to quit coughing up their dough for the church?" Dan asked.

"Some do, yes. It is in the nature of administrators to keep problems at a minimum. But," the bishop continued, "I also remember that Jesus identified himself with the Old Testament prophets who thundered about God's demands for justice and mercy and compassion. So much of Christianity today is religion without ethics, devotion without moral demand, that it saddens me to see so many of our pastors converting themselves into slick prophets of positive thoughts and sweet nothings. When the Church loses the will to pronounce moral judgment on society it has lost one of its reasons for being. I'm glad, in spite of the troubles you cause me, Dan, that you haven't abandoned your inclination to chase the bastards, as you put it."

"Don't worry, Bishop, when I lose the urge to chase the bastards I'll hand in my collar and join them, and make some important money."

Sam clapped her hands. "Danny boy, you almost inspire me to give up my atheism and join the crusade."

"Hell, Sam, join anyway. We gladly welcome atheists. Besides, you're not an atheist, you're an agnostic."

"That's what Randollph says," she told him. "I keep forgetting."

Clarence came in carrying a phone, plugged it into a jack near Randollph's chair, and set it on the table.

"I regret to disturb you, sir, but Lieutenant Casey wants a word with you. He was most insistent."

Randollph picked up the phone from its antique French cradle, which Sam had chosen to "perk up the place."

"Yes, Lieutenant?"

"There's been another one," Casey said. "I'm coming right over."

Chapter Sixteen

Rabbi Amos Lehman hung his black topcoat in his study closet. He never wore a hat, except one of those Russian fur things when the winds blew snow in from the lake, or the wind-chill index was low enough to freeze your brain. Except the yarmulke, of course. His was a Reformed congregation, which was to Judaism more or less what the Unitarians were to Christianity. Reformed Jews could eat pork and lobster if they chose—and many did so choose. He didn't so choose. He supposed that some sliver of orthodoxy, some remnant of tradition buried too deep in him to be extracted by reason, forbade him to eat what had been pronounced unclean long before Jesus walked the shores of Galilee.

There was no need, either, to wear the yarmulke in his study. But it was a Jewish tradition to wear it when at study, a custom the rabbi found to his liking. So he found the little skullcap in a desk drawer and put it on.

Actually, he was being a bit of a fake, he realized, pretending to be a wise teacher researching the Talmud. What he did in his study wasn't very scholarly. It was mostly tending to the business of running the synagogue. The temple. This whole wing of the temple should have been named "the executive suite." There were offices for three assistant rabbis. And an office for the cantor. And an office for the master of the Jewish Sunday school. And a reception room manned (womaned?) by Mrs. Shapiro and two secretaries.

Judaism, he reflected, had been corrupted—if that was the word (and he thought it was)—by the Christian culture here in the United States. The principal activity of the week wasn't the Sabbath service on Friday evening—it was what he thought of as "the preaching service" on Sunday morning. It was a rite not so very different from what one would encounter in a not-very-liturgical Protestant church. He was still Jewish enough to entertain a faint scorn for this adopted Christian custom. But he knew he shouldn't scorn it, for it was his ability to draw crowds to this service that accounted for his success as a rabbi. Plainly put, he was a cracking-good preacher. He was scholarly but interesting. He knew how to relate the insights of faith to the problems of life. He knew a good story when he saw one, and he knew how to tell it. He had a sense of humor that permeated his preaching. Not a one-liner sense of humor. A lot of rabbis (and Christian preachers) had that. His was the sense of humor of a man who had lived a little and understood that life was tragic as well as comic. In fact—or so he had been told—there was a hint of sadness in his preaching, as if he reflected the long, sorrowful history of the Jews. As if he wondered, as did the psalmists, why Yahweh so often hid His face from those He had nominated to be His chosen instrument of salvation. Since the stockbrokers and lawyers and building contractors and teachers and dentists and bankers and M.D.'s (lots of doctors) and politicians and psychiatrists and business managers who made up his congregation didn't know his personal history, they didn't suspect that his permanent, though faint, aroma of sadness had its source not in the history of the Jews but in personal tragedy.

The rabbi also knew that he was very good at running the temple. He understood money. He ought to. He'd had enough experience with it. And he knew how to ameliorate hostility, tamp down quarrelsome committees, keep the more aggressive members of the Sisterhood from running away with the ball, and from each other's throats. C. P. Randollph had told him, on that awful night of his installation, that he found administration often

a bore and sometimes annoying. Rabbi Lehman had replied that
he didn't like it or dislike it. He just did it because it was
impossible to be in charge of a religious business and not do it.
And, as long as one had to do it, one ought to do it well.

He wondered now if he hadn't been a little too self-assured
with Randollph. Randollph had been gracious. He'd replied that
he aspired to reach the level of professional competence that the
rabbi had reached, but that he had a long way to go. After all, the
rabbi reflected, Randollph hadn't ever run anything but a professional football team. The rabbi grinned inwardly. He guessed that
the style and habit of mind that it took to boss a bunch of men
with outsize bodies and outsize egos might not be so adaptable to
a church boardroom and whatever the Protestants called their
sisterhood.

But he'd been impressed with Randollph. He had a scholarly
mind—which was amazing, considering that he'd been a professional athlete. And he was a forceful and persuasive preacher, if
his short address at the installation service had been a fair
sample. Maybe he should suggest that he and Randollph trade
pulpits some Sunday morning. He gauged that Randollph was a
man of generous spirit, even though he wouldn't let that old
windbag from the Citizens for a Moral America into his pulpit.
The rabbi was one-hundred-percent solid behind Randollph on
the censorship issue. Jews knew all too well what happened
when a government chipped away at civil rights. The rabbi felt
badly that this Holy Terror screwball was after Randollph. He
thought Randollph had done a good job on that television
program. He hadn't said a lot, to be sure, but he was smart not to
debate the issue of pornography. You can't win that kind of
debate.

The rabbi wondered if he ought to call Randollph or write him
a letter about this Holy Terror business. But how do you
sympathize with a man under a death sentence? He speculated
about the motives or impulses or compulsions that made someone kill only clergymen. Kill only Protestant clergy, on purpose,
at least. He thought a moment about his late friend Bishop
O'Manny. A large-spirited Roman Catholic. He wondered why
rabbis and Roman priests usually got on better than priests and
Protestant preachers. Maybe it was because the Romans carried
around a lot of unexpunged guilt over Tomas de Torquemáda and

other stalwart Christians who persecuted the Jews with such cruelty and vindictiveness. Or maybe it was because Roman Catholic Christians and Protestant Christians were competing for the same customers, whereas the Jews were working the other side of the religious street.

Anyway, he mourned the passing of his friend, Bishop Terence Kevin O'Manny. They weren't brothers in Christ, of course, but they were partners in the struggle to keep a moral and spiritual dimension in the life of a society that was aggressively engaged in discarding it.

Rabbi Lehman removed his yarmulke to scratch an itch at the crown of his head, then put it back on and patted it in place. He wasn't sure, he admitted, that his temple was a sturdy dam intercepting the receding waters of faith. So much of what went on at the temple was peripheral to the real business of religion at best, and entirely irrelevant at worst. The Sunday school crammed a little Hebrew into the heads of indifferent pupils, and tried to acquaint them with the glories of Jewish history and Jewish spirituality. But he sometimes wondered if the congregation ever really connected their faith with their life in the world. They knew, for example, the commandments of Moses. But they cheerfully broke many of them. By observation, and through counseling, he was aware that many of his people regularly knocked over the commandments like tenpins in a bowling game. Thou shalt not covet, thou shalt not steal, and thou shalt not commit adultery were the ones that went down frequently. But the rabbi thought the most violated of the commandments was "Thou shalt have no other Gods before me." People didn't realize when they were breaking that one. They thought of it as having meaning back in the days of idol worship, a nice antique linking us to the past but no longer possessed of utilitarian value.

They couldn't see—in fact, it was impossible to make them see—that they were idolaters, that they spent their lives pursuing false gods. They were no different from their Christian brethren in their affection for luxury without character. Like their Christian brethren they surrounded themselves with the artifacts of a culture that saw no point in quality. They dressed in clothes that "made a statement" (the rabbi thought wryly of his yarmulke that he fancied gave him the look of a scholar). They had their

Cadillacs, one very much like another. They had their trips to Las
Vegas. They dined in expensive restaurants, not because the food
was superb (which sometimes it was and sometimes it wasn't),
but because these were the "in" places. (The rabbi wondered if
there were any great Jewish chefs. If there were he hadn't heard
of them. Over the centuries, ever since the Lord had poured out
an omer of manna per person on the starving Israelites lost on
their journey to Canaan, the Jews had had to make do with
whatever edibles came their way. So they'd never developed a
palate.)

Rabbi Lehman thought of two members of his congregation—
one rich and one poor (the temple didn't have many poor
members, but it had some). They were his favorite people.

David Cohen had made an immense fortune in the stock
market. Made it as a young man. He had foreseen the crash of '29
and had gotten out in time. He had a highly honed ability to pick
young companies which were destined to dominate their markets. Past eighty now, this elegant old man still lived in the Tudor
mansion he had bought as a present for his bride. It was
furnished with pieces that he had picked up all over the world,
purchased because he thought they were beautiful. And, because
he had exquisite taste, they were beautiful. It was decorated with
Rembrandts, Titians, Corots, as well as a Van Gogh or two,
several El Grecos, Monets, and—of all things—a Paul Klee. He
had once explained to the rabbi that, though his paintings had
appreciated in value more than any investments he had ever
made, he hadn't bought them as investments. He had bought
them because he liked them. Somehow, out of this eclectic
collection of furniture and art, he had fashioned a home rich in
harmony and beauty.

David Cohen had never learned to drive an automobile. He had
a chauffeur who kept Cohen's Rolls-Royce—at least forty years
old by the rabbi's estimate—in mint condition. The rabbi had
ridden in it often, and he always looked forward to the experience. That lovely tan-leather upholstery, somewhat worn now,
but still exuding the fragrance of genuine properly tanned
cowhide; the intricate, symmetrical burled walnut wood trim,
and the room in it, room for a big man to stretch out his legs, to
sink back into the leather's soft embrace without disturbing
another passenger. This was a car!

Once, on their way to lunch at Cohen's club in the Loop, he'd asked Cohen if he had ever considered the purchase of a new Rolls-Royce.

"No, Rabbi," Cohen had replied. "The new ones are designed to appeal to a taste I do not share. They are like any other automobile—cramped for room. Their luxury is applied rather than integral. They are crammed with so much wiring and so many gadgets it takes a detective to trace down a malfunction. And they are mechanically unreliable. Listen to the motor of this car—if you can hear it at all. It was constructed to run properly for a century. This car suits me. It gives me pleasure."

"Is there a touch of worldly pride in that attitude, David?" the rabbi had asked, engaging in a little gentle kidding, for they were old friends.

"No, Amos, my possessions do not possess me. I own what I own not because I can afford anything I want, but because I like the things I own. They mean something to me. When I'm gone, the paintings and the furniture will go to the Art Institute where others may enjoy them."

Lehman looked on David Cohen as a man who had lived a life of quality. The rabbi was something of a New Testament scholar (not uncommon for rabbis, especially those of the Reformed branch) and recalled that Jesus had said how hard it is for a rich man to get into heaven. The rabbi thought that, as a general rule, Jesus was right about that. But if any of the rich people in his congregation made it, he was sure it would be David Cohen.

The rabbi's other favorite among the members of his temple was a Mrs. Sarah Gold. Mrs. Gold had no money. She and her husband had escaped from Germany before Hitler had his machinery to exterminate the Jews running efficiently. Mrs. Gold's husband, dead twenty years now, had been a gardener who found plenty of work on North Shore estates. They'd lived modestly, saved a little. She got along on what he left her and what she could make as housekeeper at a rather seedy hotel.

Mrs. Gold's small apartment looked nothing at all like David Cohen's mansion. It was overfurnished, without taste or harmony. But everything in the small rooms had a meaning for her. There was a trunk which her grandmother had taken on her wedding trip. There was a large, comfortable, ugly overstuffed chair upholstered in a faded purple brocade. It had been her late husband's favorite chair. There was her collection of German and Czechoslovakian glass of no esthetic merit, but every piece connected with a memory.

Mrs. Gold's life, objectively viewed, was hard, dull and lonesome. But Mrs. Gold thought of it as rich and full. She missed her husband, but life had to go on without him. She was the most useful member of the temple Sisterhood because she could do, and did, any job no one else wanted to do. She got on well with the affluent members of the temple. She treated them as equals, not superiors, because it never occurred to Mrs. Gold that she was poor. Or that lack of money had anything to do with personal worth. Her life was at the other pole from David Cohen's life. But the rabbi thought of Sarah Gold as also having achieved a quality life.

He wondered if he had lived a quality life. It had been his aim. To be a responsible person. To be compassionate. To do something useful. To enjoy the gifts of creation. To love and be loved. To pull his own weight and more. To be a complete human being. This, he supposed, was his doctrine of salvation. Probably this kind of life could be achieved without any religious faith at all. But he was convinced that a worthy religious faith pointed the way. Certainly his Judaism provided the framework for a quality life. So did Christianity, for that matter—at least the kind of Christianity followed by Bishop O'Manny and Cesare Paul Randollph. Maybe Hinduism did too. Mahatma Gandhi had been a Hindu. Maybe Buddhism. Maybe Islam, although he had his doubts about Islam. The sons of the prophet seemed to him a bloody lot, trying to impose a pre-medieval culture on their section of the world. Maybe, though, the religion was better than its practitioners—a flaw in most faiths. Maybe Islam had just been getting a bad press lately.

The rabbi knew, though, that he was not a complete person. There was an area of emptiness in him that he could not bring himself to fill because he wasn't sure it could be filled.

The rabbi shook his head as if to clear it, to arrest his mind's meanderings. With work to do you'd better not dwell on that, he admonished himself. He buzzed Mrs. Shapiro and asked, "Rose, what's on our plate for today?"

"I'll be right in, Rabbi."

Mrs. Shapiro came in, laid two piles of letters on Rabbi Lehman's desk. The larger pile, he knew, would already be slit open. These were obviously business and professional correspondence. The smaller pile would be made up of anything that looked like a personal letter. Mrs. Shapiro left these letters unopened, pointedly, the rabbi thought, because she suspected they might be from females.

Rose Shapiro walked with the same efficiency she did everything else. No fanny twitching, none of the "Look at what I've got to offer" sway that so many women affected. She didn't rush, she didn't appear to hurry. It was just a no-nonsense kind of walk.

Yet the rabbi was aware of her sexuality. Mrs. Shapiro often said, "Aren't the forties awful! You aren't young and you aren't old." Rabbi Lehman was rather sure that Rose had passed beyond the barrier of being in her forties, but she didn't look it. Diet, exercise, and sunlamp had kept her trim and tanned. Her creamy-yellow jersey dress modestly indicated the well-formed figure it covered. The brown-and-bone paisley scarf knotted at the neck looked just right with her brown-blonde hair with a light blonde streak in it.

Rose Shapiro was a handsome woman, a pleasant and appealing woman. And the rabbi knew she was dead in love with him. He suspected that the congregation knew it too. He'd heard a few remarks about how Mrs. Shapiro was adept at keeping unattached ladies who might be seeking a closer relationship with the rabbi from poaching on her territory. He'd thought about Rose as a prospective Mrs. Lehman. It had been many years since he'd experienced the joy of a woman's body. He had affection for her that, cultivated, could grow into love. She was intelligent, witty, well read, an interesting conversationalist. But he hadn't encouraged her. He just hadn't been able to make the emotional leap into another marriage. But he'd been thinking more about it lately. Perhaps the time had come to do something about it.

Rose Shapiro ticked off the rabbi's responsibilities for the day. Speak to a Rotary Club luncheon (about Zionism); drop by the architect's office to look at preliminary drawings for the new wing of the temple; office appointments with a Mrs. Samuels (a marital problem, Rose Shapiro guessed—she could smell this sort of thing); Saul Abrahamson would drop in to talk about his son's

bar mitzvah; and then the Sisterhood's program committee
wanted an hour with him (more likely two hours, Mrs. Shapiro
said). That ought to do it for the day. His evening was blessedly
free of meetings or appointments. (Did Mrs. Shapiro put an extra
emphasis on this, implying that she would be glad to fill it for
him?)

"I'll go through the mail, Rose, and call you if anything needs
answering." The rabbi said that every morning. It was his kind
word of dismissal. Mrs. Shapiro said, "Just whistle when you
need me." She said that every morning, too.

Rabbi Lehman shuffled through the opened letters. Several
charities wanting his spiritual and financial support. A letter
from a seminary student stating that he would graduate in June
and would like to be considered for any vacancy on the
rabbinical staff. Several form letters duplicated to look like
personal letters (but you could always tell—the personal saluta-
tion never quite matched the text of the letter), all of them
wanting him to buy something, or do something for some group
or other. He made rapid, brief notations on them for Mrs.
Shapiro.

He turned to the unopened mail. The top envelope had a
typewritten name and address, but no return address. He
chuckled, thinking how Rose had assumed it was from some lady
who wished to remain anonymous. Putting it on top of the pile
was her way of saying she suspected something was going on,
something of which she disapproved.

Rabbi Lehman slit open the cheap envelope (did Rose Shapiro
think that the dime-store envelope was disguising a scented
feminine writing paper? She probably did).

But it didn't contain any fancy stationery. There was a single
page, a ruled sheet from a notepad. The message, like the address,
was typewritten.

When you pass during some nocturnal blackness, snowy
     and cold,
They'll say, "Rabbi Lehman lived furtively all these years,
He embezzled from innocent creatures, the young and
     the old,

And his wife killed herself, an act unrepaired by his
   tears."

And they'll say when your bell of quittance is heard in
   the gloom,
"He did time, and he's atoned for his fate."
But the austere tablets of Moses prefigure your doom,
You must realize how just is my hate.

Rabbi Lehman was stunned. His first reaction was how could
anyone have known? How did information nearly a quarter-
century old come into the writer's possession?

They'd been a young couple on their way up in the business
and social world. He was executive vice-president of a small but
growing bank. Katherine had been a teller, and they fell in love,
and were married before his Orthodox parents could protest his
marrying a gentile and her parents be too long upset that she was
marrying a Jew. It hadn't been easy handling two sets of hostile
parents. But he'd have suffered the rack and the thumbscrew for
her, so much did he love her. He imagined that no two people
had ever been so in love before. Not Romeo and Juliet. Not
Heloise and Abelard. No one.

He felt the pain as sharp and shattering as if it had been
yesterday when an unannounced audit had turned up a hundred-
thousand-dollar shortage in the bank's funds. It had been cleverly
done, but only two employees of the bank could have managed
it—himself or Katherine. He hadn't done it, so it had to be
Katherine. He didn't even ask her about it. He confessed to the
embezzlement, saying unwise personal investments had moti-
vated him to help himself to the bank's cash.

He'd been aware, of course, that Katherine was a compulsive
gambler. Horses, sporting events, anything on which a bookie
would take a wager. She'd been to a psychiatrist and thought she
was cured. But she wasn't. She'd ended up borrowing from loan
sharks, and when they threatened to go to her husband she'd
panicked and embezzled the money.

He remembered that awful scene when she confessed to him
what she'd done, and begged him to let her "come clean" and

take her punishment. She loved him so much. She couldn't bear to hurt him more than she had already. But he'd explained to her gently that he wouldn't let her do that. He was better able to take the punishment than she was. They had enough money to make partial restitution, and he'd repay it all when he got out of prison. He never chided her for what she had done. He considered her gambling a sickness which needed healing rather than punishment. Besides, he loved her too much to condemn her.

He'd drawn an unexpectedly heavy sentence from an anti-Semitic judge (later convicted of accepting bribes from the Mafia).

"You Jews are going to have to learn not to be so greedy," the judge had said, and handed out the stiffest penalty the law would allow. And one month after he'd gone to prison, Katherine had written him a heart-broken letter of love and remorse, then shut the garage door, got into her car, started the motor, and died.

When he got out of prison he still owed the bank fifty thousand dollars. He earned the money in six months by playing the stock market. Then he set about to remake his life. He went to Cincinnati, told the whole story to Rabbi Sidney Salzman who headed the seminary, and asked to be admitted to study for the rabbinate. Rabbi Salzman had wept and admitted him.

Amos Lehman wondered now, had wondered over the years, if he had done the right thing in taking Katherine's guilt upon himself. At the time he hadn't reasoned it out. He only knew he loved her too much to see her suffer. A sterner love might have seen that his sacrifice would only compound her guilt and self-loathing. A more objective affection might have guessed that she would be unable to handle her unexpurgated sins.

Ah, well, he'd never know. What he did know was that the ache, the emptiness had not faded with the passing years. He loved her still, with all the intensity with which he had loved her then. He longed for her with a longing that time had not abated. Rabbi Lehman didn't believe or disbelieve in a life after death. But he hoped there was one. He hoped there was some kind of existence in which he could hold Katy in his arms once more.

He sighed and took off his yarmulke. Time to go speak to the Rotarians. How in the world had that Holy Terror fellow gotten hold of his story? Well, no point in speculating on that. He had gotten hold of it.

Rabbi Amos Lehman suddenly felt at peace. Maybe this way was best. Maybe God, in his infinite wisdom, was presenting him with a gift. What a joke on the Holy Terror, though, even if he'd never know the true story. Yahweh surely had a sense of irony.

Rabbi Lehman didn't bother to call the police and report the warning from the Holy Terror.

Chapter Seventeen

Lieutenant Michael Casey refused Clarence Higbee's offer of coffee, saying that he was coffee'd up for the morning. But he would appreciate a beer. He was wearing a brown-and-white houndstooth jacket with leather elbow patches, tan gabardine slacks, brown loafers, and an eggshell-shade button-down-collar shirt with a plain brown knit tie. He was carrying but not smoking a handsome curved pipe with a meerschaum bowl. Randollph thought the casual observer would put him down for an elegant college professor.

Casey noticed Randollph staring at the pipe. "Liz gave it to me. Part of her campaign to get me off cigarettes."

"Does it work?"

"Well, I don't smoke the pipe much, but it reminds me I'm not supposed to smoke cigarettes. Do you know, did you know Rabbi Amos Lehman?"

"Fine man," the bishop said. "Is he the victim?"

"Yes." They all had known it was the rabbi as soon as Casey mentioned his name.

"Same *modus operandi*," Casey continued. "We found this poem in his desk"—he handed a single sheet of paper to the bishop—"and he was shot through the head, sitting at his desk. His secretary found him early this morning. She'd come in early to get some work out of the way. The rabbi's study door was open. He always closed it and locked it when he left. She supposed he had come in early, though he didn't do that very often. He was more likely to stay late than come in early. He was still there when Mrs. Shapiro—that's his secretary—left last night. And," he added grimly, "he was still there this morning."

"I had him on a program once," Sam spoke up. "An ecumenical thing. A priest and a Protestant, too. Chummy brotherhood stuff. I remember, I don't know how the subject came up, he said his mind functioned better at night than in the morning, so he often worked late at his study at the temple. Oh, dear, I've had every one of these, these—I've had all the victims on my program at one time or another." She looked as if she were about to cry.

"Who'd have thought Amos Lehman had once been an embezzler?" the bishop said, shaking his head. He passed the poem to Randollph.

"That's a funny thing, he wasn't," Casey told them. "We called the police where he'd been a banker—on Long Island it was. Luckily, the captain had been around for thirty years or so, and remembered the case. He said everybody knew that Lehman didn't do it. It was his wife. She was a compulsive gambler, got in with loan sharks, it's a familiar story. Lehman confessed, went to prison. His wife committed suicide. The Holy Terror didn't have his information straight."

Randollph was touched by the story of Rabbi Lehman's self-sacrifice. This willingness to suffer for a sin you had not committed in order to save someone you loved. This, viewed from the outside, looked like the noblest and finest act of which a human is capable. And yet, Randollph wondered, is that the explanation? He looked fondly at Sam. He'd gladly do the same for her. He loved her so much that he'd willingly accept any suffering if it would spare her suffering. Was this truly a selfless love? Or was it a selfish love, one that would not permit the lover to live with himself if he permitted his beloved to suffer if he could spare her the suffering by taking it on himself? Randollph bet that the late Rabbi Lehman had asked himself that question a thousand times over the years. He hadn't known the rabbi very well, but Lehman had not exhibited any symptoms of the martyr cherishing his selfless suffering. Tricky business, separating self-love from selfless love.

"I mourn his passing," the bishop said. "But I'm happy that he was not an embezzler, though God forgives embezzlers as He forgives other sinners. Still, had he been guilty, it would have shaken my confidence in my ability to judge another human being. I'd have bet that Amos Lehman had been an honest man all his life."

"What I came over for, other than to warn you again, Doctor, to be especially careful"—Casey looked hard at Randollph—"is to ask if you have any ideas, any ideas at all about what kind of a nut would want to specialize in knocking off the clergy—I suppose a rabbi is a clergyman."

"They weren't always," Randollph said.

"Then what the"—Dan Gantry looked at the bishop—"what in heck were they?"

"Originally wise men or scholars, interpreters of Scripture. And I believe they adjudicated disputes in the community where a question of Jewish law was involved. But now they aren't much different from the Christian clergy. They preach. They raise money. They administer church—temple—affairs. They plan programs. They are even ordained."

"The Holy Terror thought Rabbi Lehman was a clergyman. He fits into the pattern." Lieutenant Casey, Randollph noticed, had the scowl he always wore when he was baffled. "So who'd want to kill just the clergy? Money. Family quarrels. Sex. Stupid violence. Those are motives for most of the homicides I deal with. Those I can understand. But killing clergymen, only the clergy? That I don't understand."

"You've no doubt asked a psychiatrist for a psychological profile?" the bishop asked Casey.

"Yeah, three psychiatrists. They come up—cutting out all the professional jargon—they come up with something like this: The guy's punishing some authority figure from his childhood. Someone he hated. Could be a parent. Could be a priest or pastor. Could be about anybody. Had to be somebody he didn't dare admit to himself he hated. Probably someone he was supposed to love and respect. He's getting this subconscious hate out of his system by murdering symbols of whomever he hated."

"Sounds like a lot of Freudian horse"—Dan looked at the

bishop again—"Freudian bunk to me. Like these shrinks explaining women's psychological problems as, well, penis envy."

"That's what I think," Casey agreed. "I think it's some religious nut."

"Antireligious nut," Dan said.

"Perhaps a *mauvais prêtre*," the bishop suggested.

"A what?" Sam asked.

"A spoiled priest, an evil priest."

"Tell me more," Sam said.

The bishop reached for another cornstick, then rejected it. Clarence, who was refilling coffee cups, said, "Please have another one, m'lord."

"No, I must avoid the sin of gluttony, Clarence—and I'm on the borderline now. Would you have a cigar? I seldom smoke one, but I'd enjoy one now so I can pleasantly prevent myself from falling into the sin of overeating."

"I have a supply of Montecristos, m'lord. I fancy a good cigar myself on occasion."

"Havanas?" The bishop asked, then said, "No, don't tell me. The sin of importing illegal cigars be on your head."

"Quite so, m'lord," Clarence answered pleasantly. "My conscience is clear. When governments lay down a law for purely political reasons which would prevent us from enjoying the good things of life, I see no ethical transgression in breaking it."

"My God, Clarence, you're a moral philosopher!" Dan said.

"We're all moral philosophers, Mr. Gantry," Clarence replied. "Our conduct reflects our moral philosophy. Some people think it out, and others don't." Then, as if he'd spoken beyond his station, he said, "I'll bring the cigars immediately, m'lord," and left.

"A bad priest, Samantha," the bishop said, "*mauvais prêtre*, is a term connected with the black mass. To conduct a true black mass you must have a true priest. That is, a Roman Catholic priest who stands in the apostolic succession, who has been ordained by a bishop who was ordained by a bishop and so on, stretching all the way back to St. Peter, the first pope. But, since the black mass worships the devil, it would have to be a bad though true priest who would officiate at such a rite."

"Sounds silly," Sam said.

"It is, of course," the bishop said. "I was using the term to apply to any clergyman who had rejected God, the Church, religion. It happens, you know. What they once loved they come to hate. If that hate is strong enough, and if for some reason they suppress it, well—when it finally explodes it can do a lot of damage." The bishop selected a cigar from the box Clarence offered him, lit it slowly so the end would not get too hot, puffed a blue cloud over his end of the table, and said "Ah!"

"The guy's got to be a head case," Dan said. "A kook, a kink. He's a minus."

"Mike, does it mean—this new murder—does it mean that the H.T. has decided to pass up Randollph?" Sam sounded like a little girl asking for something she was pretty sure she wasn't going to get.

"Don't count on it," Casey said. He turned to Randollph. "You have any further thoughts on this nut's motives, Doctor?"

"Yes, but I doubt it would hold together under careful scrutiny."

"Tell us about it. Let us pick it apart."

Randollph sipped some of Clarence's excellent coffee. Clarence ground it every morning using a mix of beans from various countries according to his own recipe. It was rich and strong and aromatic. Randollph looked forward to that coffee every morning.

"You can bet that I've pondered this, the motive that makes the Holy Terror the Holy Terror, probably as much as you have, Lieutenant. I'd like to save my own hide. He may not be a spoiled priest. Or he may be. I think of him more as a reversed version of St. Francis of Assisi, or St. Augustine of Hippo."

Casey looked puzzled. "How so?"

"You know all about St. Francis and St. Augustine, Lieutenant." It wouldn't hurt, Randollph thought, to affirm Casey as a college man, a man who lived in the brutal world of homicide investigation, but who could converse about the gentler topics of life. "Ask yourself, what were the characteristics of Francis and Augustine, or of any bona-fide saint, for that matter."

Casey sucked on his empty pipe and corrugated his brow. "Well, dedication to what he believes. An intensity of purpose. Passionate devotion to his cause. Willingness to suffer, if need be, for his faith." Casey took the pipe out of his mouth and scratched his nose, satisfied that he had delivered a succinct and erudite answer to Randollph's question.

"Exactly. And what are the characteristics of the Holy Terror's behavior?"

"About the same," Casey said.

"You've lost me," Sam said. "St. Francis I know, but who was St. Augustine of Hippo? They didn't teach about him in Presbyterian Sunday school."

Randollph looked at Casey. "You tell her, Lieutenant."

"It's your field, Doctor."

"I tell her things all the time. It'll be a refreshing change for her. And you know as much about Francis and Augustine as I do—good Catholic that you are."

Casey was obviously pleased. "O.K. Feel free to correct me. Both Augustine—who lived in North Africa in the fourth century—and Francis, who lived in Italy in the twelfth or thirteenth century—"

"A little of both," Randollph said.

"Thanks. Both of them were what you might call young men about town—they lived, that is, they got around, if you know what I mean."

"Like some of the sports at the television station," Sam said.

"Yes. Well, both of them were converted, or became serious Christians. They turned their lives around, all the way around. Augustine became a bishop, a great theologian, and is recognized as the greatest doctor of the Church. Pardon me, Doctor, I mean my church, of course. There wasn't any other church back then, was there, doctor?"

"Not really. A few dissident sects."

"And St. Francis founded the order of Franciscans—mendicants, little brothers of the poor. Both of them put the same energy into living the Christian life as they had in living the high life. Doctor Randollph's point is that the Holy Terror might have been brought up a strict Christian and turned his life around by hating and attacking the Church. Murdering servants of the Church, clergymen."

"Deconverted," Dan said.

"Well, I deconverted," Sam said. "But I didn't all of a sudden hate religion and the Church. I didn't, I don't hate it. I'm not hostile. I just thought it was kind of dumb. I just got bored with it. I'm sorry, Randollph."

"Don't be," he said. "I got bored with it, too."

"Then how the hell did you turn out to be a preacher?"

"I fought my way through the boredom. If you can do that you get to a level where religion, Christianity, becomes infinitely interesting. But it's a long story. I'll tell it to you as a bedtime story sometime."

"Ha! You don't ever have religion on your mind at bedtime."

"Hear! Hear!" Dan said.

The bishop, who tried to ignore these remarks, continued. "Lieutenant, have you considered that there is a moral thread running through all these killings?"

"You mean he only kills clergy who have"—he looked at Randollph—"who have, uh, something he thinks is bad about them?"

"Yes. What does that suggest to you?"

"That's he's a religious nut. That he sees himself as a righteous avenger. He's punishing clergy who have"—Casey looked at Randollph again—"who have betrayed their calling."

"Don't be so diffident about my supposed moral shortcomings," Randollph said. "This is where my theory about the Holy Terror breaks down."

"How so?"

"Because all the other victims, save the accidental victim, of course, had records of legal and ethical offenses. This Holy Terror—H.T. as Samantha calls him—isn't stupid. He's pretending that his murders are a form of moral judgment. But he reads the papers. He must know that his case against me is flimsy. He must know that I am not guilty of anything but belief in the Constitution. And even if I were guilty of liking salacious pictures or literature, that is hardly to be classed, morally, with thievery and manslaughter."

"A nut's a nut," Dan said. "They don't have to make sense in what they do."

"Where does he get his information?" the bishop asked.

"That's got us stumped," Casey answered. "Some of it would be easy to come by. That fellow who wrote the newspaper column—"

"John Wesley Horner," the bishop said. "One of ours. It will be years before that church he was serving gets over it."

"Yes. Well, his trouble in Phoenix was not so secret. You must have known about it, Bishop."

"Yes, Lieutenant, I'm afraid I did. I knew of his shady record. The bishop of Arizona asked me to find a place for him. Our man at Alexandria Hills wasn't cutting the mustard, and I had to find a place for him. And I happened to know that the bishop of Tennessee was trying to unload a chap he didn't like—the fellow was something of a fearless spirit and constantly challenged the bishop's policies. Rightly, too. The bishop of Tennessee is rather stupid and a bit of a dictator, but that's beside the point. So the incompetent from Alexandria Hills went to Chattanooga. The strong-minded fellow from Chattanooga went to Phoenix. And I took Horner. Yes, I knew all about him."

"Sounds like you just traded problems," Dan said. "Is that any way to run a railroad?"

"No and yes," the bishop, not at all offended, answered. "No, we ought to do better in matching our men to their parishes. Character, strength of personality, commitment, scholarly and persuasive preaching skills—these ought to be the criteria for selecting a man to fill any pulpit, and especially a large pulpit. But we seldom have that opportunity. A certain number of our pastors—like Horner—will, in spite of their success, or the desirable position they hold—will have character flaws which sometimes get them in serious trouble. Others may be clerical rascals. Perhaps they don't get caught outright, but after a time a congregation may smell out the truth and, even if they can't prove it, ask the bishop to move the brother. Some of our pastors are good and capable, but just don't fit the congregation they are serving. The chemistry's wrong. So they need to be moved. So, Dan, no, this isn't any way to run a railroad, but, yes, this is the way you have to run a railroad. I'm afraid I've talked so long my cigar's gone out."

"Is this how bishops run my church?" Casey asked.

"I expect that it is. I don't want to disillusion you, but the Roman Catholic Church is, after all, a human institution."

"We're taught that it is a divine institution," Casey said.

"Well, yes. But the divine purpose is carried out through fallible human beings. We have this treasure in earthen vessels, as St. Paul said. But this isn't helping you solve the problem of the Holy Terror's sources of information."

"Wouldn't a newspaper's morgue have bios on these guys?" Dan asked.

"Yes, they have material on them. All these men were prominent enough to rate space in the morgue. But remember, the scandalous stuff was covered up. We've looked. Just the usual biographical sketch the fellows—the victims—wrote up themselves. And pictures and news stories about their careers since coming to Chicago. They were prominent, but not big names"— Casey nodded to Randollph—"except Dr. Randollph, of course. His file is pretty fat."

"Mostly clippings from the sports pages, I expect," Randollph said.

"Mostly. This Holy Terror could have dug up all the scandalous information about his victims from old newspaper files and police records. But he'd have had to research the records in Newark, Long Island, and some hick town in Alabama. The odds against that are way too high. He didn't get his information that way."

"He could have, Mike," Sam said.

"Tell me how."

"He could have picked out these, these victims, in advance and run checks on them. That wouldn't have been difficult."

"You mean pick three names, and it turns out all of them have scandal in their past? That would be hitting the jackpot."

"Well," Sam persisted, "he could have picked a bunch of names and researched them, and three out of the bunch—or maybe more—had bad records."

"Possible. But highly improbable. He'd have had to hire private detectives, or gone to all those places himself. He'd have left a trail. We've checked that out. No sign of a trail."

"Oh," Sam said.

"The only one he didn't have to research was Dr. Randollph," Casey continued. "Which might mean that the doctor was the real victim, the one he actually wanted to kill, and the others were just covers for his actual purpose. Diversions. Red herrings."

"Oh, God," Sam moaned.

"Except for one thing."

"You mean the flimsy charge against me?" Randollph asked.

"There's that. But Horner was killed before Sad Tad Barry in your church got after you about pornography."

Casey thought a minute. "Of course, he could have had the

finger on you all the time. Thought he had something bad about you, but this flap over pornography was better, or more current. Is that possible?" It was a general question, but Randollph knew it was aimed at him.

"Do you mean is there some unsavory secret in my past, Lieutenant?"

"We could talk about it privately if you like."

Randollph laughed. "I appreciate your tact, Lieutenant, but that won't be necessary. The only police records on me you could find would be speeding tickets. I've committed no felonies. I've never killed anyone. I have never embezzled money, unless you count the Sunday-school collection. I used to put my dime in the plate and take out a nickel."

"I don't think the Holy Terror could make anything out of that," Casey said with a smile.

"He might have found stories in my file linking me to a number of actresses—some accurate and some just dreamed up. I haven't always led an entirely godly life."

"Now he tells me," Sam said. But she was smiling.

Randollph laughed again. "You knew. I told you."

"Yes, dear Cesare Paul Randollph, I knew. But you'd better keep your hands off any other dames now or it will go hard with you. And them."

"So Lieutenant, you are telling us—you are telling us you have no hint as to who the Holy Terror may be, and no way of getting a lead to his identity?" the bishop asked.

"That's about it. A lot of murders are solved by information we get from an anonymous tip, or—"

"Stool pigeons?" Dan asked.

"Yeah. Stool pigeons. Street people who give us information for money, or for favors. But they're no help on something like this. It's like Son of Sam, or those psycho rapists who carve up their victims. We know there is some nut out there. But if we can't establish some connection with the killer and his victims we can't check alibis, or find personal motives. We go through police routine, but it doesn't help."

"Great, just great!" Sam said. "Meanwhile we have to live with this thing hanging over us. How long do you think we can stand that, Mike? How long will our nerves hold out?"

"I wish I could tell you." Casey looked as if he were suffering from very low spirits. "We'll solve it, of course. He'll make a mistake. Someone will notice something. It usually happens that way."

Sam had hold of herself now. "Mike, do you think the fact that I interviewed all the victims—is that, does it mean anything? Randollph doesn't think so, but what do you think?"

"I honestly don't have any idea. It seems like a left-field idea. I might talk to some of the people at your station, see if they have any ideas. Not very promising, but I haven't got any place else to start. Will you set it up for me?"

"Sure."

Casey rose to go. "By the way, Doctor, I didn't recognize that poem the Holy Terror sent to the rabbi. I mean, he's always copied, more or less, some established poet's style. Do you recognize it?" Casey's tone implied that it was unlikely that Randollph would recognize it either.

"Yes," Randollph told him. "It's roughly modeled on Thomas Hardy's poem 'Afterwards.'"

Casey, he thought, had used up one day's ration of opportunities to display his intellectual accomplishments.

Chapter Eighteen

"How do I look?" Sam did a model's turn, showing her plain deep-green wool suit from all angles.

"Smart. Understated."

"Not very sexy, huh? And get your feet off that coffee table or take your shoes off."

Randollph slipped out of his brown loafers and put his feet back on the coffee table. "I don't know why women are convinced that they have to be half naked to stimulate lustful thoughts in a man. A well-groomed, well-turned-out woman can be more exciting than a striptease."

Sam bent down and kissed the top of his head. "Thank you, C.P. I don't need to be sexy for a bunch of old dames in the Women's Guild, anyway."

"They aren't all old dames."

"That's nice. What does a woman's guild do? I mean, does it have some reason for existing like raising money to buy underwear for heathens and things like that? Or does it just serve tea?"

"Actually, the Guild in this church is a coalition of various women's groups. We have a Christian Women's Society, a Young

Professional Women's Society, a Women's City Missionary Society. And another one or two."

"When someone says Women's Guild I get this image of a bunch of Helen Hopkinson biddies sitting around nibbling cookies and swapping stories about their children. Do I have to go to all the meetings, Randollph?"

"You don't have to go anytime, lady. You don't even have to go tonight if you don't want to."

"Oh, hell, Randollph, that would be rude, skipping the reception for the wife of the pastor. My God, I can hardly believe that's me."

"Some of it may be boring, Samantha. I don't know, since I don't go. But I have a lot of respect for what the women do. They influence the thinking of the Church—the whole Church, not just this one—more than most men do."

"Great. But I'm not a believer. Do I have to pretend that I'm a sweet little pastor's wife who thinks whatever her lord and master thinks?"

Randollph laughed at her. "Come on, Samantha, you know the answer to that. Don't pretend anything. Although," he added, "you might make an effort to curb your use of mild profanity when you're exasperated."

"Damned if I won't try, Randollph. Will I have to make a speech?"

"I don't know. They'll probably ask you to say something."

"What'll I say?"

Randollph pretended to deep thought, then said, "On the whole, I think you should confine your remarks to what a wonderful husband you have."

Sam scooped up a small pillow from the sofa and threw it at him. "So what are you going to do, buster, while I'm being received?" She looked him over. "Slacks, sport shirt, loafers. Don't you have a meeting to go to?"

"Nope. I'm going to sit here and read this trashy spy novel."

"That'll be bad for your mind, Randollph. Shouldn't you be reading the Bible, or some dull book about theology?"

"No, I shouldn't be reading the Bible, or theology. Preachers need to read some fiction. Not many of them do. You can get intellectually lopsided just reading in your own field. Not," he added, "that I expect this novel to improve my mind."

"Is there any sex in it?"

"I'm sure there is. I haven't gotten that far into it yet, but that's part of the formula for a book like this."

"You said on my show that you didn't like dirty books."

"So I did. But I didn't say I never read them. The kind of sex you get in a book like this isn't very erotic. Clinical in its description, probably, but not erotic."

"If you don't approve of pornography, like you said on the program, shouldn't you, hadn't you ought to skip, not read, that is, any sexy stuff?"

Randollph took his feet off the coffee table and laid his book aside. "I feel a little guilty about that, Samantha. I should have made the distinction between a novelist, or a movie for that matter, employing, using, what do I want to say? Including sexual passages that are germane to the story, the motivation, and just dropping in prurient material for the heck of it."

"You did make the distinction."

"Only in passing. I should have pursued it."

"That kind of distinction is way too subtle for an old poop like Tad Barry—or for the antiporno people in the audience."

"That's true enough," Randollph said. "I'd guess Jack Dan Lancer would understand it. He isn't stupid. But he'd have to pretend he didn't understand it. It's in his interests not to understand it."

"Does the Holy Terror understand it, Randollph? Oh, I'm sorry." Sam sat down by him and put her head on his shoulder. "I'm trying not to think about that monster. I don't want to start you thinking about him."

Randollph stroked her hair. "Don't be sorry. He's a reality, and you can't convince yourself that reality isn't real. Not if you want to stay sane."

Sam snuggled closer. "I'm trying, Randollph. I'm trying to live like a normal person, doing what I'm supposed to do, work, go to this damned reception. But it isn't easy." She sat up. "If I knew who he was I'd shoot the son-of-a-bitch myself. He's my enemy! He's trying to steal my happiness! He's got no right! Oh, damn it, if I cry I'll ruin my makeup."

Randollph thought about what Samantha had said. There was a faint tapping at the door to the left side of his brain. It was saying, "Let me in. I have information for you." But then it quit.

Randollph tried to comfort her. "Don't cry, Samantha. We can live with it. We've been doing it."

"O.K., Randollph. I'm holding up pretty well." She smiled at him. "I come from tough Calvinist stock, you know. Got a Kleenex?"

He handed her a man-size tissue. "You asked whether the Holy Terror understands the distinction between dirty sex and sex that is essential to a story. I'd bet he does."

"Why? He certainly isn't giving you the benefit of the doubt?"

"No. I've thought a lot about that. He's obviously clever—something of a literary type—knows poetry anyway."

"You could say that about almost any college graduate—from a halfway decent college, that is."

"True enough. And if he understands the distinction, understands that you don't measure pornography by counting four-letter words, then why does he pretend not to understand it? Because he wants me for a victim? That would make him like the Lord's Lancer—he understands that I'm not pro pornography, but it is in his interests to pretend that I am."

Sam got up. "I gotta go or I'll be late for my reception." She kissed him. "Try not to think about it. I'm going to put it out of mind." She headed for the door. "Thea Mason's been invited. She'll give me moral support and a lot of wisecracks about women's guilds—she saw enough of them when she was growing up."

"Anyone taking you in charge, someone from the Guild?"

"A Mrs. Fosterman, Susan Fosterman. What's she like?"

"The perfume lady? You're in good hands."

The Women's Guild of the Church of the Good Shepherd normally met in an exclusively furnished church parlor. But not tonight. Tonight the crowd was too large. Almost all the members of the Guild had wanted to be in on this meeting. And most of them had brought guests, friends, and acquaintances who were eager to meet a local celebrity, to see what Sam Stack was really like.

So they were meeting in the gymnasium. The trustees had included the gym in the plans for the church on the grounds that "It'll give our kids something to do, keep 'em out of trouble." They had not envisioned the subsequent flight of the congregation to distant suburbs, where their kids could get into trouble or stay out of it in more elegant surroundings. The gym had been little used for a generation or so. But now Dan Gantry had a busy basketball and volleyball program for kids from the slum areas not very far from the church. Once, when some of the trustees had grumbled about the expense of light and heat to keep the gym open, Dan had replied, "It's damn near the only thing we do for people who live around here."

The Guild had prettied up the place for Sam's reception. There were lots of flowers. There were two long serving tables with cutglass punch bowls, lace tablecloths, and crystal and silver. Hattie Carmichael, the church hostess, had done her best. But it was still a gym. Despite the aroma from the flowers and generous sprayings of scented deodorant, the smell of perspiration, chlorine, and unwashed jock straps prevailed. It was more a place for sweaty struggles and the obscenities of street language than welldressed ladies getting together for punch and polite devotions.

Mrs. Fosterman had been waiting by the penthouse elevator in the hotel lobby when Sam got off. She introduced herself and said, "I'm your keeper for the evening. You're even prettier in person than on television."

Sam, who was on a first-name basis with movie stars, television personalities, and nationally known politicians, was almost overwhelmed by this elegant lady. She wondered where Mrs. Fosterman found that simple deep blue frock that had no flaw in it, either of fit, color or design. How did one acquire that selfassured presence entirely free of stuffiness or condescension? Would she, at Mrs. Fosterman's age, have achieved Mrs. Fosterman's dazzling handsomeness and air of being totally at home in the world? She hoped so.

"I hope you won't be bored," Mrs. Fosterman said as she led Sam toward the gym. "It won't be as exciting as your daily work."

"Don't worry, I won't be bored for being nervous."

Mrs. Fosterman seemed surprised. "You, nervous? You meet the public all the time."

"As a television reporter, interviewer. As myself. As Sam Stack. But tonight I'm Mrs. Randollph."

"That bothers you?"

"Not bothers. I just don't have any experience borrowing my identity from someone else." Sam found it easy to talk to Susan

Fosterman. "I guess I'm saying I don't know how to play the role of the pastor's wife. In the little Presbyterian church I grew up in, the lady of the manse—that's what they called the minister's wife in our congregation—was supposed to be gracious and pious and teach Sunday school, a lot of things."

"Two employees for the price of one," Susan Fosterman suggested. "Good business. Bad Christianity, but good business."

"I'm not like that at all. To tell the truth, I'd rather not be a minister's wife. Only Randollph is a preacher, and I want to be his wife."

"Matilda Hartshorne—her husband was your husband's predecessor—struck me as not being overly keen about being Mrs. Hartshorne, but she loved being the wife of a prominent pastor. She was a pain. I like your order of priorities better. Have you told your husband how you feel? Not that it's any of my business."

"Yes. Sure."

"Does it bother him?"

"No. He says to be myself. That the church didn't hire me as pastor, and he doesn't need a wife to tell him how to run it."

"Good for him. And this church doesn't need a lady of the manse to act out a role." Mrs. Fosterman pushed open a door to the gym. "I'm taking you in the back way so we won't be caught in the crush. Well, hitch up your girdle and onward to the battle."

Sam was surprised to see over three hundred women milling around the gym. Big women. Small women. Fat women. Slender women. Old women. Middle-aged women. Youngish women. Young women. Beautifully dressed women. Women not well-turned-out. Sam wondered how many of them were strong on being good Christians, how many weren't very religious but devoted to the church, how many were here out of curiosity, and how many belonged to the Guild and attended because they were fighting the loneliness and indifference of the big city and this was a place to meet other human beings and be reassured, for an evening at least, that they were persons. How many of them, she wondered, were virgins? And how many of the virgins wanted it that way? And how many wished they weren't but, because of some early experience or teaching or trauma, were unable, emotionally, to give themselves to a man? And how many wished they had a man, but had been unable to find one that suited them, and had too much taste and self-respect to settle for one-night stands? And how many of them had lovers? And how many were carrying on affairs? And how many were widows who had loved once and would never love again? She shuddered. The Holy Terror wanted to make her a widow, the bastard. She couldn't imagine what her life would be like without Randollph. She didn't want to imagine it. She put the thought out of her mind.

Above the soprano chattering Sam could hear music. Mrs. Fosterman steered her firmly through the crowd to the front of the gym. When they got there she saw that an ensemble of piano, violin, cello, and flute was making the music. And Tony Agostino, the church organist, was playing the flute! The man who made that great organ rumble with power and beauty was producing light, lilting sounds by blowing delicately into a long silver pipe. Sam thought it was incongruous but nice. She guessed that the other players, all young, were some of Tony's private students.

The focal point of the room, for tonight, was a table and a lectern. There were a lot of women around them, including Thea Mason. Thea was wearing a carmine Chinese-style dress slit well up the thigh, large gold pendant earrings, and was smoking a cigarette in a long holder. Sam supposed Thea's costume was a gesture of contempt for churches and church guilds. Others might dress and comport themselves appropriately for the occasion, but not Thea. Thea was a well-educated woman, Sam thought, and had enough experience of the world to have some maturity. But she was being childish, pouting at her unhappy life in her father's parsonages. Sam wished Thea wouldn't behave this way, then caught herself. She had no right to criticize. Wasn't she determined to be herself instead of the pastor's wife? Wasn't she, like Thea, rebelling against the religion of her youth? Anyway, she was glad Thea had come. She needed all the moral support she could get.

Susan Fosterman greeted Thea as an acquaintance of some years. Then she said, "Mrs. Randollph, may I present Heather French, president of the Guild, Jane Exeter, secretary-treasurer, and Bella Campbell, chaplain."

President French was tall, large-boned, and about Susan Fosterman's age. Jane Exeter was small, in the neighborhood of fifty, Sam guessed, and wore half-moon glasses with which she had been inspecting a folder of papers. Bella Campbell was a heavy, soft forty-plus wearing an expensive but abominable-looking yellow dress. Heather French, Sam guessed, was domineering. Jane Exeter was no nonsense. And Bella Campbell she put down as a gusher.

President French banged a gavel three times. Tony Agostino's ensemble cut off in the middle of something by Bartok. Three hundred women hastened to the section of folding chairs that had been set up in front of the podium. When most of the ladies had found places, President French banged the gavel again three times and said into a microphone: "This is, as you know, a reception for our pastor's wife. But it's also a business meeting. So let's get the business out of the way before the festivities. Jane."

Jane Exeter, looking a little put out at being gotten out of the way, read minutes, distributed mimeographed financial reports, and answered a few questions from the floor. None of this meant much to Sam, though she peered at the financial report as if she would find wisdom and inspiration in it.

Thea, masking her mouth with the mimeographed sheaf of papers, whispered, "You're faking it good, Sam. You really look interested."

Sam whispered back, "Don't make wisecracks. Don't make me laugh. And for heaven's sake, don't make me mad. I might cuss."

"That'd be a nice item for my column."

President French rapped with her gavel to silence the scores of low-voiced conversations which had broken out as soon as Secretary-Treasurer Exeter had been gotten out of the way. "Chaplain Bella Campbell will now conduct our devotions," she announced.

Chaplain Campbell carefully placed a Bible and some papers on the lectern, folded her hands on top of them, and bowed her head for a moment. Then, granting the assembled ladies what she probably thought was a beatific smile, she said, "Our subject tonight is prayer." She then read from the Gospel of Matthew's accounts of Jesus instructing his disciples to pray, "Our Father, who art in heaven . . ."

"Now," she said. "Ella Emerson of our church choir will sing 'Sweet Hour of Prayer.'"

Tony Agostino's ensemble backed the slim, pretty black woman as she sang. Sam positively despised this syrupy hymn that she'd heard a thousand times as a girl growing up in a small-town church. But she had to admit that Ella Emerson made it sound pretty good.

"Now," Chaplain Campbell announced, "we're going to ask you to participate in our devotions. I'm going to ask some of you to tell us—and this is spontaneous, no one has been told in advance that they'll be asked—I'm going to ask some of you to tell us your prayer secrets. Let's begin with the question 'When do you pray?' I think it would be nice, since this meeting is in her honor, to begin with our pastor's wife." She beamed at Sam. "Mrs. Randollph, when do you pray?"

"I don't," Sam said. Omigod, she thought, I said it. I didn't intend to say it. I didn't want to say it. It was stupid to say it. I just reacted. Oh, Jesus, what's going to happen now?

Chaplain Campbell looked as if, in the midst of her sweetly pious thoughts, someone had smacked her in the face with a lemon-meringue pie. The room was deadly quiet. She just stood there with her mouth open.

Susan Fosterman left Sam and went to the lectern. "Bella," she said, "I was supposed to introduce Mrs. Randollph later in the program. But if you don't mind, I think I should do it now." Chaplain Campbell took her seat, still looking stunned.

"Mrs. Randollph, I don't need to tell any of you this, is Sam Stack whom you know as the hostess of *Sam Stack's Chicago*. Or, if you prefer, women's answer to Phil Donahue." That got a titter from the crowd. Mrs. Fosterman continued. "Sam—Samantha's her name, a lovely name—and I had an opportunity to talk before the program." She extended her hand toward Sam. "Samantha, would you join me at the podium?"

Sam somehow felt secure joining Susan Fosterman in front of the crowd. She didn't know much about Mrs. Fosterman, but she sensed that this lady carried a lot of weight with this crowd.

"Ladies," Susan Fosterman said when Sam had joined her, "I present to you your pastor's new wife, or your new pastor's wife—it works either way."

That broke the tension. The audience laughed and clapped. Susan Fosterman, with a few words, had turned them around.

"Now, Samantha," she said, "I think we ought to talk about

your answer to Chaplain Campbell's question, don't you? I think I understand it, but I've had a chance to talk to you and these ladies haven't. Do you want to enlarge on it?"

"I think I'd better," Sam said. She was drawing strength from Susan Fosterman. She felt at ease, just as she felt before a studio audience.

"My answer was involuntary," she told them. "If I'd thought about it, I'd have probably, well, come up with a polite evasion. I didn't mean to be rude." She nodded toward the still-stunned Bella Campbell. "I apologize to the chaplain." The chaplain managed a weak smile of acknowledgment. "So let me come clean. I wish I could tell you that I'm a good Christian lady who agrees entirely with her husband. I guess I wish it. But I'm not and I don't. I hadn't been near a church for years until I met Randollph—Dr. Randollph. I grew up in the Church—Presbyterian Church. I was bored with it. I decided I was an atheist"—this got a suppressed "ooh" from the crowd—"but my husband said an atheist wasn't a bad thing to be. He said the early Christians were accused of being atheists. He said an atheist is a person who doesn't accept the popular god or gods of the current culture." Sam paused a moment. "That's what I think he said. So I switched to being an agnostic. At least C.P.—Dr. Randollph—says that's what I am. That means I'm not sure there is a God or not, and that even if there is I'm not sure that we can know it. So if I'm not sure, it would be dishonest of me to pray. And it would be worse to not pray, but tell you that I did. And that's why I said I don't."

The audience clapped more lustily for this. Sam felt in control.

"I, for one, appreciate your honesty," Susan Fosterman said. "Samantha, perhaps it would be nice if you answered any questions our ladies might have—that is, if you don't mind."

"I don't mind." This was her turf. This was what she did. This was what she was good at. Susan Fosterman, she suspected, knew that.

A woman in prim pink stood up. "Mrs. Randollph, does your, eh, your being an agnostic bother your husband?"

"I asked him that," Sam answered. "He said he didn't marry me because of my theology." More laughter.

"But doesn't that, your belief, isn't that a handicap to him, in his work, I mean," the pink lady persisted. "Shouldn't a minister and his wife be a team?"

"Maybe," Sam said. "Maybe that's the ideal, I don't know. But I'm his wife first. And I'm a person with an identity of my own. I told Mrs. Fosterman before the meeting that I was nervous because I didn't know how to play the role of minister's wife. Well, you've seen how rotten I am at it. So I guess I won't try."

The pink lady sat down.

"Is it true that you have a butler? I'd love to have a butler. And will we ever get a chance to see the parsonage?" This from a trim young matron in the third row. Apparently, the problem of their pastor being married to an agnostic was less interesting to her at least than the domestic arrangements in the parsonage.

"He's not exactly a butler, though he dresses like one. Clarence Higbee is his name. He's an Englishman, and a delightful person. He may be the world's best chef—cook. Since I work, work hard, and sometimes irregular hours, we have to have someone. And I'm glad you mentioned about seeing the parsonage. It's your parsonage, and you ought to be able to see it. I'll arrange for an open house soon. I'll get right at it." More clapping.

One of the younger women, a girl in her mid-twenties, Sam judged, dressed in high-fashion jeans and a white silk shirt, stood up. "Is Reverend, is Dr., your husband, is he sweet, does he say nice things, is he—"

"You mean is he a good lover?"

"That's it." The girl blushed.

"If you were closer to the front," Sam said, "You could see the stars in my eyes." The ladies whooped and cheered. I think, Sam said to herself, that I've brought it off. Thank you, dear God.

It was Sergeant Garboski's shift on the elevator detail. Sam had seen him a number of times, but never without his vaguely gray hat, years out of style, with the sweat-stained hatband. And where did he find that untidy purplish-brown suit, she wondered.

"Miss Mason I know," he told Sam, "but you'll have to identify this other lady. Orders." The sergeant was striving to be polite.

"This is Mrs. Fosterman, a friend of mine."

"If you say she's O.K., then go ahead." Garboski gestured

toward the elevator. "No offense, ma'm," he said to Mrs. Fosterman. "Just orders."

"No offense taken," Susan Fosterman assured him. "I'm comforted to know that the police are taking every precaution to protect Dr. Randollph."

Clarence opened the door to the penthouse. Sam had a key, but since the advent of the Holy Terror a sturdy deadbolt had been installed and was always in place when anyone was in the parsonage. It was impossible to conceive how the Holy Terror could get to the penthouse door without riding the elevator but Lieutenant Casey had insisted on this protection even if it appeared to be superfluous.

"Good evening, madam, Miss Mason," Clarence said.

"This is Mrs. Fosterman," Sam said. It had taken several gentle instructions from Clarence to convince Sam that domestics, however affectionately regarded by their employer, were not introduced to guests.

"So you're the famous Clarence," Mrs. Fosterman said.

"Famous, ma'm?" Clarence seemed puzzled.

"You're to address the Claude Bonnet Society, aren't you?"

"That is true, ma'm."

"What's that?" Sam asked.

"Oh, a very exclusive dining club. Started over a hundred years ago by a wealthy Frenchman living in Chicago. Dedicated to the preservation of fine dining. Bonnet left a sum in his will to provide for an annual dinner at which only the most respected chefs were to be invited. They lecture, then prepare the dinner."

Thea Mason fumbled in her bag for a notebook. "That's an item for my column. How did you know about it?"

"I'm a member," Mrs. Fosterman said. "There are two ways to become a member. You inherit membership. I inherited mine from my father. Or you can be elected. But it isn't easy. No one who has ever been seen devouring a sixteen-ounce sirloin with french-fried potatoes need apply."

"Clarence, why didn't you tell us?" Sam demanded. "An honor like that! Let us share in your glory."

"I hadn't found the moment to mention it, madam." Clarence, Sam thought, was probably blushing beneath his permanent tan.

"He's going to lecture on the proper preparation of veal," Mrs. Fosterman informed them. "Ellman Otis, our club president, says

Clarence has no peers in the Chicago area when it comes to veal dishes. What are you going to prepare for us, Clarence?"

"I shall demonstrate several dishes, ma'm. For the dinner I've yet to decide between roast leg of veal with cherries—that's with fresh cherries inserted in the meat, seasoned with cinnamon and cardamom, and roasted in a sauce of veal stock, cherry syrup, and madeira, then—"

"Stop right there," Mrs. Fosterman said. "I vote for that. Then I can say that I made the selection. Will you do that, Clarence?"

"Of course, ma'm." He was pleased by her interest. "Though Filet of Veal Vézelay is also a worthy dish. Veal lends itself to many modes of preparation."

"I'll look forward to it," Mrs. Fosterman assured him.

"So shall I, ma'm. Dr. Randollph is in the drawing room if you'd care to join him."

Randollph hastily got his feet off the coffee table, into his loafers, put his trashy novel aside, and stood up as the ladies entered. Sam went to him, planted herself in front of him, and said, "Well, husband dear, I let the cat out of the bag tonight."

"Oh? That requires explanation." He thought she looked like a little girl who'd done something naughty but was determined to brazen it out.

"I told them I was an agnostic."

"And how did they respond?"

"Very well, I'd say," Mrs. Fosterman told him. "I think they appreciated her honesty. I know I did."

"I'm sorry—good evening, Mrs. Fosterman, Thea. Samantha made her announcement before I had an opportunity to greet you."

"Aren't you going to scold her?" Thea Mason asked. "If my mother had told the Ladies' Aid she was an agnostic—if she'd even just told my father—he'd have jumped up and down and yelled at her, and then he'd have had her on her knees praying for forgiveness. Only she wouldn't have been praying, he would. Long and loud. 'O Lord, show this miserable sinner the error of her ways,'" Thea mimicked. "'Snatch her from the pit of hell with your powerful arm, O God, set her feet in the paths of righteousness, and teach her to confess the name of your dear son as her savior.' He could be a mean old bastard." Randollph thought Thea was near to tears.

"I didn't mean to do it, C.P." Sam seemed subdued. "I just got in a box where I either had to lie or tell them."

"It's nothing to get excited about," he said. "And it should be a relief to you. Now you don't have to worry about what people would say if they found out."

"I just didn't want to hurt you."

"I'm sure you did no harm. You aren't hired to preach the gospel here. I am."

"This ought to be an interesting marriage," Thea Mason said. "A preacher husband and an atheist wife."

"Agnostic," Sam corrected her.

"Atheist, agnostic, most people don't know the difference."

"I'm sorry to disturb you," Clarence announced from the doorway, "But there is a call for Mrs. Randollph."

"Excuse me," Sam said, and left.

"May I prepare some refreshment for you?" Clarence asked.

"I'm full of punch and cookies," Mrs. Fosterman said.

"Me, too," Thea agreed.

"Dr. Randollph?"

"I'll make myself a snack later," Randollph said.

"You will find steak tartare in the fridge," Clarence said.

"You fixed steak tartare!" Randollph was amazed.

"No, I did not prepare it. You are acquainted with my convictions about the ingestion of raw meat. It was sent by a new purveyor of choice meats who is soliciting our custom. They sent some steaks and Rock Cornish game hens. And the tartare."

"Perhaps I can modify my barbaric tastes under your tutelage, Clarence, but in the meantime I'll look forward to that tartare."

"Oh, damn!" Sam came back looking stormy. "Oh, damn! We're going to have a visitor."

"Anyone I know?" Randollph asked.

"No. Her name's Maryanne Bostwick. I was in school with her."

"That empty-headed little fluff?" Thea Mason said. "That dizzy caricature of high society? That dumb blonde?"

"That's the one."

"You were chums?"

"Not on your life!" Sam was vehement. "I hardly knew her. She's just curious to see where we live and meet my husband."

"She say that?" Thea looked surprised.

"No. But it didn't take any psychic powers to figure it out. Something to talk about at her next cocktail party."

"Calls herself Mimi," Thea said. "Mimi. Can you imagine what kind of woman would willingly call herself Mimi? She's always trying to get her name in my column. A pest, a bore."

"I know her," Mrs. Fosterman said. "She'll be wearing mink or sable and carrying that foolish little poodle. She should have lived in the jazz age."

"Mrs. Colbert Van Horne Bostwick the third, madam," Clarence announced. Clarence did not announce guests who were known by Sam or Randollph. Mrs. Colbert Van Horne Bostwick the third must have instructed him to announce her, Randollph thought. Clarence wore his usual impassive expression, but Randollph bet that he was suppressing a chuckle. Clarence would have instantly classified her as a social pretender. Her mink was no pretender, though. Randollph was not familiar with the price of mink but that creamy fur looked expensive even to the uninformed eye. The well-barbered head of a white poodle poked out from beneath its mistress's arm, surveying this new scene with quick, jerky movements of its neck.

Mrs. Bostwick rushed over to Sam and kissed her. "How nice to see you again, Sammy."

"Nice to see you, Maryanne."

"Mimi. That's what all my dear friends call me. Why, Theodora, I didn't expect to see you here. A lovely surprise."

"Thea," Thea said. "All my dear friends call me Thea."

"Oh, yes, Thea. And Susan Fosterman! You sell perfume, don't you?"

"You bet I do! Lots of it."

"This is my husband, Dr. Cesare Paul Randollph," Sam said.

"Oh, I'm so glad to meet you at last!" Mimi extended her dogless arm as if she expected Randollph to kneel and kiss her hand. "You're the famous football player."

"Was a football player," Randollph replied. "I'm a preacher now."

"How strange. That's what my husband says. Why would Con Randollph want to quit when he was a star, when he had many good years left? That's what my husband says. He's a big football fan. I think football's boring, but I'm glad to meet a star. Star of anything. Being a preacher must be boring too. We belong to St.

Stephen's Episcopal. Very exclusive congregation. The rector's a bore, though. Why did you quit, football I mean?"

"It would take too long to tell," Randollph said.

"Are you a star preacher?" Without waiting for an answer Mrs. Colbert Van Horne Bostwick the third looked around the penthouse living room. "What a cosy apartment. Small, of course. We have such a large place. We do so much entertaining, you know. You must come to one of our parties sometime. You don't do much entertaining, I suppose, not in a place this small."

"We are very selective in the guests we invite," Sam said with wicked pleasure. "Clarence, our majordomo, is the finest chef in Chicago. He prefers to serve only guests with a discriminating palate. We can't invite just anybody."

"That funny little man who let me in? Is that him? He's a fine chef?"

"The best," Mrs. Fosterman volunteered. "He's been invited to lecture at the Claude Bonnet Society annual dinner. And prepare a dish, of course. The entrée."

"Ooh." Mimi was impressed. "I'd like ever so much to belong to that club. So exclusive! Do you know anyone who's a member? If I could get a member to recommend me—us, my husband wants in, too—I'm sure they'd want us."

"I'm a member," Mrs. Fosterman said. Randollph thought he saw a gleam in her eye.

That stopped Mimi for a moment. Then, in a respectful, almost pleading voice, she asked, "Could you get us in? I mean, well, money's no object. I'm sure they'd be glad to have us. Could you?"

"It doesn't cost anything to join," Mrs. Fosterman informed her.

"It doesn't?" Mimi digested this. "How can it be so exclusive if it doesn't cost money?"

"You have to qualify."

"How?"

"By being recognized as a person with a discriminating palate." Randollph felt he could no longer suppress a loud guffaw, so he blew his nose lengthily.

"I like pâté de fois gras, and I think truffles are lovely. Would that do? However do you afford a chef on a preacher's salary?" she asked Sam.

"We take in washing." Sam said.

"Oh. Oh, you're teasing me. You always were a tease, Sammy." The poodle, either bored or uncomfortable, let out a little yip. "Oh, dear, Mimi Junior's hungry. Her name's Mimi Junior," Mimi Senior explained unnecessarily. "After me. She's mamma's darling! All this talk about food has made my little darling hungry. It's past her nighttime snack. Would you have any nice raw meat, Sammy? No dog food. Only the best for Mimi Junior. You have prime meat, I hope?"

Randollph saw this as a chance to escape. "If Mimi Junior will follow me I'll find her something tasty."

Mrs. Bostwick put the poodle on the floor. "There now, darling, follow the nice man. He's going to feed you." The little dog trotted after Randollph. Maybe, thought Randollph, she wants to escape, too.

Randollph opened one door of the huge refrigerator Clarence had installed in the kitchen. He saw the steaks, cherry red and white, laid out on wax paper. He looked at the dog.

"You couldn't handle one of these, old girl. It's bigger than you are. You'd gorge yourself, and probably die of the bellyache, and Mama would be hysterical." He thought of a hysterical Mrs. Bostwick and shuddered. Then he saw the steak-tartare balls. "I don't know whether you can appreciate all the good stuff in these or not," he told the attentive little dog. "But I bet you'll like it. Would you care for a little buttered pumpernickel with it? That's the way I like it." Mimi Junior yipped again and tried to stand on her hind feet. "What a ridiculous-looking creature you are," Randollph said. "Your very existence proves that God has a whimsical side to His nature. Else why would He have created you? You reveal to us something of the Divine Personality. You serve a theological purpose. How do you like being a source of revelation? Does it fill you with false and overweening pride?" The dog whined. "You live a soft life," Randollph lectured the poodle sternly. "You probably have no moral fiber left in you. Did you know that none of the prophets lived a soft life? None of them came from the fertile crescent. They all came from the rocky hill country where life was hard. Oh, we might have to except Isaiah—the first Isaiah, that is. Were you aware that there were three Isaiahs?" The little dog was watching him intently. "I see that you didn't know it, but that you are interested. Well, at least three guys had a hand in writing the book of Isaiah. Not counting the various editors who may have stuck in some of their own ideas. You've read the book, of course. Didn't you notice how the style of writing changes, and the ideas? The second Isaiah—only his name probably wasn't Isaiah, we don't know who he was—he was the important one. He came up with the idea of the suffering servant. Absolutely marvelous writer, too. A poet." The dog whined again. "Oh, you think it is time for class to be over? You're probably right. Since you've been such a good listener, I'll get your supper."

The steak-tartare balls were on small squares of wax paper. He selected one. "Don't you think the teacher ought to have the first one? Pecking order, you know." The dog went up on its hind legs again. "Oh, you don't think so? You think because you are a revelation of the whimsical side of God's personality you ought to be first? Maybe you're right." Randollph put the paper containing one tartare ball on the floor. The dog jumped and yipped.

"There, you greedy little bastard," Randollph said. "Don't eat the paper, too. Might interfere with your bowel movements." He watched while the poodle gulped the tartare ball in one swallow, then turned back to the refrigerator. "It's my turn now," he said. "I've been a good host and served you first. Now it's my turn." He selected another tartare ball. "I think I'll eat this one without any buttered pumpernickel," he said, more to himself than to the poodle. Before he ate it, he turned his head to look at the poodle. Mimi Junior was lying on her side dead.

"Cyanide crystals," Lieutenant Casey said. "These tartare balls are full of them. The lab will have to check it out, of course, but I've seen enough cyanide crystals to recognize them. Besides, the dog smells of cyanide."

"Why didn't the steak-tartare balls smell of them?" a shaken Randollph asked.

"Because they don't smell until they turn to gas. As long as they're cold you can't smell them."

"They must turn to gas very quickly when they're ingested," Randollph said.

"Very, very quickly. Can you get that dizzy dame out of here?

I've got to talk to Clarence, and I can't do it with her shrieking and moaning about her poor baby. Is she nuts?"

"Just stupid, I think. I'll see what I can do."

Casey and Randollph went back into the living room. His wife, Randollph saw, looked completely stunned, in another world. Thea Mason sat in glum silence. Mrs. Fosterman was trying to comfort the moaning Mrs. Bostwick.

Randollph went to Mrs. Bostwick. "I'm so sorry about your dog," he said. Of course, he wasn't sorry. He was grateful for Mimi Junior's untimely departure from this life. If it hadn't been for the hungry little dog he'd be lying on the kitchen floor dead. "Mrs. Bostwick, I'm sure Lieutenant Casey can provide you with transportation home."

"Yes, of course," Casey agreed.

Mrs. Fosterman stood up. "I'll take her home. I have my car, and it's not much out of my way. Come with me, Mimi."

Mimi got up. "I want my little Mimi Junior," she sobbed. "I want to take her with me. We've already selected her plot in God's Precious Pets Memorial Gardens." She turned to Randollph. "Do you think our rector would conduct the services?"

"I'm afraid I couldn't speak for him," Randollph told her uneasily. He knew that the rector would not. But he wouldn't want to be the rector when he had to say no.

"We'll see that your dog is returned to you after the lab has finished its tests," Casey said with uncharacteristic gentleness. Perhaps, Randollph thought, he didn't want to start Mimi off on another round of shrieking and moaning.

"You won't hurt her?" Mimi pled with him. "You won't cut on her or anything like that?"

"No," Casey lied. He'd have to tell the lab boys to do an extra-neat job. Mrs. Fosterman led Mimi away.

"Now," Casey said, "I need to talk to Clarence."

"Do you want me to leave?" Thea Mason asked. "I'm the press, you know. I want to stay."

"Stay if you like," Casey said. "No point in trying to keep this out of the papers. Might not hurt if someone reported it accurately."

"Thanks, Lieutenant."

When Clarence came in he looked stricken but under tight control of himself.

"May I say how terribly sorry I am that my negligence permitted this to happen," he said to Randollph.

"Let's clear up one thing right now." Randollph spoke to Clarence with a sternness and authority that, under less extreme circumstances, he would never have found it in himself to use. "This was in no way your responsibility. You did the normal thing. You've done it dozens of times. You had no reason whatever to do other than what you did. It isn't going to help you, and it certainly isn't going to help us, for you to assume a guilt which you did not earn."

Clarence's face seldom registered any emotion. But Randollph could see it relax with relief. "Thank you, Dr. Randollph. It is very kind of you to look at it that way."

"Tell me, Clarence, how this meat got into the house." Casey asked.

"It was sent by the Chicago Fine Meats Company."

"How was it ordered? You call them and specify you wanted some steak tartare?"

"No. No, not at all. I would never order steak tartare, much less prepare it." Clarence's tone of voice implied that no civilized person would do such a thing.

"Then how'd it get here?"

"I received a call from the company. Would I accept a package of prime steaks, Rock Cornish game hens, and steak tartare. They'd appreciate my opinion of the quality of their meats. The tartare, the caller said, was one of a number of specialties they were planning to prepare for a catering business they were launching. It sounded plausible."

"And you accepted?"

"Yes. I hesitated about accepting the tartare. Dr. Randollph knows my antipathy toward human consumption of raw meat. But I knew he was fond of the, of steak tartare. So I accepted."

"Wasn't it strange, a company calling you to give you an expensive, I suppose expensive, gift like that?"

"Not at all, Lieutenant. It is a frequent occurrence."

"Why?"

Clarence hesitated. "I have a modest reputation in culinary circles. If I find the product of a particular purveyor to be of uniform excellence, then I'm likely to tell others who follow my trade. A majordomo in a gentleman's household does all the purchasing of comestibles. There is a very substantial business in this city for suppliers of meat that is of a grade not obtainable in the markets."

"I see." Casey scratched his head as if he could cull some brilliant insight from it. "Is there actually a Chicago Fine Meats Company?"

"Oh, yes," Clarence said. "An old established company. Recently under new management, I've heard. I've never had occasion to utilize its services."

"Did you save the wrapping this stuff came in?"

"No," Clarence answered. "It never occurred to me that it might be of use. I like to dispose of trash as soon as possible."

"Do you remember anything about how it was labeled, the package?"

"I gave it only a passing glance, Lieutenant. There was a rather small company identification as I recall. Printed. The address was typed on a regular mailing label. It was a rather large box. Packed in dry ice, of course."

"Was the company label pasted on?"

"Yes, come to think of it, it could well have been."

"Could it have been the logo, you know, the stuff a company prints at the top of its stationery? Could someone have just cut it off a sheet of stationery and pasted it on?"

"Yes, I suppose so. As I said, I only gave it a passing glance. The package had already been opened, of course. Your men check all packages designated to this address."

"For bombs," Casey said. "Letters too. We don't read them—the letters, I mean," he hastily assured Randollph and Sam. "Just check."

"One of your men called me to ask if I was expecting a package of meat," Clarence said.

"I'm glad to hear they are on their toes. Do you remember the voice that called to ask if you'd accept the gift from the, the—"

"The Chicago Fine Meats Company," Clarence supplied. "Yes, it was a woman."

"Oh?" Casey raised his eyebrows. "Anything distinctive about it?"

"No." Clarence thought a moment. "Pleasant, a voice that was accustomed to persuade, I'd say."

"A professional," Casey said. He sighed. "We'll have to check all this out, of course. But I can tell you now what happened."

"I'd be interested to know," Randollph said.

"This meat never came from that company. Someone snipped off a company letterhead logo and pasted it on. They hired a telephone-answering service to call you, Clarence. Probably sent the message and payment by mail. Then they hired a delivery service to deliver it to the desk. That would take a little doing for the sender, but I can think of several ways it could be done. By the way, Clarence, did you check, did you, well, make a judgment about the quality of the meat?"

"Yes, of course." Clarence appeared to be surprised that Casey would ask. "Any majordomo would, as a matter of course, see that he was receiving what had been promised."

"And?"

"The steaks were of good quality, but not exceptional. Not what I would select."

"And the game hens and tartare?"

"I am not the best judge of Rock Cornish game hens, Lieutenant, as I do not rank them high on my list of desirable poultry. As to the steak-tartare balls, it would be difficult to judge their quality without tasting them." Clarence shuddered.

"The whole package, then, the meats you could buy at any meat market?"

"I would think so, Lieutenant. The tartare balls are a specialty item."

"Probably made them himself." Casey turned to Randollph. "You are real fond of tartare?"

"I confess—confess with shame in Clarence's presence—that I am."

"Never tried it myself. Who knew you liked the stuff?"

"The whole world," Thea Mason said. "The world of Chicago, that is. I had an item about it in my column. That was right after Johnnie DeBeers's farewell party. I thought our football hero was putting on a he-man act, eating those tartare balls like they were M and M's. But he said no, he loved them, but Clarence frowned on the stuff and he seldom had a crack at any. I thought that was funny, so I put it in my column."

"Well, there goes another lead," Casey said, looking annoyed. "Can't run down every reader of "Thea Hears" and ask them if they put cyanide crystals in Dr. Randollph's steak-tartare balls."

"Perhaps the cyanide crystals would be a lead, Lieutenant," Randollph said. "I assume you can't just walk into any drugstore and buy them off the shelf?"

Casey gave Randollph a look that said don't try to tell me my business, bub. But he spoke pleasantly. "They aren't easily available, but there are any number of ways they can be obtained. It would take the Army, and maybe the Navy, too, to run down that lead."

"How would he get hold of them?"

"Oh," Casey said, "fake a purchase order, or swipe them, or bribe some corrupt pharmacist in some city where he wasn't known. That'd be my bet. And that's why I don't have enough men to check it out. In these days of fast transportation he could have gotten the stuff in San Francisco or Miami or London."

"So this, this mess this evening, doesn't get you any nearer to finding this Terror monster than you were before?" Sam was trying to keep the hostility out of her voice and almost succeeding.

"Not much nearer," Casey admitted.

"Does it occur to you, Lieutenant," Randollph asked him, "that this latest attempt confirms—or strengthens anyway—the supposition that I am the primary target?"

"How's that?"

"Because the Terror is going to extraordinary lengths to do away with me—especially since the sins of which he accuses me are, to any reasonable mind, several shades less scarlet than those of his victims to date."

"Who says he has a reasonable mind?" Thea put in. "Sad Tad Barry would think the sin of favoring pornography more crimson than murder."

"Perhaps," Randollph said. "But I give the Holy Terror credit for being smarter than Barry."

"Maybe we'd better research your personal life," Casey said. "Maybe there's some scandal there that would give us a lead to someone with a motive to murder you." He smiled as he said it, but it was clear that he was serious.

"Believe me, Lieutenant, if I could think of someone, anyone, with a motive to do me in, I'd tell you only too gladly."

"Even if it would reveal something, something that would embarrass you in your present position?"

"I would prefer to risk the embarrassment of a past indiscretion than a murderer's bullet or poison." Randollph sounded very sincere.

"No women scorned, say, that might have had their hatred triggered by your recent marriage?" Casey turned to Sam. "I'm sorry. I have to ask. The Holy Terror could be a woman, you know."

"I understand, Mike." Samantha, Randollph thought, had let fear subdue her hostility toward Casey for not having found the Terror.

"None. None at all," Randollph said. "Most of them were"—he hesitated—"passing fancies. At all events, I can't recall a parting that wasn't amicable."

"I really didn't think it would be something like that." Casey, Randollph thought, was apologizing. "Did the item in your column mention whether Sam, Mrs. Randollph, liked steak tartare or not?" Casey asked Thea Mason.

"Yes. I said that Sam hated the stuff."

"Then the Terror could send poisoned tartare confident that no one in the household but Dr. Randollph would eat it." Casey reflected on this for a long time.

Thea Mason got up. "I'd better get going if I want to get this story in tomorrow's paper. Any objection, Sam, C.P.?"

"No." Randollph said.

"Go ahead," Sam said. She didn't sound very enthusiastic.

"Anything you want me to get in the story, C.P.?"

Randollph pondered this, then smiled. "You might write that theology saved me."

Thea looked blank. "How's that?"

"I was lecturing the dog. I pointed out to him, to her, that God's creation of such a ridiculous-looking thing as a poodle proved that God has a whimsical aspect to His personality—"

"I still don't see," Thea interrupted.

"I was going to eat the first tartare ball. But Mimi Junior"—Randollph grimaced—"hopped up and down so frantically that I told her that maybe, since she was a revelation of God's whimsical nature, she deserved first crack at the food. So you can say that my little lecture to the dog, a theological lecture, no matter how frivolous, saved me."

"I'll be damned!" Thea said.

"I don't think my pastor at St. Aloysius would approve of that theology," Casey said with a chuckle. "I'll try it on him. Come to think of it, though, he might like it. He thinks all theology is a lot of nonsense. Go to mass, practice birth control, and support the parish financially—that's what he believes in."

"Two of the three are important," Randollph said. "I'd except the item about birth control."

"I don't buy that one, either," Casey said. "And even if I did, Liz wouldn't."

"Thanks for letting me stay, Mike," Thea Mason said as she put on her coat. "This will be a real scoop, as they say in *The Front Page*. I'm sorry it has to be about an almost-tragedy happening to my friends." She kissed Sam, shook hands with Randollph and Casey, and left.

"Mike," Sam asked after Thea Mason had gone, "have you thought any more about the fact that I had all the, all the Holy Terror's targets on my show?"

Casey shrugged. "Yeah, I've thought about it. Even went over there and questioned some people."

"Who?"

"Oh, John DeBeers—senior and junior. Adrian Holder. That anchorwoman, anchorperson—"

"Marva Luscome."

"That's her. Looks like an angel."

"She isn't. Not by a hell of a sight." Sam was very positive.

"Treated me very nicely."

"She would!"

Randollph thought it was time to get on with it. "Did you find out anything?"

"Not much, except that Marva Luscome looks like an angel. And Adrian Holder, though a pleasant guy, got in trouble for beating up on a priest."

"I didn't know that!" Sam was startled.

"Not the sort of thing one advertises about himself. He didn't want to tell me about it, either, but . . ." Casey let the sentence dangle, implying that professional skills or methods of interrogation best not described could elicit information from the most reluctant of witnesses.

"And the others?" Randollph asked.

"Oh, I found out that Johnnie DeBeers is carrying a torch for Sam. That's why he's taking this job in California. It's like he's joining the French Foreign Legion to get away from his past. But that's no news to you."

"And John DeBeers senior?"

"Well, I found out that he's a very affable man. But a troubled one, I'd say."

"Troubled about his wife?"

"Yes, that. She's in a blue funk over Johnnie leaving Chicago. He seems at his wit's end to know how to help her. I'd say he's very much in love with his wife but—how does that song go? 'I don't know how to love you.' She's something of a religious nut, I gather. Getting worse." Casey seemed to examine this thought, then discard it. "Also, I get the impression that John senior is pretty unhappy himself about Johnnie leaving. He's an only child." Casey stopped again as if weighing and calculating. "All of which adds up to more or less interesting information, I guess, and not much else."

Sam spoke up in a small voice. "Mike, have you found out yet how the Terror got his information about Horner and Pierce and Gropius and the rabbi?"

"I wish to hell I had," Casey said. "If I knew that, I'd have it figured out, who the Terror is, have it figured out in no time."

Sam's answer was in an even smaller voice. "I think I know where the information came from."

Casey shot out of his chair. "Good God, Sam, why haven't you told me?"

"I just now thought of it, Mike."

"Well, tell me, tell me!"

She told him.

Casey headed for the door. "I'll be in touch with you tomorrow," he flung back over his shoulder.

After he'd shut the door Sam and Randollph sat in silence for some time. Then Sam started to cry. She got up, went over and sat down on the sofa by Randollph, and buried her face in his shoulder.

"Pray God it isn't so," she sobbed. "Oh, God, don't let it be so!"

Chapter Nineteen

"Where," Randollph asked, "do you find fresh melon and red raspberries this time of year?"

Clarence set the iced silver bowls in front of Sam and Randollph. "It is my responsibility to know what is available at the greengrocers'," he replied.

"Beautiful!" Sam said. She surveyed the pale-yellow half melon cupping the mound of glistening red berries. "The berries look like rubies set with pinpoint-size diamonds. Beautiful!"

"I dust the berries lightly with sugar before I chill them. The sugar crystallizes. That gives the effect of diamonds. I do think the way the food is presented can add so much to its enjoyment. Will you be ready in about ten minutes for the next dish?"

"What is it?" Sam asked.

"Don't tell us," Randollph ordered. "I like to be surprised."

"Oh, all right. Surprise us," Sam said. "We'll be ready."

When Clarence had departed to the kitchen, she said, "Randollph, since last night I've been saying to myself, 'I will not be sad, I will not be furious. I will keep my nerve. I will not come apart. I will hold myself together.' You know, I think it's helping. I'm even hungry. Last night I thought I would never want to eat again. But now I'm hungry."

Randollph marveled anew at the resilience of the human spirit. Here he was, just a few hours from narrowly escaping life's final curtain, digging vigorously at a bowl of melon and raspberries. Perhaps Norman Vincent Peale, not—in his opinion—the profoundest interpreter of the Christian faith, had a genuine Christian secret in his theology of positive thinking. He finished before Sam and picked up the morning paper Clarence had placed in a rack by the table.

"I was there," he read aloud.

"What?" Sam muttered through a mouthful of raspberries.

"That's the head on Thea Mason's story about last night. It's a three-column box in the upper-right corner of page one."

"What'd she say?"

"Hmm. 'I was there when the little dog died. Had it not been for his theology, the Reverend Dr. Cesare Paul Randollph, pastor of the Church of the Good Shepherd, would have died instead of the little dog.' Hmmm. 'Dr. Randollph, current target of the killer known as the Holy Terror.' Hmmm."

"Quit hmming," Sam instructed.

"Read it later," Randollph advised.

"See if she mentions it in her column, C.P."

Randollph noted the page for "Thea Hears" in the front-page index, then dutifully turned to it. After quickly scanning the column he said, "No, she doesn't mention it. She does mention that Clarence is addressing the Claude Bonnet dinner, though. That's the day after tomorrow. The night after tomorrow. At the Playboy Club in Wisconsin?"

"Yes. Didn't I tell you? Clarence will have a chance to see all the little bunnies."

"Somehow, Clarence doesn't strike me as the typical Playboy customer."

"You might be surprised, dear. Those little bunnies have tails. Oh, do they have tails!"

"He'll be gone all night?"

"Yes. With plenty of time to play after cooking the dinner—his part of the dinner."

Clarence wheeled in a serving table with an oven beneath it and a pan over a chafing-dish burner on top. He quickly pulled two round dishes from the oven and set them before Randollph and Sam. "Soufflé Vendôme," he announced. He turned to the pan, lifted the lid, and poured hot fat into an empty dish, then splashed liquid from a bottle into the pan. "Bourbon bacon," he explained. "This is that splendid lean bacon cured to my specifications by one of our farm suppliers." He deftly struck a match, held it over the edge of the pan, withdrawing his hand just as the pan shot up a curtain of blue flames. "Whiskey," he said. "Straight bourbon whiskey. One-hundred proof." He rapidly transferred four strips of bacon each to two warmed plates he had snatched from the oven. "I've never prepared this dish before. I've done Soufflé Vendôme previously, of course."

"What's in it—the soufflé, I mean?" Sam asked.

"Poached eggs, madam," Clarence said. "I put about half the soufflé mixture in the bowl, then add poached eggs that have been allowed to cool, cover them with the remainder of the mixture, sprinkle it with cheese, and bake."

Clarence, Randollph surmised, had gone to an extra effort for this breakfast as an expiation for lingering feelings of culpability for his part in the near-tragedy of the night before.

"And the butterscotch rolls of which you are so fond, madam," Clarence said as he whisked them out of the oven. "May I serve you?" he asked.

"Indeed you may," Sam said.

"Clarence, Randollph—Dr. Randollph and I were having a debate. When you get done with your duties at the Playboy Club up there in Wisconsin, will you go and watch the Playboy bunnies?"

"Bunnies, madam?"

"Girls. Girls in rabbit costumes. You see a lot more of the girls than you do the costumes. A lot more. Randollph says that wouldn't be your cup of tea. I say he's wrong."

Clarence replaced the pan of rolls in the oven. "Though a confirmed bachelor, I have always considered the well-nourished female figure one of God's masterpieces and a delight to the eye."

"Well nourished?" Randollph asked.

"He means fat," Sam said.

"Fat is not a precise term, madam. Are you aware that, by estimate, not one lady depicted on canvas in the Louvre Museum weighs less than eleven stone?"

"How much is eleven stone?"

"Approximately one hundred and fifty-five pounds, madam."

"Wow!" Sam said. "Hefty. I doubt that any of the bunnies will weigh eleven stone, but they do fill out those costumes."

"Perhaps, if time permits, I shall make my own appraisal." Clarence left.

"A good exit line," Sam said to Randollph. "I know a lot more about men than you do, Randollph."

Clarence reappeared bearing a telephone. Randollph had once asked him why he didn't just leave the phone in the dining room.

"It would disturb the ambience of the room," he answered. "A telephone is a symbol of the outside world intruding itself into the privacy of the dining room, thus creating a discordant note in what should be an atmosphere of serenity. I prefer to bring in the phone if the call is of sufficient importance to warrant the interruption of a meal."

Clarence plugged the cord into the jack and set the phone in front of Sam. "A Mr. Holder for you, madam," he announced. "He is most insistent."

Sam picked up the receiver. "Yes, Adrian, what are you in a dither about?"

"I had to catch you before you left, Sam. Pack your bag. You're going downstate for three days."

Sam said, "What was that slogan the war-resisters used—'Hell no, I won't go.' That's my answer, Adrian."

"Afraid you'll have to, Sam."

"Just why?"

"Sammy, dear," Adrian Holder's voice pled, "You know that we're on cable downstate now. You know that means big bucks to us. What you don't know is that some of these cities that get us think we are interested only in Chicago. They want some specials done on their communities. And they all want Sam Stack, star reporter, to do them. We've lined up Champaign, Bloomington, and Peoria—all strong markets. It'll only take three days. Counting today. We need you. Bad. Please say yes."

"I don't want to. I hate these rush assignments. You know that. I don't want to be away from my husband at—at a time like this. You can understand that, can't you, Adrian?"

"I understand. But please."

Sam let out a big sigh. "O.K., Adrian. O.K. But you owe me one. A big one. And I'll collect. You can bet on that."

"Thanks, Sam. And stop by to see me on your way to the airport. I've got all the stuff you'll need."

Sam put the phone down and looked at it blankly.

"From what I overheard, you're going to be away for a few days," Randollph said gloomily, missing her already.

"I'm sorry, C.P."

"Why the rush job?"

Sam thought about it. "Adrian didn't really make it clear why it had to be right now. This is a crazy business, run by crazy people."

"And Clarence will be gone, too. I'm feeling lonesome already. Samantha, did Adrian Holder ever have a crush on you?"

"A crush?"

"Was he in love with you? Make a pass at you? Ask you to marry him?"

"Yes," she said. "Yes, yes, and yes."

Chapter Twenty

"I've called this meeting at Dr. Randollph's request," Lieutenant Michael Casey announced. Casey, Randollph noticed, was elegant in a camel-hair jacket. "I've called it here at the bishop's office because I don't want anyone wondering, around the police station, what's going on," Casey continued. "Captain John Manahan is here," Casey continued, "because he is my superior." Casey stressed "superior" so that it sounded like he meant "ridiculous as that may seem to you." But this was probably too subtle for Manahan to catch, Randollph decided. And, anyway, the captain was busy skinning the cellophane hide from a fat cigar.

"The bishop is here because he is Dr. Randollph's superior, and we need his approval for what Dr. Randollph wishes to propose to us. Dan, Reverend Gantry, is here at my request, and the reason will become apparent." Casey paused, probably for dramatic effect, Randollph thought, then stated in a flat voice, "Dr. Randollph believes that he knows the identity of the Holy Terror."

Captain Manahan, in the process of sucking in smoke, burst into a fit of coughing. "Who? Who the hell—" he gasped.

"The Lord be praised!" the bishop exclaimed. "At last. At long last."

"Son-of-a-bitch!" Dan said, apparently forgetting the presence of the bishop.

"Now," Casey went on briskly, ignoring his sputtering superior, "we can't be sure. Dr. Randollph has a list of three possibilities with a strong leaning to one name on the list. And we have no proof—not yet. In fact, the chances of finding proof strong enough to arrest, let alone indict, are slim to nonexistent."

"Then what—" a partially recovered Captain Manahan managed to get out.

"You're going to set a trap," the bishop said.

"That's right. That's what Dr. Randollph is proposing." Casey didn't waste words.

"I want to know who this Holy Terror guy is, I gotta right to know, Mike—"

"How?" The bishop asked Casey.

"Dr. Randollph." Casey said.

"For a variety of reasons, which I won't go into now, I expect another attempt to be made"—Randollph hesitated—"on my life tomorrow night. In the parsonage—the penthouse."

"Can't be done. Impossible, way we got it guarded." Captain Manahan spoke with the certainty of the expert. "You figured out how he can get in there? Can't be done."

"This Holy Terror has already demonstrated his resourcefulness." The bishop spoke thoughtfully. "He's imaginative. He apparently enjoys challenges. He's actually made a kind of game out of his grim business. A deadly game. He has an intricate mind, diseased though it may be. He'd like to show you how he can do the impossible. But I confess I don't see how to do it. Do you, C.P.?"

"Yes."

"How, then?"

"By simply announcing to the police guarding the elevator the name of someone I know and wouldn't suspect. They'd call me and I'd say, 'Send this friend of mine right up.'"

"Well, I'll be God"—Captain Manahan looked at the bishop in his episcopal purple rabat and quickly made a rhetorical retreat—"it could be done that way, little luck. Good disguise—"

"Especially with some help and cooperation from the police,"

Casey filled in. "Or, rather, a little planned negligence. The idea is to let the Terror in and—"

"And nab the twerp," Dan said.

"Won't that be terribly dangerous?" The bishop asked. "Suppose this Terror has a gun and shoots C.P.—Dr. Randollph—as soon as he opens the door?"

"We've thought of that," Casey answered him. "Dr. Randollph will be wearing a bullet-proof vest."

"He could shoot him through the head, Mike," Captain Manahan said. "That's how he shot the others." Manahan, Randollph reflected, wasn't as stupid as his oafish manners made him seem.

"Yes, Captain, that's a possibility. But picture the scene. The Terror will be standing on a level with Dr. Randollph when the door opens. It would be unnatural to point the gun upward at the head. The normal thing to do would be to shoot straight ahead. At the area of the heart."

"I don't like it," the Captain said. "Somethin' could go wrong, Then I gotta explain how I let the doctor here get murdered."

"There's a chance, I admit. I don't like it either. But Dr. Randollph wants to do it."

"I don't really want to do it," Randollph explained. "But I'm infernally weary—and scared—of being a target for a determined killer. It's ruining my life. My wife's a strong lady, but it's driving her toward a nervous breakdown. I do my work—in a sense my work has been my salvation. But always with this threat on my mind. I'm tired of living this way. I'm willing to gamble on bringing it to an end."

Casey let Randollph's statement sink in. Then he said, "Now here's the plan—"

"Just a minute, Mike." Captain Manahan got up from his seat at the bishop's long conference table. "This is your case. I have confidence that you'll make th' right decision." He looked at a heavy waterproof watch on his wrist. "Gotta 'nother meeting. Important. Gotta rush. Leave it to you." He departed hastily.

After Manahan had gone, the bishop said, "The good captain is no doubt beating a bureaucratic retreat."

"How's that?" Dan Gantry asked.

"Why, if the plan fails he can say it was Lieutenant Casey's plan, that the lieutenant was acting without his captain's approval," the bishop explained.

"And if it comes off?"

"Then he'll take the credit," the bishop answered. "The first principle of survival in a bureaucracy is to never leave your flank exposed. Always be sure, when laying out a program or a plan, that you maneuver some poor chap into a position to take the blame if things go wrong. And," he added, "in any kind of bureaucracy, things go wrong more frequently than they go right. I speak from experience."

"That's not very reassuring, Freddie—Bishop." Randollph accompanied his remark with a smile.

The bishop returned the smile. "There's another bureaucratic principle, C.P., that says when you are ninety-nine-percent sure that a program is going to be a big success, a program proposed by one of your subordinates"—he nodded toward Casey—"you maneuver yourself into a position in which the entire responsibility is squarely at your office door. You exclude the possibility that your subordinate who thought up the program can claim any credit at all for its success. In this case," the bishop continued, "though I haven't heard all the details of the plan, if I were in Captain Manahan's shoes, I'd take it over and make it my plan. I wouldn't give the lieutenant a chance to claim even a smidgen of credit. I believe it will work."

"That's reassuring," Casey said.

"That how the church bureaucracy works?" Dan asked.

"I'm afraid it is," the bishop said. "It's bad practice. Without laying claim to any special righteousness, I don't follow the practice. I'm convinced that the only way to make an organization work properly is to find the ablest people you can, then give them full credit for their accomplishments."

"I wish you were the police commissioner," Casey said. "As to the rest of the plan, there's not much to it. Tomorrow, early afternoon, Dan here will go up to the penthouse, along with a fellow he's recruited—"

"Sticky Henderson," Dan said.

"Yes. They're both big guys. They'll go up separately. I'll have them get on the elevator from one of the upper floors of the hotel. Then, a little later, I'll do the same thing."

"Why not a contingent of policemen?" the bishop asked.

"Because I'd have to brief them. They'd have to call their wives or something, let it out some way. Possibility of a slip. Farfetched, I know. But I want this airtight."

"I see."

"Dan and Henderson will be behind the door. When the Terror steps in—"

"Are you sure the Terror will step in?" the bishop interrupted.

"Reasonably so. What's that word you used, Doctor?"

"Hubris," Randollph said.

"Ah," the bishop said, "excessive pride, arrogance, an unrealistic self-confidence."

"The doctor says that's what the Terror has," Casey explained.

"I think the Holy Terror's the kind of person who will want to gloat over me a bit," Randollph added. "The Terror's worked hard to win this victory. That's likely to bring on a desire to explain, to boast."

"So the Terror steps in," Casey said. "Henderson—he's a big guy, like I said, and with fast, sure hands—"

"Very quick," Randollph said.

"Henderson will strip the Terror of the gun, and he and Dan will pin—"

"And where will you be, Lieutenant?" the bishop asked.

"In the coat closet, out of sight—with a gun. That's the second line of defense. If anything should go wrong with the first plan—and I don't think it will—Dr. Randollph has instructions to drop to the floor, then I shoot the Terror. I'm a very accurate shot."

"Where will Clarence and Samantha be during all this?" The bishop asked.

"Samantha is already on her way to Champaign on a three-day special assignment," Randollph informed him. "And Clarence will be at the Playboy Club in Wisconsin."

"Clarence—at the Playboy Club?" The bishop was astounded.

"Lecturing the Claude Bonnet Society or Association—a group dedicated to fine dining. He said he also might take a look at the bunnies if he has the time."

Dan laughed. "Clarence, watching the bunnies? Why, the old goat!" The bishop simply murmured, "Will wonders never cease?"

"The Terror knows Clarence will be absent," Casey explained. "Thea Mason had a note about it in her column. The coast will be clear."

"How will the Terror know that Samantha won't be there?" the bishop asked.

"The Terror will know," Randollph said.

* * *

After Dan and the bishop had gone, Casey said, "I could kick myself for not figuring out the source of the Terror's information. So obvious."

"You can kick me, too," Randollph said. "Samantha thought of it. I didn't."

"Well, that's the key that unlocks the old puzzle. Let's get down to business. What do you want me to do? You said there were a couple of things."

"Yes." Randollph drew a paper from the inside pocket of his jacket. "Here are three names. The three names. I don't think we really need bother with two of them, but we could be wrong." Casey did not miss the "we." Randollph was already transforming his plan, his solution, into their plan. Casey did not doubt, once it was over, Randollph would have transformed it further into Casey's plan.

"So what do I do?"

"Call their colleges. You'll have to find out what they are. Can you do that?"

"Can do," Casey nodded.

"Find out if they took a course in English lit—literature. A course that had a section on poetry. Find out who the professor was. Run them down if they're retired or have moved on. Ask the teacher the question I've written here."

"What good will this do?" Casey wanted to know.

"It will confirm our suppositions," Randollph told him. "It will tell us for certain whom to expect tomorrow night."

"You said there were a couple of things you wanted me to do. What's the other one?"

"Reassure me that this plan is going to work."

"It'll work." Casey was very positive. "I'll bet my promotion to captain on it. It'll work."

Chapter Twenty-one

It came, as Randollph expected that it would, in the morning mail. He had wondered if he was wrong, after all, when it wasn't in the mail that Clarence had put on a silver salver beside his breakfast plate of grilled ham and fluffy scrambled eggs. ("A simple breakfast, Dr. Randollph," Clarence had apologized, "but I'm in a rush to get off to Wisconsin.")

But it was on his office desk, where Miss Windfall had left two mounds of mail—one, the usual collection of promotional letters; and two, a smaller collection of personal epistles.

It was in pile two. Same cheap envelope. Same typed address. No return address. Same single sheet of typing.

I'm sure you've known you'd always get done in
Because I am so desperate keen to kill.
You've done quite well, trying to save your skin,
Luck's on your side, but luck won't stop my will.
Men worse than you, my football-player friend
Have had to suffer judgment at my hands
You've done your job, aware your day neared end.
The clock ticks down—no cheering from the stands.

Goodbye, old jock! Remember me to God,
And tell Him that I did what must be done
To make some morbid sense out of this sod
On which He placed me—it hasn't been much fun.
You're not a bad sort, wish you could be spared,
But something in me will not let it so.
A demon maybe, or some truth I've at last bared
Within my soul. No matter, it is time to go.

Now it was all but certain that the Holy Terror would be putting in an appearance at the penthouse tonight. And Randollph now had no doubt as to who it would be.

He tossed the poem aside. The Holy Terror might be coming. The stock market might crash. Revolutions were no doubt starting in distant lands. And Chicago, as usual, was teetering toward bankruptcy. No matter. Come Sunday, he'd be standing before twelve hundred people expecting him to rightly divide the word of the Lord, or at least entertain them for twenty minutes.

He attacked his sermon with vigor and enthusiasm. His mind was clear. The decision had been made. The game plan agreed upon. It was like preparing for a football game. Once you had done everything you could do to prepare, you relaxed and left the outcome to the fates.

The sermon was going so well that he worked right through the lunch hour. By the middle of the afternoon he'd finished. He asked Miss Windfall to get him Lieutenant Casey on the phone.

"Lieutenant," he said, "I got a poem in the mail."

"That pretty much ties up the package, doesn't it?" Casey said. "You going up to the penthouse now?"

"Right away."

"I'll be there in an hour or so. Gantry and Henderson are already there. And, by the way, I ran down those English teachers. Found the one you especially wanted me to question."

"And?"

"You were right."

Randollph normally summoned the elevator to his parsonage to the hall outside his office. But, because the police didn't want it out of their sight these days unless they were certain as to who would be on it, he took one of the regular elevators down to the hotel lobby. Randollph bought an afternoon paper and a *New Yorker* magazine at the hotel news stand, then went over to Sergeant Garboski who, apparently, had been assigned guard duty for the rest of the day. Garboski, in shapeless brown suit and sweat-stained gray felt hat several seasons out of style, was a reassuring figure to Randollph. He looked like a grade-B movie version of a plainclothes cop.

"I'll be going up now, Sergeant," he said.

" 'Kay," Garboski said. Then, as Randollph was about to close the elevator door, the sergeant said, "Doctor. Luck."

So Garboski had been briefed already. "Thank you, Sergeant," Randollph said. "I'm sure that fickle lady will be true to us tonight." As the doors closed Randollph enjoyed watching the puzzled expression on Garboski's face.

Randollph found Dan Gantry and Sticky Henderson in the kitchen. Henderson had found one of Clarence's aprons, and was arguing with Dan the merits of several possible menus for an evening meal.

"Elmer Gantry here wants a steak," Sticky Henderson complained. "I plannin' to show you cats some fancy cookin'. Ain't as good as Clarence, maybe, but I ain't no fry cook."

"Sticky, lad, solid food's the ticket for tonight. Nothing sets better on a man's stomach than steak."

"O.K., O.K., I'll fix steak. You my friend, so I defer to your plebeian taste," Henderson grumbled.

Randollph could see that they were just blowing off a little nervous steam. Sticky Henderson had on a sweatsuit. Dan was wearing worn slacks in an outrageous plaid—no doubt left over from his predress-for-success days, Randollph guessed—and a black turtleneck sweater. They were, as Casey said, both big guys. They were ready for action.

The phone rang. All three of them jumped!

Randollph thought, oh no! It's too early. And Casey's not even here yet.

It was the bishop.

"C.P.," he said, "I want to be there for—what's the phrase?—the action."

"Freddie, this isn't your kind of action."

"Now, C.P." the bishop said pleasantly, "I'll not take that as you probably meant it—that I'm too old and out-of-shape to be of any assistance. You're probably right, of course. I'll stay in your study with the door closed until, ah, you've bagged your prey."

Randollph thought about it. Casey wouldn't like it. But it was, after all, his house. And Freddie was his bishop. "If you'll settle for staying upstairs in a bedroom until it's all over, it's a deal."

"Splendid! How do I get in? I assume your elevator's closely watched."

Randollph thought again. The bishop and his wife lived in a suite in the hotel. "I'll have Sergeant Garboski bring the elevator to your floor and pick you up," he instructed the bishop. "Are you ready now?"

"I'm ready."

"He'll be right up."

As he hung up the phone, Randollph said, "Sticky, you've got another mouth to feed. The bishop's coming."

"Hope he likes steak," Sticky said.

"Everybody likes steak," Dan said. "And don't forget that Lieutenant Casey will be here."

"I ain't forgettin'. Glad to have a little law around, time like this. Plenty food. I been through everything, beggin' your pardon, Con. This place like a restaurant, Michelin Guide probably give it three stars. Now if you gentlemen will excuse me, I must be about my duties. Ain't that the way that Clarence cat talks?"

It was a strange dinner party, Randollph thought. A black professional football player. A white football player turned preacher. His associate pastor, a big, muscular guy. A dumpy middle-aged bishop in a purple rabat. And a cop.

"Damn good!" Dan Gantry said, munching his way through a section of french bread filled with pink slices of top-grade sirloin. "My compliments to the chef."

"Thank you, Elmer." Sticky Henderson looked pleased. "Secret's in puttin' a little fresh-squeezed garlic in the butter I spread on the bread. Told you I ain't no fry cook."

"It is indeed excellent!" The bishop also praised the chef. "Lieutenant, what time do you expect this visit from the Terror?"

"Can't tell. Eight to nine o'clock, probably. Not too early, not too late."

"We got time to kill, if you'll excuse the expression," Sticky Henderson said as he cleared away the dishes. "How about a little poker? I got cards."

"What'll we use for chips?" Dan asked.

"I got chips, too, We play us some poker, the bishop don't mind."

"Ah, I'd like to sit in," the bishop said. "It's been many a year since I played, but in my undergraduate days I was quite good at it."

"Huh? A bishop that plays poker?" Sticky Henderson was surprised.

"If you'll hand me the cards I'll deal while you get out of your apron, Mr. Henderson." The bishop peeled off his black coat and hung it on the back of a vacant chair. "Dealer names the game?"

"Sure." Henderson was still astounded.

The bishop took the cards, riffled them expertly, then dealt one card to each player, face down. "This will be straight stud," he announced. "The serious gambler's game. My winnings will be contributed to our City Mission Society."

They played silently and steadily. But Randollph and the bishop won consistently.

"Never knew you played such a mean game with the pasteboards, Con," Sticky Henderson complained.

"I don't play cards, I play people," Randollph said.

"What that mean?"

"I've figured out when you're bluffing, and when you've got the cards, Sticky. Dan, too. The bishop's too cagy, but I'll figure him out, too."

"No you won't," the bishop said, turning up his down card, a queen. "Pair of ladies, and a pair of nines. You thought I was betting on the pair of nines I've got showing. You've got a pair of jacks."

"So I have," Randollph said ruefully.

The bishop raked in the pot. "Nice little contribution to missions," he said.

The phone rang. It was 8:17 by the kitchen's digital clock.

"Up the stairs, Bishop," Casey commanded. "Dan, Henderson, let's all get out of here. Don't want anybody sneezing when Dr. Randollph's talking."

Randollph waited till they were all out of the kitchen. Then he picked up the phone and said, "Randollph."

Randollph thought he could detect tension in Sergeant Garboski's voice, but maybe that was his imagination. "Fellow here in a dog collar wants to come up," Garboski growled. "Says his name is Amory Allen—the Reverend Doctor Amory Allen."

"Does he speak with a Scotch burr?" Randollph asked.

"What? You mean does he talk funny?"

"Yes."

"He talks funny."

"That would be Dr. Allen. Yes, he's a friend of mine. You can send him up."

"O.K." Garboski expelled a sigh of relief before he hung up the phone. Acting, Randollph supposed, was not one of the sergeant's accomplishments.

When the door chimes sounded Randollph took a deep breath to calm his nerves and quell the fear he felt rising in him. Now I've got to play a part, he thought, and I'd better put on a good act.

It didn't go exactly as planned.

Randollph rehearsed his set speech in his mind, then opened the door. "Come in, Dr. Allen, glad to—why, you aren't Amory Allen—"

"No, I'm not," the figure in clerical garb and a black hat, said. "This is a gun pointing at your heart. Now back in carefully, Doctor. Back away from me. Not fast. Slowly." Randollph backed carefully. He could see Dan and Sticky behind the door, and it took a powerful act of will not to shift his eyes toward them. Suddenly, the Terror halted. It was as if he'd smelled a trap. Randollph didn't even think about what to do—he just hit the floor rolling sideways. He heard the splat sound of a shot, then the sound of glass shattering. Sticky Henderson slammed the door hard, knocking the Terror into the door frame, then he and Dan piled onto the bogus Amory Allen. Sticky had him in a bear hug, and Dan jerked the gun out of his hand.

"Ain't no point strugglin', Terror baby," Randollph heard Sticky say. "You quiet down now or I break your goddam arm." Then Casey quickly had handcuffs on the Terror.

Randollph got up. "Come on in, John," he said. "As you can see, we've been expecting you."

John DeBeers, in clerical garb, black hat, heavy black-rimmed glasses, and a brown wig which appeared to be his natural hair, didn't look at all like John DeBeers. With hands cuffed behind him and Lieutenant Casey's gun pointing at him, he looked stunned.

"I—" he stuttered.

"Hold it!" Casey cut him off. "I've got to read you your rights."

He read them. Then he said, "If someone will hold this gun on him a minute, I'll call down to the lobby and get some of my men up here. Then off to the slammer."

"Don' need no gun," Sticky Henderson said. "Terror baby ain't goin' nowhere. Hope he try. I like to bust him up some." Sticky, Randollph reflected, apparently relished his role as goon in a righteous cause.

"I'll hold the gun," the bishop said, stepping into the foyer of the penthouse. "After hearing all the noise down here I just had to come down and see what was happening."

"You were supposed to stay upstairs until I called you," Casey accused him.

"I know, Lieutenant. But we can talk about the ethics of it later."

"Can you use a gun?" Casey asked doubtfully.

"Oh, yes. I abhor handguns. They are only good for target shooting and killing people. And, of course, police work. But I know how to use one." He didn't explain how he knew. "Who have we here? Don't tell me the Holy Terror is a clergyman. A spoiled priest?"

"No," Casey explained as he handed his gun over to the bishop. "This is Mr. John DeBeers, whom you met at Dr. Randollph's wedding."

"My word! I'd never have recognized him. I can't imagine why Mr. DeBeers would want to murder all those clergymen, let alone C.P. Why?"

DeBeers spoke for the first time. "Because," he said, "religion ruined my life."

"Religion ruin his life? Don' make no sense to me." Sticky Henderson said. They were sitting in the living room of the penthouse waiting for Lieutenant Casey to return. He'd asked them to wait.

"I thought it was something like that," Randollph said.

"Still don' see how," Henderson persisted.

"You aren't familiar with his personal history," Randollph told him.

"What that got to do with it?"

"John DeBeers was the son of a strict Dutch Calvinist father," Randollph explained. "He was brought up to obey and revere his parents, which he apparently did. His concept of God was probably quite similar to his picture of his father."

"Not a fun guy, huh?" Sticky commented. "My church, we think God pretty strict, but He understand we human, we gotta kick up our heels some. We go too far, He forgives us an' lets us start again with a clean slate."

"Although I might not put it exactly that way, that's very sound theology," the bishop said.

"Somewhere along the way, DeBeers revolted against his religion and against his father," Randollph continued. "He told me that. He refused to become the Dutch Reformed clergyman his father insisted he become. He refused to marry the girl his father had picked out for him. He went into journalism and married an Italian Roman Catholic girl. His father apparently then rejected him. That was, for him anyway, like being rejected by God."

"That hardly seems a sufficient motive for murdering several clergymen, and especially trying to murder you, C.P." the bishop said.

"No, but it was, well, what you might call the psychological seedbed out of which his career as the Holy Terror grew."

"So what make him become this Holy Terror cat?" Sticky asked.

"His marriage went sour. He told me that, too. Apparently he loved his wife very much. But the love she had once given him—as I make it out from the sketchy conversation I had with him—was gradually transferred to God, or at least a growing and irrational love of religious devotion. And to their son."

"So this time, instead of being rejected by God he was rejected for God," the bishop said softly. "I'm beginning to see."

"Why he pick on you, Con?" Sticky asked.

"Because I married Samantha."

"He want her?"

"No, but his son Johnnie did. If she'd married Johnnie—as he pleaded with her to do—then Johnnie would have settled down and stayed in Chicago, and his mother would have been happy. But Samantha never had any romantic interest in Johnnie DeBeers. She rejected him and married me—a clergyman. As DeBeers saw it, another defeat for him at the hands of religion. I think that's when he snapped."

"Boss, didn't Johnnie DeBeers start out to be a priest?" Dan

Gantry asked. "Then he flunked out, or got some girl pregnant, or something. That would be religion defeating him again, wouldn't it?"

"I expect DeBeers had mixed feelings about that," Randollph answered. "I doubt that he was enthusiastic about his only son becoming a priest in a faith he did not share. But without doubt Mrs. DeBeers's reaction was to withdraw farther from DeBeers. In that sense, he may have perceived it as another defeat by religion. Once he'd started thinking along the lines that religion had shattered his life, he probably lost all rational perspective on himself."

"The old lady probably thought Johnnie'd be the first American pope. And her a lush. A Christian lush. Funny combination."

"Not unprecedented," the bishop said. "The whiskey priest is a stock character in fiction. Why not a whiskey priestess?"

The door chimes rang. Randollph thought how lovely it was to once again be able to answer the door unafraid. He excused himself with "that's probably Lieutenant Casey."

When Casey joined them, Dan Gantry asked: "Did you get anything out of him, Mike?"

"A little. Can you imagine a guy who made a game out of killing priests, ah, clergymen?" Casey shook his head. "It got to be a game with him. He actually got—what did he say?—a relief, a sense of relief and even exhilaration after he'd done one of his jobs."

"But I was the original target," Randollph said.

"Yeah, what he said was kind of garbled, but what I make of it was he decided you had to go, you were the last straw or something—"

"But he needed to cover that."

"That's right. Then, one evening when he was waiting for Thea Mason, waiting in her apartment—he had the key—he got to rummaging around in her files—"

"Thea Mason?" the bishop sounded astonished.

"Yes, Bishop. He was"—Casey thought a moment for the right way to say this to a bishop—"he was, well, seeing her. And he found a lot of files on Chicago clergymen. She has files on everyone of any importance."

"I hope that includes me," Dan said.

"Quiet, Elmer, let the man talk," Sticky said.

"Well, he found she had some dirt on nearly everyone. Must

have put out the kopeks to plenty of private investigators. I guess it's a gossip columnist's business to know the dirt on everybody. Anyway, DeBeers found these files on prominent clergy with all the bad stuff, and that was the idea he needed."

"Knock off the nasty guys, huh?" Sticky Henderson said.

"That was his idea. He could kill them and feel that it was good riddance. That was about what he told me. He didn't seem to feel any regret over it. Felt like he was God, he said. Although he was terribly upset when I told him Rabbi Lehman wasn't guilty."

"That's the trouble with playing God," Randollph said. "We never have all the information God has."

"Thea Mason's files. Who'd have guessed?" The bishop said.

"Sam—Mrs. Randollph—guessed," Casey said. "She'd been in the apartment. She'd seen the files."

"She was afraid Thea was the Holy Terror," Randollph said. "Her good friend."

"John DeBeers was her good friend, too," Dan observed. "You called her yet?"

"Yes," Randollph answered. "She's flying back as soon as she can get a plane. It wasn't easy to tell her. How do you mix gladness and sorrow?"

"How come this Terror cat write all that poetry?" Sticky Henderson asked. "He tell you that, officer?"

"Like I said, it got to be a game with him. He wanted to be clever. He wanted to defy the world. He babbled something about having to outwit God. He's chagrined that he couldn't even outwit Dr. Randollph."

"How you get on to him, Con?" Sticky asked.

"Lieutenant Casey and I talked it over. We decided that the vital questions were who had access to Thea's files, and why was so much care taken to protect Samantha?"

"Protect your lady? How he do that?"

"He knew—anyone who read Thea's column knew—that she hated steak tartare. And he had Adrian Holder order Samantha to go out of town on a rush assignment. That clinched it. That's how the lieutenant and I knew he'd be here tonight."

"Don't forget the poems, doctor," Casey said.

"Oh, yes, Lieutenant Casey got hold of DeBeers's college teacher of English literature. He was fond of poetry—"

"You called it 'man's poetry,'" Casey reminded him.

"Don't tell my wife I said that," Randollph admonished him. "She'd say I was being a sexist."

"I won't," Casey promised. "Anyway, DeBeers, as a student, liked to write poetry using well-known poems as models. Said it sharpened his wits, according to his teacher."

"Jesus, what a creep!" Dan Gantry said. "And to think I went to a lot of trouble to find him a slug of Scotch at the boss's wedding reception." He shook his head in disgust.

"Surely a number of people must have had access to Thea Mason's files. I gather that she's a lady, ah, not stingy with her favors." The bishop, Randollph saw, was still trying to unravel that clue.

"Oh, yes," Casey answered him. "Adrian Holder. He once asked Sam to marry him. We considered him. After all, he's the one who ordered Sam on this hurry-up assignment. We guessed DeBeers told him to do it, but we didn't dare ask."

"Johnnie DeBeers had a few recreational evenings in Thea's apartment, too." Dan said. "I just happen to know."

"We knew that," Casey said.

"How come you select old man DeBeers from all them alley cats sniffin' round this bitch in heat, Con?"

"You've got your animals mixed, Sticky," Randollph said. "If you mean why the lieutenant and I thought John DeBeers was the most likely candidate among the possibilities, I suppose because we decided that it would take a bright, complex, highly moti-vated, unhinged personality to manage it. And because there was a—well, a moral dimension to all the murders. He seemed to need the reassurance that—in some sense—he was performing a moral act. It's rather complicated."

"Not to me it isn't," Dan Gantry said. "A nut. He didn't have all his screws tightened."

"Religion ruined my life," the bishop murmured. "What a sad statement. But true. Sad but true. The history of religion is replete with examples. I suppose your knowledge of church history— plus John DeBeers's personal history—helped you to think of him, C.P."

"Lieutenant Casey is also familiar with church history," Randollph said. "He's had a good Catholic education. He's familiar with, with the erratic religious personality." Casey, he thought, looked both pleased and uncomfortable, if that were possible. "We both understand how, well, religion has the potential to distort reality."

"Religion can bless or hurt," the bishop said. "We clergy, the church, don't like to admit that it can hurt. But it can. It's like an explosive. It needs to be handled with reason and care." He sighed, as if this were a heavy burden for a bishop to bear.

Casey looked as if he had to perform an unpleasant duty. "Dr. Randollph is giving me more credit than I deserve. He's the one who put the finger on DeBeers, not me. I'm going to make that clear to the press." Randollph thought that the lieutenant would probably like to lie about it, but was blocked by a sturdy Catholic conscience. It was up to him to clear Casey's conscience.

"Don't you dare! That's an order, Lieutenant."

"Why not?" Casey asked, grasping for moral straws.

"For one thing, it won't do my career as a pastor any good to be known as the clerical sleuth. I'm already tagged with being an ex-jock. That's enough. So save me the embarrassment."

Casey muttered something, but he was looking more cheerful.

"On the other hand, it won't hurt my career a bit if the papers say, 'Casey solves another one,' or some such garbage. I'll feel guilty about that."

"Catholic guilt," the bishop said. "Where would writers like Graham Greene be without it? I think C.P. is right about it, Lieutenant."

"You're giving me absolution in advance for taking the credit?" Casey was smiling. "Can a Roman Catholic accept absolution at the hands of a Protestant bishop and expect it to be, to be—"

"Efficacious? A nice theological point, Lieutenant." The bishop was smiling too. "I'd say in this case you should take the broad ecumenical view."

"You could say two Hail Marys and throw in a paternoster if it will make you feel better, Mike," Dan Gantry suggested.

Randollph said: "How about this? You tell the press that Dr. Randollph made some very helpful suggestions. Will that clear your Catholic conscience?"

"It might—along with the bishop's absolution. By the way, doctor, did you recognize the model for the Terror's last poem to you?"

"Yes. It took its inspiration from Siegfried Sassoon's 'To Any Dead Officer.'"

Casey shook his head in wonderment. "How you can know all that stuff beats me."

He's overdoing it, Randollph thought. I'll bet a nickel he knew the poem.

"Is this part of your absolution too, Lieutenant, this modest acknowledgment of my superior command of English literature?"

Casey just grinned. "Not to change the subject, doctor, but John DeBeers asked me to ask you if you'd visit him in prison."

Randollph was surprised. "A plea for forgiveness," the bishop said.

"DeBeers said to tell you that the New Testament says it's a Christian's obligation to visit the prisoner," Casey went on.

"Cheeky bastard!" Dan said.

Randollph thought about it. "Yes, the New Testament does say that. Right now I'm not feeling much charity toward the Holy Terror. I feel more like beating him up—"

"I'll help, Con." Sticky Henderson was enthusiastic.

"Me, too," Dan said.

"But," Randollph continued, "when my unchristian tempers toward him have cooled, and I remind myself that he wasn't really trying to kill me, he was trying to kill something inside himself—well, maybe."

The commuter airlines terminal at O'Hare airport is a building with all the architectural charm of a huge quonset hut. It squats next to the wing of O'Hare's vast main building which accommodates the international terminal. The international terminal receives the traffic from London, Stockholm, Paris and sundry cities whose very names excite the imagination and stir hopes in the least romantic breasts that someday they may board one of the enormous 747s or 707s to adventures in another world. Most of them know, though, that if they fly at all it will be out of the commuter terminal, in small two-engine propeller planes, some of them quite odd-looking, to places like Peoria and Dubuque and Madison. There is nothing romantic about the commuter terminal.

Randollph was pacing around just inside the door of the terminal which admitted passengers from incoming flights. A twin-engine Beechcraft scudded around a corner, diminutive beside a KLM monster lumbering toward its dock at international. It braked and shut down the engines. The door opened, retractable steps unfolded. And nine passengers hurried out, hardly listening to the hostess's professionally cheery "have a nice evening." The sixth to debark was Samantha.

When she saw Randollph she hurled herself into his arms, clutching him as if, were she to let go, he would disappear.

"I think I was hysterical on the plane," she said without lifting her head from his shoulder. "I sobbed, then I'd smile, then sob some more. The passengers must have thought I was a head case."

Randollph didn't say anything.

"I'd think about how you were safe, and I'd smile—even laugh. Then I'd think about John DeBeers, and burst out crying. I ought to hate him. I ought to want him dead. He did such awful things. But he was my friend. My boss. He was good to me." She looked up into Randollph's eyes. "Is it wrong of me to cry for him?"

"No," Randollph said. "I think it's quite proper."

"There was a preacher on the plane," Sam rattled on. "He was fat and had bad breath. He saw I was upset, so he came and sat beside me, and said, 'Little lady, I see that your soul is troubled. The Lord Jesus is the answer to your problem. I'll just say a prayer that you might give your heart to the Lord Jesus—'" She stopped.

"And?" Randollph said.

"I told him to buzz off."

"Those were your exact words?"

Sam put her head on his shoulder and giggled. "I won't tell you exactly what I said."

"Did he—"

"Buzz off? He sure did."

Randollph found a taxi. The expressway was not so crowded at night, and the driver made good time. Sam sat huddled against him, and they talked in low voices.

"I feel like—I don't know what I feel. It's like something has come to an end, and I have to put life back together again. And I don't know how to do it."

"Rejoice that we are free of the Holy Terror," Randollph told her. "Sorrow for John DeBeers. And then do what you always do.

Your job. It's still there, and you're good at it. And keep on loving me."

She pressed closer. "I like that last part."

"I'm hungry," he said. "Clarence won't be back until tomorrow, but let's warm up something he's left in the fridge, then—"

She smiled up at him.

"Let's," she said.